# The Best of Adam Sharp

# GRAEME SIMSION

## The Best of Adam Sharp

ST. MARTIN'S PRESS ☙ NEW YORK

THE BEST OF ADAM SHARP. Copyright © 2016 by Graeme Simsion. All rights reserved. Printed in the United States of America. For information, address St. Martin's Press, 175 Fifth Avenue, New York, N.Y. 10010.

www.stmartins.com

Lyrics from "Angel of the Morning" by C. Taylor copyright © 1967 EMI Blackwood Music Inc. For Australia and New Zealand: EMI Music Publishing Australia Pty Ltd (ABN 83 000 040 951), Locked Bag 7300, Darlinghurst NSW 1300 Australia. International copyright secured. All rights reserved. Used by permission.

Designed by Anna Gorovoy

Library of Congress Cataloging-in-Publication Data

Names: Simsion, Graeme C. author.
Title: The best of Adam Sharp / Graeme Simsion.
Description: First edition. | New York : St. Martin's Press, 2017.
Identifiers: LCCN 2017001936| ISBN 9781250130402 (hardcover) | ISBN 9781250130426 (ebook)
Subjects: LCSH: Married people—Fiction. | Marriage—Fiction. | Domestic fiction. | BISAC: FICTION / Contemporary Women. | GSAFD: Humorous fiction.
Classification: LCC PR9619.3.S497 B47 2017 | DDC 823/.914—dc23
LC record available at https://lccn.loc.gov/2017001936

Our books may be purchased in bulk for promotional, educational, or business use. Please contact your local bookseller or the Macmillan Corporate and Premium Sales Department at 1-800-221-7945, extension 5442, or by e-mail at MacmillanSpecialMarkets@macmillan.com.

Originally published in Australia in 2016 by The Text Publishing Company

First U.S. Edition: May 2017

10  9  8  7  6  5  4  3  2  1

*This book is—again—for my wife, Anne,*
*my inspiration, collaborator, and first reader.*

*It is also a nod to the music and musicians*
*that contributed so much to the life of my*
*generation. If you don't know the songs in this*
*book, I encourage you to download them and*
*listen as you read—there is a playlist at the end.*

# BEFORE THE DELUGE

If my life prior to February 15, 2012, had been a song, it might have been "Hey Jude," a simple piano tune, taking my sad and sorry adolescence and making it better. In the middle, it would pick up—better and *better*—for a few moments foreshadowing something extraordinary. And then: just na-na-na-na, over and over, pleasant enough, but mainly because it evoked what had gone before.

A day that began in my childhood bedroom in Manchester, boxed in by photograph albums and records, was always going to evoke the past.

My walk to the station, through streets gray with drizzle and commuters huddled into their coats and plugged into their phones, did not so much remind me of days gone by as stir a longing for them, for a summer under blue skies half a world away, where the music of boom boxes competed with the laughter of carelessly dressed drinkers spilling from the pub onto the footpath.

The route took me past the Radisson Hotel, once the Free Trade Hall and scene of a seminal moment in popular music. May 17, 1966. A heckler shouts "Judas!" to the young Bob Dylan, who has returned after the interval with an electric guitar, and he responds with a blistering rendition of "Like a Rolling Stone." My father was there, in the audience, eyewitness to music history.

And on the station concourse, a teenage girl in a light blue anorak and a beanie like mine was singing Adele's "Someone Like You," a song about glory days, regrets, and the passing of time. It might have been just a pretty tune had there not been the memory of another young woman, twenty-two years ago now, to give substance to the observation that love only sometimes lasts.

I leaned against the wall opposite the busker. Passengers passed between us, a few of them tossing coins into her keyboard case. She was singing without a microphone, leaving it to the acoustics of the enclosed space to do the work. Her playing was basic but she had a good voice and a feeling for the song.

I allowed it to wash over me, letting music and performance take the simple sentiments to a higher plane, indulging for a few minutes in the sweet sadness of nostalgia, so different from the everyday gloom I had woken to in my mother's house.

I tossed in a two-pound coin and earned a smile. There was a time when I might have done more: put a tenner in to get her attention, offered to accompany her so she could stand up to sing, made a little personal history. That time was gone. These days I was taking more from my bank of memories than I was putting in.

The day might come when I had nothing but memories, and the choice of whether to indulge my romantic side and wallow in them, or my cynical side and reflect on their reliability.

Had I painted the Australian skies a deeper blue because they were the backdrop to my Great Lost Love?

Did they really jeer Dylan at the Free Trade Hall? A month ago, I had pulled the bootleg from my dad's vinyl collection, and my mother had thrown her own handful of mud into time's ever-rolling stream.

"Your father had a ticket to that concert. But he didn't go. He had his own job to do and a family to look after."

I would have backed the original version. My mother was constantly recasting my wayward dad as a responsible breadwinner and role model, more so lately since I did not have "a proper job." Which was why I was able to travel halfway across England in the middle of the week to take her to medical appointments.

No matter now. I would soon have more immediate matters to occupy my mind. Later that day, as I continued my engagement with the past, scouring the Internet for music trivia in the hope of a moment of appreciation at the pub quiz, a cosmic DJ—perhaps the ghost of my father—would lift the needle on the na-na-na-nas of "Hey Jude," say, "Nothing new happening here," and turn it to the flip side.

"Revolution."

# Part 1

**1**

I was back home in Norwich, reading up on Pete Best, the Beatles' forgotten first drummer, when the e-mail popped up in the bottom corner of my screen.

> *From: angelina.brown@tpg.com.au*
> *Hi*

That was it. *Hi*. After twenty-two years, twenty without any contact at all, out of the blue, Angelina Brown, my Great Lost Love, decides to change the world and writes *Hi*.

There was a song to mark the moment. "My Sentimental Friend," a hit for Herman's Hermits in 1969, was, thanks to the physics of headphones, playing in the middle of my skull. It would now have a place in the jukebox musical of my life, with the line about the girl he once knew who left him broken in two. Not quite Wordsworth, but sufficiently resonant that, when the message arrived, I was thinking about its sender.

Was this the first time she had thought about me, letting her mind drift to a time when "Like a Prayer" was top of the charts, wondering what happened to that guy she met in a Melbourne bar and fell in love with? Just a browse of her contacts list and a casual *Wonder what he's doing now?*

Click on Adam Sharp, type two letters, Send.

There had to be more to it. For a start, I would not have been in her contacts list. We had not been in touch since e-mail was invented.

The address suggested that she was still in Australia. I checked the World Clock Web site: 1:15 P.M. in Norwich was a quarter after midnight in Melbourne. Was she drunk? Had she left Charlie? Had he left her? Maybe they had split up fifteen years ago.

She was still using her maiden name. No surprise there. She hadn't changed it the first time around.

I knew barely anything about Charlie—not even his surname. In my mind it was the same as hers. Charlie Brown. The little bald cartoon character in his baseball mitt: *It's a high fly ball, Charlie Brown. Don't miss it, Charlie Brown.* In real life, I was the one who had missed it.

One night, after a few pints, I had Googled her. I got nowhere. Angelina shared a name with an equal opportunity commissioner and a newspaper columnist, and finding her among the litigation and opinions had been too much for my beer-addled brain. Unless I searched images. I stopped myself. Angelina was—*had been*—an addiction, and the only way to deal with an addiction is abstinence.

Maybe. Time passes. Every alcoholic wants to prove they're cured. Surely, after twenty years in a committed relationship, I could exchange an e-mail or two with my ex-lover, who had, as the Americans say, *reached out.*

She might have a terminal illness and want to tie up the loose ends. I could blame the breakfast conversation with my mother for that thought. Perhaps she and Charlie just wanted advice on holiday options in Northern England: *Looking for somewhere cold and miserable to get away from this interminable sunshine.* What would it say about my relationship with Claire if I felt too vulnerable to respond to an innocuous query?

I let Angelina's e-mail sit until the evening. I was still weighing my options when Claire arrived home. Our conversation was shouted between my room and the bottom of the stairs, but I could picture her in her important-meeting gray suit with the green scarf and the chunky-heeled boots that brought her up to a neat five foot four.

"Sorry. Meeting went a bit over. Dinner smells good."

"Jamie Oliver. Chicken casserole. I've had mine."

"Do you want a glass of wine?"

"Ta—bottle open in the fridge."

"How's your mum?"

"Haven't got the results yet. I think she's a bit scared."

"Did you give her my love?"

"Forgot."

"Adam . . . better not have. Have you fed Elvis?"

"You'd know if I hadn't."

That was a fair snapshot of the relationship that Angelina's e-mail might test. We were a functioning household. We didn't fight; we enjoyed meals together on the weekends; we looked out for each other. Good friends. Nobody writes songs about those things, but there is a lot to be said for them. We had done better than my pub-quiz teammate Sheilagh and her husband, Chad, who cared for everyone except each other. Or our friends Randall and Mandy, whose battle for custody of their IVF twins had left casualties from San Jose to Liverpool. Or my parents, for that matter.

But the last few years had seen a fading of what was left of the romance. Two months earlier, I had purchased a single bed for my study, ostensibly because of my snoring and Claire needing her sleep because she had a lot going on with the prospective sale of her software company. Our sex life had followed me out of the bedroom and I didn't miss it as much as I thought I would. I wasn't sure if that was a good or bad thing.

Our situation was probably not so different from that of many couples our age. It would be a stretch to blame any shortcomings on a relationship that had ended twenty-two years earlier. I didn't think about Angelina when I was deep in a database-tuning problem, or trying to recall the name of the Bonzo Dog Doo-Dah Band's lead singer, or giving Claire a kiss on the forehead as she left for work. It was only when I was listening to music or on the rare occasion I played a song on the piano. For those few minutes or hours, I would be back in 1989.

I was playing in a bar—not a pub, a *bar*—in Melbourne, up a staircase off Victoria Parade in the inner-city suburb of Fitzroy. It was one of the few places that stayed open late, drawing a mix of yuppies and baby boomers. In those days, a baby boomer was a person born shortly after the war, not someone like me who came along almost twenty years later.

Most nights the boomers outnumbered the yuppies, and my sixties and seventies repertoire got a good workout. There was a steady trickle of customers early in the evening, but it only got busy with the after-dinner crowd and the stragglers from the pubs shaking out their umbrellas, piling their winter coats and woolen hats on the stand, and ordering an ice-cold lager. It was early July, midwinter, and Australia had yet to deliver on its promise of sunshine.

The place would not have won any prizes for interior decoration. There was a bar that seated eight or ten on stools, a dozen small tables, a couple of leather sofas, and old movie posters on the walls. No meals—just bar snacks. But once a crowd built up, with more patrons standing than sitting, the noise and smoke provided enough atmosphere to compensate.

I had been in Australia three weeks. A local insurance company was implementing a new-generation database and I had landed a fifteen-month consulting assignment that would give me a tour of its branches around the world. I was twenty-six, barely five years out of a computer science degree, riding a wave of technology that the old-timers in their thirties had failed to catch. Computing was my passport out of my lower-middle-class, comprehensive-school origins—after I had abandoned the more obvious option of becoming a rock star.

In my first week in Melbourne, I tagged along to the bar with a few workmates to celebrate one of them becoming a father and ended up playing a couple of songs on the piano. I remember doing "Walk Away Renée" in homage to the new arrival, who had been given that name. The barman, a knockabout bloke named Shanksy, gave me a half pint—a *pot*—of lager. I thanked him for letting me use the piano and he said, "Anytime, mate."

I took up his offer and the bar became my social life. Shanksy looked after my drinks and I put a tip jar on the piano. I did all right with it, but money was not the motivation. My day job paid well and included an accommodation allowance, which covered a warehouse apartment above a vegetarian restaurant in Brunswick Street, a fifteen-minute tram ride from work and a ten-minute stagger from the bar.

I got to know the piano well. It was a locally made Beale, old, but with a nice sound, and there was even a microphone and a small amplifier. I would drop in on the way to work or after my morning jog and entertain the cleaners with my scales.

In the evenings, it made all the difference. Without it I would have been a loner paying for my own drinks, with no reason to talk to anyone and no reason for anyone to talk to me. And too much time to think about the hole in my life.


I didn't see her walk in. I saw her when she came over to the piano. In a town that dressed in black, she was wearing a white woolen dress and high boots. Mid-twenties, shoulder-length dark brown hair against light skin, maybe five foot seven with the heels.

She had a pink cocktail in her hand. We were in what was technically a cocktail bar, but this was Australia and most people drank beer, wine, and simple mixed drinks unless they got into downing shots—B52s and Flaming Lamborghinis. The collection of liqueurs behind the bar was more for show and Shanksy's cocktail repertoire was limited. But tonight he had produced a pink one. With a cherry and an umbrella.

I was playing Van Morrison's "Brown Eyed Girl" and she stood to one side of the piano, close enough to let me know she was there, sipping her cocktail.

When I had finished, she clapped, walked up, and asked: "Do you know 'Because the Night'?"

I had a chance to look at her more closely and was struck by her eyes: big and brown, and, under the right one, a streak of mascara tracking halfway down her cheek.

I don't usually notice perfume unless it has just been applied. Perhaps hers had been, because it was strong and distinct. For the record, it was Obsession by Calvin Klein. Ever since, I have been able to detect it at twenty paces. A woman steps onto the bus and I pick it up, along with all the memories attached to it. Proust's madeleines.

"It's by Patti Smith," she said, while I was wondering if I should say something about her mascara.

"And Bruce Springsteen."

"Say that again," she said, and laughed.

"Bruce Springsteen. They wrote it together. Springsteen never did a studio recording, but it's on his live album."

*"Root i' togevver, eh? Loovely."*

Her impression of my accent would have placed me closer to Glasgow than Manchester but it was accompanied by a light-up-the-room smile.

I gave her a look of mock offense.

"Sorry," she said. "I didn't mean to be rude. I just love your accent."

I decided to take the risk of being rude myself and drew my finger down my left cheek.

We had an exchange of touching our faces, nodding and laughing as she got the message, wet her finger, rubbed the wrong cheek, then managed to turn the streak into a smear on the right one.

"Hold on," I said, and walked to the bar, where there was a pile of paper napkins. On the way back, I realized that the place had gone quiet, and not just because the piano player had taken a break. Everyone—from Shanksy behind the bar to the couple standing in the doorway still wearing their coats—was watching me. Watching us. I had no desire to play out in public what I had begun to imagine as a tender moment, nor to draw attention to the fact that she might have been crying.

I blew my nose on the napkin, stuffed it in my pocket, and sat back at the piano.

"So, 'Because the Night,' was it?"

She wiped her cheek with the back of her hand, then looked around the room.

"It's okay," I said. "You got most of it."

"Would you mind if I sang?"

In general, the answer to "Can I sing with the band?" is a polite "No," a response based on experience and the advice of my dad. He used to have—he said—a firm rule that nobody, but *nobody*, got to sing or play with whatever band he was in.

"If Eric Clapton comes in and wants to play, I'll tell him he can bugger off. Because if the owner decides he likes Clapton better than us, then he's got our gig and we don't eat."

He delivered his lesson in job security so many times that, despite the improbability of Mr. Clapton deciding to settle for the audience and financial rewards of the King's Head in Manchester, it became family history as an actual event.

"You know," my mother would say, "your dad once told Eric Clapton to bugger off—'scuse the French, but that's what he said—so he could get on with earning a living. There's a lesson there."

My dad may or may not have said "bugger off" to God, but I would be prepared to bet that his response to the young woman with the big brown eyes would have been the same as mine, even without the pressure of a bar full of people waiting for something to happen.

"What key?"

She was not bad, and the crowd loved her. I mean, they *loved* her. She was in tune and giving it all she had, but it was a sexy song and she was more Olivia Newton-John than Debbie Harry—or Patti Smith, for that matter.

Who was I to judge? She got a standing ovation and calls for more. After one five-minute performance she owned the place, and I was a part of it. I had no idea what was going on.

"Would you like to do something else?" I asked.

"'Daydream Believer'?" She laughed. "That's your accent, isn't it? Davy Jones."

She had a good ear. And a commendable familiarity with popular music from before her time.

"What number is this, Jim?" I said, mimicking Davy Jones.

That smile again: "Seven A." A *very* commendable familiarity.

"Do you know 'Both Sides Now'?" she said.

"Never heard of it."

I played the intro. This was not going to be as stimulating as having her standing three feet away hoarsely asking someone to touch her now. But the Joni Mitchell song was probably closer to what her singing teacher would have recommended, and she did it nicely.

She had looked at clouds and love and had begun looking at life when a short, sharp guy in a blue pinstripe suit with red braces and gelled hair came up on her other side and stood there, radiating impatience. He was about thirty-five and studiedly good-looking in a Michael Douglas sort of way. Gordon Gekko in *Wall Street*.

I did an extra reprise of the final chorus, which he responded to with a glare and pursed lips in case his folded arms were not sending the message. As soon as she had sung the last line, he dropped a coin in the tip jar. I wound the song up and thought that would be the end of it. Gordon Gekko began to walk away, but my singer stayed where she was, right beside me.

"Do you know 'Angel of the Morning'?" she said.

I hit an A chord and raised my eyebrows to see that she was happy with the key, which I guessed would test her upper range. She responded by singing the first line a cappella.

I automatically brought my heel down to begin counting the beat. If you tap your toe, the rhythm stays in your foot; tap your heel and you feel it through your body. I felt more than that. She put her hand on my shoulder and pressed gently in time with me. It was an extraordinarily intimate gesture, given that we were not just in front of, but surrounded by, an audience: *I don't care if anyone's watching—let's do this, just you and me, and thank you for being here and on my side.*

The loud cough and dirty look from her minder said: *Play another chord and I'll break your arms.*

I played an E. I was in a bar in Melbourne, not the South Side of Chicago, and the pretty guy in a suit was no Leroy Brown.

He looked at me. My singer looked at me. They looked at each other. Then they walked toward the door. She still had a faint black mark on her cheek.

I should have just let them go. They were customers, and had done nothing to provoke me beyond the insulting tip.

It was, in part, a reaction to him pushing her around, and to her acquiescing, only a few minutes after having the courage to take on a challenging song in front of a bar crowd.

It had also been a bad day at work. I'd been dubbed Seagull, after a joke that consultants fly in, do a lot of flapping and squawking, shit all over everybody, and fly out. I had probably earned it, trying too hard to make an impression that justified being paid three times what the permanent employees were getting. I was technically up to the task, but still green at the consulting game.

And there *was* the tip. Gordon Gekko had no way of knowing about my well-paid day job. I may have been channeling my late father when I gave him a Lennon–McCartney send-off.

"You're Gonna Lose That Girl."

They both turned around. It was too dark to read their expressions. I had to finish the song, to maintain the pretense that the choice was coincidental. It took me further than I had intended. They were both stopped in the doorway, listening as I sang about making a point of taking her away from him, yeah.

Yeah, yeah, yeah. In the end it was me who lost the girl.


*Hi*, said the computer screen.

*Meow*, said Elvis, rubbing against my leg.

*Mum*, said my phone, switched to silent.

One thing at a time.

"I've got the results," said my mother. "I'm afraid it's bad news."

I knew her better than to respond with anything more than a neutral "It's late in the day to be getting results." It was after ten P.M.

"I've had them for hours. I didn't want to spoil your dinner."

"Oh."

"They couldn't find anything. So we still don't know what it is."

An outpouring of relief that my mother did not have cancer would only have prompted a homily on misplaced optimism, likely illustrated with a story from my childhood that I had chosen to forget.

*Hi* was still looking at me. A link to my past and a chance for a reality check. Nothing more than that. She was ten thousand miles away. One little drink couldn't hurt.

I filled the cat's water bowl and walked back to the computer. Claire had gone to bed.

Reply to Sender.

*Hi*. As my finger hovered over the mouse, I saw her again, standing by the piano, tear track down her cheek, trying to hide her nerves. Enlisting me as her ally: "I just love your accent."

Backspace.

*Ay up lass*, I typed.

Send.

# 2

As I was emptying the tip jar, having played through to closing time, Shanksy walked by with his bucket and mop.

"You know who that was, don't you?" he said.

"Who do you mean?"

I was kidding, of course. It had been a quiet night for young women with beautiful brown eyes walking into the bar and singing "Take me now."

"Sergeant Carey from *Mornington Police*. Angelina Brown."

My singer did *not* look like a cop. Why would I recognize a police officer from out of town anyway? And was her name Carey or Brown?

Shanksy cleared up the confusion, which was due to my recent arrival in the country that had given the world *Neighbours* and *Home and Away*. "Carey" was in fact "Kerrie": only on television are police sergeants referred to by their first names. Ms. Brown was an actress, which explained the special reception.

"Who was the boyfriend?" I asked.

"No idea. I've never seen her in here before. Not a bad set."

"Thanks," I said. "You liked the Beatles song?"

He laughed. "'You're Gonna Lose That Girl.' Sailing close to the wind, mate. Lucky everyone else was thinking the same thing."

Except everyone else knew who she was and that she was out of my league. I must have been the only person in the bar who had felt it might be the beginning of something. There is a particular magic when people play and sing together, and it had been there at the piano, along with the tease about my accent and the moment with the mascara. But my ungracious parting shot would have blown any chance I might have had.

Perhaps there was an element of self-sabotage. My move to Australia had been prompted by more than the promise of money and sunshine. There had been a relationship—my first serious relationship—back in the UK. After eighteen months together, nine of them sharing a flat and a cat, Joanna wanted to have children and I was not ready. Trouble was, I wasn't sure I would ever be ready. I couldn't put a date on it. It had ended with me catching a plane to the other side of the world. Now I wanted to work myself out before I let anyone else down.

Even if I had been looking for a new partner, I would not have chosen a well-known actress who should have been free to sing a couple of songs without being stalked by the pianist. In any case, she apparently had a boyfriend. For all those reasons, I didn't do anything about it.

Angelina did. A fortnight later, she walked into the bar, alone. It was six P.M. and the place was empty. Normally I would not have been there so early, but I had asked one of the admin staff from work out for dinner, my first date in Australia. Angelina was indirectly responsible. She had awoken something, even if it was just my mother's mantra of getting on with it.

The obvious way to begin my date with Tina was with some special attention at *my* bar. We had come straight from the office, so I was in suit and tie, with my hair cut and beard trimmed for the occasion.

The absence of other customers detracted a little from the effect I was aiming for, but we took a table near the bar and had just ordered drinks when Angelina walked in.

She was showing none of the self-confidence that had fueled "Because the Night"; rather, the uncertainty that had undermined its credibility. She looked younger than I remembered her. She caught my eye, saw Tina, and turned to leave. Then, one table away from the door, she sat down.

It took a few moments before I allowed myself to believe that she might have come to see me, and a few more to realize that this was exactly what her actions had signaled, right down to deciding that she didn't want to confirm my suspicions by walking out.

When Shanksy walked over to take her order, Tina said, "Isn't that Angelina Brown?"

Normally I would have responded by showing off my recently acquired knowledge: "From *Mornington Police*. She plays Sergeant Kerrie, doesn't she?" Instead I said, "Who?"

"She's an actress in a soapie. I watched it once or twice, you know, just to see what it was about. She plays the smart one, not the hot one, but seeing her here in person, she's quite attractive. You think so?"

I took the opportunity to look at her again.

"She's okay," I said. I thought she was the most beautiful woman I had ever seen.

"She's always solving the crime or counseling people, and she seems really together, but she's actually having an affair with a pathologist. She's not married but he is, and he's a slimeball, and everyone wants her to get a grip and go with the detective sergeant who really likes her but who's too shy to say anything. . . . Anyway, like I said, I don't really watch it."

At least Tina was giving me time to think. Why had Angelina left it so long? What about the boyfriend? How was I going to connect with her before she walked out of my life again?

I could hardly ask Tina to make herself scarce so I could pursue another woman. Even putting aside basic decency, it would have been career suicide to insult the woman who ran the office football tipping competition and was thus connected with everyone in the department. I could have claimed to have met Angelina before—friend of a friend— or, God forbid, told the simple truth that she had sung at the piano one night, but I had effectively stated that I did not know her. There was no practical way I could give Shanksy a message to deliver in front of Tina.

Behind the bar, he poured Angelina an orange juice. She was not going to stick around. Somehow I had to get a message to her. And in that thought lay the answer. It was a clunky answer, but it would have to do.

I intercepted Shanksy on his way to Angelina's table.

"Tina, this is Shanksy. Tell her what I do here."

"He's the piano player. When he feels like it."

"No way," said Tina.

I signaled to Shanksy to refill her glass and walked to the piano, now having an excuse to play to the empty house.

I was struggling to think of the words to the Bee Gees' "I've Gotta Get a Message to You." *The preacher tortured me?*

I was at the piano, about to regale a beautiful woman with a fudged impression of the brothers Gibb, when inspiration of sorts arrived.

"You Are So Beautiful."

It was more of a one A.M. last-drinks-stagger-off-into-the-night closer, but the sentiment was on the mark.

I was under way before I had time to consider the rest of the song. It was not a total screw-up, like singing "Go Away Little Girl," but the lyrics needed Joe Cocker's voice to offset the schmaltziness.

I did my best. I tried to keep looking toward Tina rather than Angelina, singing about a woman being everything I'd hoped for, the joy and happiness she brought me, a gift from heaven, and then I realized that Angelina might think I was singing it for my date. So, as I growled the last drawn-out "to me," feeling a complete idiot, I turned to Angelina and gave her what I hoped was a meaningful look.

She was laughing.

I went back to my table and could tell something was wrong. Surely one look had not given me away? I had focused on Tina for most of the song.

That turned out to be the problem—and the solution.

"Adam, that was lovely," she said, "but . . . wow. Just a bit heavy. I mean, we don't really know each other yet. I'm just getting over a relationship, and I'm more about—you know—having a good time."

Being taken to an empty bar and serenaded with a full-on love song at six P.M. was probably an unnerving start to a first date with the new guy in the office.

"Hey," I said, "me too."

"I wish that were true," said Tina, "but it's obvious you're looking for something more. Would you be really upset if we just called it a night now? I can get the tram, and then it's like nothing happened."

I began to stand, but Tina stopped me.

"It's okay. We can finish our drinks. You seem like a really sensitive person. It just wasn't what I was expecting. After the way you are at work. No offense."

While Tina finished her drink, Angelina walked to the bar, settled her account, and disappeared down the stairs.

Shanksy waited until I had paid—"Playing one song for your girlfriend doesn't get you two free drinks"—and allowed me to get halfway to the door before calling me back.

"Almost forgot. Your girlfriend left you this."

He gave me an envelope, with *English Piano Player* written on the front. In another pen, Angelina had added *and friend*. She had probably just been planning to drop it in, not expecting I would be there so early in the evening.

It was a photocopied invitation to a farewell party for Jenny and Bryce, strangers to me. They were "off to England," probably to live in Earl's Court, work in a bar, and save for a hitchhiking trip around Europe. Or, more likely, to get some up-to-date experience in database design so there would be no need for overpaid imports like me.

The party was accordingly themed "Bring a Brit." It was hardly insulting—even a little more respectful and euphonious than the "Bring a Pom" that my workmates would no doubt have written—but I had allowed my imagination to run to something more personal.

# 3

The following Friday, I fetched up just after ten P.M. at a double-story house in the eastern suburbs. It was a big party, maybe seventy guests, mostly in jeans, although more stylishly dressed than I would have expected of twenty-somethings. Actors and crew, perhaps: cooler than the IT crowd.

Angelina was standing in the living room with a group of women of about her own age. She was wearing a bright burgundy jacket with a short skirt, a beret, and quite a bit of makeup: striking, but distinctly different from her look in the bar when she delivered the invitation, which in turn was different from that first night singing. The perfume was the same.

She opened a gap for me, touched me on the arm, and smiled a silent welcome. I took the opportunity to check her left hand: no ring.

They were deep into a conversation about tactics for defending a drunk-driving charge, and Angelina managed to convey without words that she was pleased that I had come and if I could put up with her friends' rudeness in not pausing to let her introduce me, she would do so in due course. Although she might like to contribute to the discussion first. And, in the meantime, don't go away.

I smiled. I wasn't going anywhere.

The conversation was lighthearted, but it was apparent that the young woman on the verge of losing her driver's license was struggling to appreciate the more outrageous suggestions, most of which were coming from a Jayne Mansfield look-alike with an irritatingly childish voice.

Angelina offered the first serious suggestion. "How long does your probationary license have left to run?"

"Why?"

"Because they go by the date of the court case, not the date you got booked."

"Are you sure?"

"Pretty sure. If you're on a full license on the day you go to court, you'll only get a suspension. If you're nice to the magistrate."

"Nice to the magistrate" set Jayne Mansfield off again, and left me to conclude that Angelina must have some experience with the law—in the negative sense. The wild, law-breaking actress.

She had still not managed to introduce me when a familiar figure materialized. He was wearing black slacks, a black rollneck sweater, and polished shoes. He looked older than most of the other guests.

He gave me a quick appraisal, raised his eyebrows, but did not acknowledge me directly.

"Richard!" said Jayne Mansfield to the man formerly known as Gordon Gekko. "Miranda got booked at point-oh-eight. There's some way she can get off, right?"

"Pass. I leave my work at the office." He smirked. "Like Angelina. She only does sex at work."

Okay. It seemed they were a couple. He was apparently a lawyer. And unquestionably a first-class arsehole.

Jayne Mansfield responded with a giggle that went on longer than it needed to. I looked directly at Richard, and his expression made it clear that his joke was meant to contain a barb.

Angelina stood there, taking it. I was familiar with the dynamic and not just from the night she had sung at the bar. My father had a coruscating wit that would have left Richard in the shade. As a child I had spent too much time listening to him use it on my mother.

Richard gave the lie to his statement about leaving work at the office by launching into an anecdote about a judge's daughter who had been charged with soliciting.

I squeezed Angelina's arm, I hoped discreetly, and walked to the dining room. A few moments later she followed.

"What was that about?" I said.

"She didn't mean any harm. She's just a bit of a ditz."

"I didn't mean her."

"Too much to drink. Don't worry about it. Not your problem."

I waited, and she added, "We broke up. A week ago. It's still a bit raw for both of us."

"Can I get you a drink?" I said.

"I'd love one. Thank you. You're being very sweet."

On my way to the kitchen, I realized that she didn't know my name, which was probably why she hadn't introduced me. By the time I found vodka, orange juice, and ice, she had wandered off.

I eventually spotted her at the top of the stairs. There was a handwritten sign at the base: *No guests upstairs please.*

I took her drink up. "I didn't feel like any more conversation," she said. "With anyone else, I mean."

"Hard to have a conversation without anyone else," I said, and she smiled at the lame joke. "I'm Adam."

"That's a shame. I'd hoped you'd have an *uh* sound in your name, to go with your accent."

"Like Gus? Or Duncan? Or Douglas?"

"Dooglas." She laughed. It was an attractive laugh, a little tipsy but not drunken, and I liked being the cause of it. "Sorry. You're not offended, are you?"

"You can call me any name you want." Even a Scottish one.

"All right, Dooglas," she said. "What did you do with your girlfriend?"

I told her the Tina story, at length, throwing in a few Mancunianisms to go with the accent, and she laughed through it. I was enjoying myself, too.

"It was a nice choice of song," she said. "I don't get called beautiful too often and it's what everyone's looking for in my world."

"You have to trust the spontaneous song test. It's like word asso-ciation. Never lies."

"Come on," she said. "That night I sang with you. I saw myself in the mirror afterwards. Mascara everywhere. I looked like Alice Cooper."

"You realize I'll never look at Alice Cooper again without think-ing of you. I may decide he's the sexiest man on the planet."

The music from downstairs had stopped for a few minutes, but it came back with a roar: Joe Cocker singing "You Can Leave Your Hat On." Angelina smiled and touched my arm, starting a nonverbal con-versation that seemed to go:

*I'd like you to kiss me.*

*You're not really saying that, are you?*

*I'm really saying that. That's why I haven't let go of your arm.*

*No, you can't be. Not to me. Not to Adam Sharp, the database guy from Manchester.*

*I'm standing here with my face turned up toward yours, and it's going to be awkward for both of us if you don't kiss me.*

I had not kissed anyone for a while. I closed my eyes and fell into it: the softness, the openness, the unreality of who she was. I didn't want to stop but we were out in the open, visible to anyone who chose to look up from the base of the stairs.

We pulled each other down the hallway, and there was a bedroom—the master bedroom by the look of it, with family photos and an en-suite bathroom. No lock on the inside of the door, so after I closed it, I leaned against it while I kissed her again.

After a few seconds she broke the kiss, turned us around so she had her back against the door, and said, "See, I don't only do sex at work." It could have been a sultry come-on, but her tone was more defensive than seductive. For a moment I wondered if she was referring to what we had done already, if she had made her point, but then she pulled me into her again.

There was not a lot of foreplay, and that was her fault as much as mine. It was straight to hitched-up, unzipped, and pushed-aside clothes, with Angelina sandwiched between me and the door. I was no longer feeling overwhelmed. We were two people making love, and the rest didn't matter.

Then, out of the blue, she let go a series of gasps that morphed from ecstasy to apparent surprise that it had happened so quickly. But before either Joe Cocker or I could finish, Angelina disentangled herself, picked up her handbag, and made a dash for the bathroom. She was still wearing her beret.

She was gone a good ten minutes, time I used to mentally kick myself for taking it too fast. My fears were confirmed when she emerged: she went straight to the door with an expression that said *What have I done?* I picked up our glasses and followed her downstairs, took a detour at the bathroom to clean up the lipstick that had found its way onto my face, and then could not find her.

Richard was still in the living room. He peeled off from a conversation with Jayne Mansfield as I walked past. If he had had too much to drink before, he was now comprehensively leathered.

"Sorry, *my friend*, gone. Gone home without you. I have some advice for you, *choom*."

I thought he was about to warn me off, threaten me. Jayne Mansfield looked excited at the prospect.

Richard managed to string another sentence together. "In the words of the immortal bard, all that glisters is not gold."

There were plenty of comebacks to that, but there was no point getting drawn in.

The hostess confirmed that Angelina had left, and let me use the phone to call a taxi. But not before she had commented on my Union Jack sweatshirt.

"Nice to see a man who's proud of his heritage."

"Just a nod to the theme of the party."

"What theme?"

# 4

That could have been the end of it. Not exactly something to tell the grandchildren, but a memory to bring a smile whenever I heard "You Can Leave Your Hat On." Or "Because the Night." Or "Both Sides Now." Or "You Are So Beautiful."

Everything suggested a one-off, and I suppose a reasonable person might have concluded that this was not the first time a woman on the rebound would pick up a random guy for a quick encounter and toss him aside afterward.

It didn't sit. My head told me that she would not have gone to the trouble of inventing and delivering an invitation to satisfy a passing fancy. My gut told me that there was something more between us. And in the bedroom: I had no sense that she was using me. I replayed her hurried exit and saw embarrassment rather than disconnection.

That said, I was still Adam Sharp and she was Angelina Brown.

When I was at school, there was the usual drama of dates for the end-of-year dance. Those of us without girlfriends were in the awkward position of having to ask someone out—and the girls were in the more awkward position of saying, "No, I'd like to wait for a better option, but if things get desperate . . ."

There was a girl named Sarah. I liked her a lot, but she was drop-dead gorgeous—unfortunately for me, because I had convinced myself that, alone among my classmates who fancied her, I appreciated her finer qualities. Her looks put her out of my reach. It was only a couple of days before the dance, when I had organized to go with another girl, that Sarah asked if I would partner her. She had been waiting for me to ask. *Everyone* had thought she was out of their reach.

That was a time I would have liked my dad—not the dad of my early teens who was never home but the version of him who taught me to play piano when I was a child—to have been around to give me some words of wisdom. Perhaps, eight years on, fate was offering me a second chance.

It took three phone calls to locate Angelina's agent.

Australian-posh female voice: "A personal message? If you have a fan letter, you may send it care of our office. And you might want to make certain that you have the right person. Miss Brown plays the sergeant, not Constable Danni."

"I'm not a fan. I work in a bar. She left something here the other night."

"I can take care of that. What did she leave?"

"A record. 'Because the Night' by Patti Smith."

"I doubt she'll be too concerned about a record. I'm sure you can keep it."

"It's signed. *To Angelina—from Patti.* That's how we worked out who it belonged to." Genius.

"Very well. I'll come and collect it myself."

No point backing down now. "Lovely. We'll keep it behind the bar." I gave her the details, and briefed Shanksy to tell her that the record had disappeared if she turned up.


The agent didn't turn up. Nor was there any contact from Angelina.

In the absence of a life beyond work and the bar, I spent a bit of time contemplating what to do next. In the middle of the night, some of my ideas seemed inspired, but in the light of day they all risked making me look like a stalker. Angelina had given no indication that she wanted to see me again. She knew where the bar was.

Looking for a solution only increased my desire to see her again.

She had been interested enough to invite me to the party and then upstairs. There was chemistry: I had felt it at the piano and again at the party—not to mention in the bedroom. And while Richard might have had the edge on me in looks and profession, he seemed intent on poisoning the well rather than recovering the relationship. I couldn't shake the feeling that something momentous had happened and that she had felt it too. Maybe, just maybe, if I played it right, I had a chance.

The bar had a television that was only used occasionally. Shanksy was prepared to turn it on in the early evening when the bar was quiet, and for the next three Mondays we watched the weekly episode of *Mornington Police.*

Richard's jibe about Angelina doing sex at work had some basis in reality. Her character, Sergeant Kerrie, was the smart and stable one at the station, but, as foreshadowed by Tina, she was pursuing a relationship with the district pathologist, a married man. It was family viewing, and there was nothing too explicit. Nevertheless, I hoped the actor who played Dr. Andrews did not go on to international success, as I had taken a deep dislike to him.

The surprise was Danni, the hot one, who was tasked with patrolling the beach in plainclothes, a brief that the costume department had interpreted liberally. She was played by the woman I had dubbed Jayne Mansfield, and was about as interesting on-screen as in real life.

I made a note of the production company and decided to try one more time. My approach had to be confident but not arrogant, admiring but not sycophantic, about her but also about me. Dramatic, perhaps, given her profession. Creative, to match her Bring a Brit invention. And intelligent. It was going to take a fair bit of intelligence to meet all the other requirements.

The florist sold me a dozen roses—seven white and five red—and I arranged them in the form of a piano octave on a length of cardboard, the red roses doing duty as the black keys. We punched holes and fastened the flowers in place with wire ties.

Over the florist's protests, I flattened three of the rose heads with the side of my fist to make an A chord, the triad I had played to introduce "Angel of the Morning," the song her boyfriend had not let her sing. A for Angelina. And Adam. Could I pack any more meaning into crushed roses?

I could. I squashed the white G rose to make the chord a natural seventh—a lead-in, tension, anticipation.

The florist agreed that a card would be overkill.

I had never done anything like this before: a bunch of roses on Valentine's Day was my previous benchmark. It was probably a good thing I had not confided in anyone but the florist, who had a vested interest, or I would probably have let myself be talked out of it.

I was in the bar until closing that night. And the night after that, living on nuts and cheese twists while I twisted myself into a knot, turning around after every song to scan the bar, running through scenarios of what I might say.

On the third night, I finished by playing the Tom Waits song generally known as "Closing Time" (correct title: "I Hope That I Don't Fall in Love with You") to an almost empty room and when I looked up there she was, in the half-dark, sitting alone with a green cocktail, dressed in jeans and a loose sweater. The song was apposite, if too late. It would be some time before I acknowledged that I was in love with Angelina, but the feelings were all there at that moment.

I went to the bar, more to compose myself than anything else.

"What's she drinking?" I asked Shanksy.

"It's called a Fallen Angel. Gin, lemon, crème de menthe. Smells like mouthwash."

"Better make me a nine-inch pianist."

He just looked at me.

"It's a joke. A genie offers a guy one wish . . ."

"I know the joke." He pulled me a beer. "Be nice. She's as nervous as you are."

Nervous or not, the piano man is as much a student of human behavior as his coworkers behind the bar. I reminded myself that the biggest hurdle had been getting Angelina to turn up. Things would be relatively straightforward from here on.

She spoke before I had time to sit down.

"I'm not staying. I just wanted to say thank you for the roses—it was really sweet, and very clever, and I love your accent, but the thing at the party was a mistake. I've never done anything like that before. I'm married. To Richard. We've separated, but I'm not ready for anything new. I'm sorry if I gave you the wrong idea."

Speech over, she began to stand. Her glass was still half full. And I was suddenly empty, drained.

Deep breath. Smile. "No problem. You didn't give me the wrong idea. But finish your drink. It's fine."

"Thanks. I was feeling terrible. I mean, I love your accent. . . ."

The bloody accent again. What about the piano, the sparkling wit, and the athletic but considerate sexual performance?

She sat down. She was wearing wedding and engagement rings. She saw me looking.

"I should have told you at the party. I just assume everyone . . . I went there straight from work and I don't wear my rings when I'm filming. And I'm not ready to take them off yet. Which I guess must tell you something."

"You must have got married young," I said.

"I was twenty-two. I'm twenty-three now."

A short attention span. Or a bad decision.

She read my mind. "I don't want to jump from one relationship to another. I'm not even sure this one is over. So I am definitely, absolutely not available."

"But you like my accent."

"I looove your ahk-cent."

"But not enough to be me regular bonk, eh?"

She laughed and drained her glass. "I don't want to be anyone's regular anything at the moment. I need to get my head straight."

She got up again. I was about to move toward her to give her a kiss good-bye, while trying to think of how to buy some time, when I realized that she was considering something.

"Can I ask you a question?" she said.

I gave her what I hoped was a reassuring and encouraging nod.

"You promise you'll answer honestly?"

"Any reason I wouldn't?"

"Yes. That's why I need you to promise. And that you won't tell anyone I asked."

"Spit it out, lass."

She half turned away, then swiveled back. "Was I okay? I mean . . ."

I knew what she meant. And if I were to answer honestly, I would have had to say: "How the hell can I tell in sixty seconds, while I'm trying to concentrate on staying upright, not dropping you, and wondering if the banging on the door was your husband or just us? Plus, wanting to do it well enough that you'd want to do it again with me. Which apparently I didn't.

"On the other hand, when you're twenty-six and haven't had sex for three months, all sex is good, let alone sex with the most beautiful woman you've ever met. But if you want to know if you're good in bed, you'll have to audition properly."

I said, "I'll get us both drinks and then I'll answer."

Which I did. I told her the truth, with a subtle emphasis on the part about auditioning properly, and she laughed. With a drink to keep her there, I asked my own question.

"So what's this all about, then?"

"You really want to know?"

"I really want to know."

She folded her arms. "I never slept with anyone before Richard."

"Nothing to be ashamed of," I said. "Personally, I think you're quite attractive."

"Stop it. You ask me what it's about, I tell you, and then you make fun of me. Anyway, it was the opposite problem. Which is not as much fun as you might think it is. Too many creeps."

I was wise to have abandoned my less-sophisticated plans for contacting her.

"What about before. At school?"

"I went to a girls' school. They weren't big on helping us find boyfriends. My parents . . . my mother is very straight. No living together, no sex before marriage. I didn't sign up to that, but I suppose it made me a bit cautious."

"You were living at home?"

"Even after I got the part in *Mornington Police*. You know that's what I do, right?"

"I do now. I didn't when I met you."

"It's pretty demanding. I do classes and singing lessons as well: it gives you more options. I wasn't avoiding relationships but this is what I really want to do, and I didn't want to let myself down by not making the most of my chances. And I don't look like Nicole Kidman, so I have to work harder."

"Given a choice . . ."

"Don't. Anyway, Richard came along. I was twenty-one, so it wasn't as if I'd spent years waiting to meet someone."

No one-night stands before twenty-one? My tally at that age had been two, and I was living away from home and trying hard. I was more surprised that she had not had a steady boyfriend.

Whether as a result of inexperience or unreasonable expectations, it had not gone well with Richard, but he seemed adept at deflecting the blame onto Angelina. His dig at the party was closer to the bone than I had realized.

"So you decided to get an independent assessment?" I said.

"No!" She was a little tipsy. Shanksy had gone home, leaving me to close up, after provisioning us with a bottle of sparkling wine.

She topped up her glass. "All right. When you're constantly being told you're no good, but the other person isn't doing anything to try to make it better, you start to wonder. I was pretty upset with him that night."

"You'd broken up. You didn't need an excuse. And you don't need to feel guilty about it."

"I do, though. It was only a week, and I was hoping he'd apologize. I guess I still am. But I'm starting to think it's me who should say sorry."

"What did he do that needed an apology?"

"Had dinner with someone else. He wouldn't tell me who."

"Just dinner?"

"Supposedly. But he'd already lied about it. He said he was working late."

"Cut and dried. His fault. His apology. And he should tell you who it was."

"He said he needed someone to talk to. About us. Which is what I'm doing now, right?"

"You're single."

"He wouldn't have needed to talk to someone if we hadn't had problems. So it comes back to me."

"Is that why you invited me to the party, then? Someone to talk to? And don't tell me you needed an Englishman to get in the door. It took me all day to find that sweatshirt."

She laughed, then spent some time playing with her drink. "I just wanted someone in my corner," she said at last. "I didn't want to go, but I thought, screw it, I don't want this problem we're having stopping me saying good-bye to Bryce and Jenny."

"They were real people?"

"Of course. It was great that you came, but I'm still hoping Richard and I can work it out."

I raised my eyebrows.

"It's not as bad as it sounds," she said. "I thought that if we got through the problem with sex, *my* problem with sex, a lot of the rest would go away. He always said that. We have a lot of good things. What happened at the party . . . It was something I should have done before I got married, obviously."

"So, all sorted then? Seriously, did it help at all?"

"In a way."

"Go on."

She laughed uncomfortably. "This is really between you and me?"

"I told you."

"I said I had problems. Real problems. I've never been able to . . . get there. Not with Richard. And, like I said, there hasn't been anyone else."

Not in a year of marriage in bed at leisure with the man she supposedly loved, but up against a door with a virtual stranger in less time than it took Joe Cocker to give instructions on undressing? Sex is a strange and wonderful thing. Whatever transpired, she would have a reason to remember me. But was she sharing too much, giving me that openness you allow yourself only with strangers whose judgment doesn't matter because you won't see them again?

"So, thanks," she said. "I feel a bit better about myself. Not completely hopeless."

"You were a long way from hopeless. I wouldn't have chased you all over Melbourne otherwise."

I could have put it better, but she smiled. "Thank you. I really appreciate it. Really. In a year's time . . ." She set her glass down on the table. "I have to go."

"Where?"

"I'm staying with my parents. The house is Richard's. I was the one who left."

"I'll play you a song," I said, standing up.

"I've really got to go."

"One song." I walked to the piano. "Bob Dylan."

"No. You are not going to sing 'Lay Lady Lay.'"

She laughed, but I made a quick switch. I played the first verse and the chorus of "If You've Gotta Go, Go Now," and she stood beside me, almost against me, still laughing. It's a funny song, as rock songs go, and it was late and we'd had a bit to drink. I heaped on the accent, purely in the service of comedy, of course.

"Are those my only choices?" she said after I had wound up with a dramatic, if hammy, solo. "Go now or stay all night? I really do have to go home, but . . ."

I stood up and looked straight into her big brown eyes to confirm that I had understood her correctly. Then I put my hand under her chin and said, "Will you have dinner with me?"

It was not the response she was expecting, and I could not tell if she was disappointed or relieved. Both, I hoped. I let her think about her reply while I thought about what I had said no to.

"Why?" she said.

"To finish the conversation. We were just getting started."

"How long are you here?"

"Three more months. Until the end of the year. Then it's New

Zealand, Singapore, Hong Kong, South Africa, Zimbabwe, and back home to finish up. I'll be a road warrior till August next year."

"Sounds like a great job."

"It's brilliant. But not if you're looking for a long-term relationship. That time on the road is locked in, nonnegotiable."

"I really, really don't want a relationship. I mean that."

"Me neither. There was someone back in the UK. So I know where you're coming from."

"All right," she said. "But no relationship. No falling in love. Nobody getting hurt."

"I'll take that as a yes."

"One date. Dooglas."

# 5

Melbourne is a sprawling metropolis. I had not come to grips with how sprawling: my longest foray had been to North Balwyn, a thirty-minute taxi ride on the night of the Bring a Brit party, and I thought that I had been near the outer limits of suburbia. I assumed that the destination for my One Chance with Angelina was within that same compass.

Angelina set me straight as I gave the address to the taxi driver.

"*Lilydale!* Do you know how far Lilydale is?"

My inexperience with the city was working against me. The fine spring day had turned into a miserably wet evening, rain sheeting down in the falling light. It had taken me twenty minutes to flag down a taxi across three lanes of Victoria Parade traffic after Angelina met me below the bar.

I should add that she looked take-your-breath-away stunning. Yes, I had seen her in the bar, at the party, and on TV, for that matter, after the professional costume and makeup people had done their work. The dark blue dress with its padded shoulders, slit sides, and two vertical strips of fabric running from her neck to the waistband was striking, but it was more than that: she looked the way that only a woman in her twenties who has dressed up for a big occasion can look. I kissed her. She kissed me back. I could have stood there all night. It might have been a good idea, because it was downhill after that.

A bus pulling into the gutter had drenched her dress as she'd run to the taxi. And now we were on a journey of . . . how long?

"In this weather, this traffic, an hour and a half. I'm not promising anything," said our driver.

"It'll give your dress time to dry," I offered, in a feeble attempt at humor.

"Where are we going, exactly?"

I had put some thought into the evening. For better or worse, my trump card with Angelina was my accent. A search through the Yellow Pages had turned up a British-themed restaurant with live entertainment. Comedy, to boot.

"It's called the Mock Tudor."

"You're joking. We're going to Lilydale to a . . ." She stopped. She must have realized that I had tried hard. "Hey, sorry. I'm being a prima donna. It'll be fun. Like being kidnapped."

It was fun to the extent that actually being kidnapped would be fun. The driver's refusal to promise anything was well judged and we were in his company for almost two hours. Angelina did her best to give me a running commentary on the scenery, but there is only so much to be said about appliance stores and car yards in the rain.

The Mock Tudor stood alone on a busy road, with signage that screamed cheap night out. Inside were wooden chairs and benches that would not have been out of place in a boarding school, alternate service of beef and "mock pheasant," and an interpretation of the Tudor court consisting entirely of wanton wenches.

We were the only couple. In deference to my instructions that this was a special date, we did have the best table in the house, in theory, but that meant we had no relief from the entertainment on the stage directly in front of us.

The restaurant was about a third full, thanks to two large groups. I guessed the average age of the first at around eighty, with the exception of the carers. Only a few of them seemed to be responding to the show, which was under way when we arrived. It was essentially a one-joke stand-up routine, titled *Chop and Change*, delivered by a middle-aged comic dressed as Henry VIII, with contributions from the wenches when they were not serving tables. Two elderly women were making their views clear by shouting "No!" to the most offensive punch lines.

The customers at the other long table were all women, of working age and noisily disengaged from what was happening onstage. A girls' night out, or perhaps some female-dominated profession who had left it to the receptionist to organize their event.

One of the staff—forties, portly, checked jacket, probably a better match for Henry VIII than the comedian—hovered near our table, evidently fascinated by Angelina. He may have recognized her, though her dress was enough to make her stand out.

The overall effect might have been funny, in a train wreck sort of way, if I had not been on a special date. Angelina was doing her best to be enthusiastic.

"I didn't even know this place existed."

"I didn't even know places *like this* existed. Or I'd have made a different choice."

"And you'd have missed a unique part of our culture."

Our serving wench made no attempt at Middle English. "What can I get youse to drink?"

Angelina smiled hard. "I'd love a martini."

"We don't do cocktails. I can do you a gin and tonic."

"Are you sure you couldn't manage a martini? Just—"

"There's only what's on the list."

The authentic Tudor drink would have been a pint of English ale, which was absent from the *carte*, but our wench did not need any more aggravation. It seemed she'd had enough already because she added, "I'll come back when youse've made up your minds," and headed for the next table.

She didn't make it that far. Our man in the checked jacket intercepted her, and there was what might politely be called an animated exchange before he walked toward us.

"It's okay," said Angelina. "I won't make a fuss."

He was all smiles. "Good evening, I'm the manager. My apologies for any confusion. I understand the lady would like a martini."

A few times in my life, I have been manipulated by the sexual power of a woman. "Could you help me with my assignment?" *I'll do it for you.* "I don't know why they've given me a middle seat." *Take mine.* "I thought the trains would still be running." *Let me drive you home.* No promises, no offers, nothing expected in return.

It was interesting to be on the other side. I wondered what it was like for Angelina. Could she turn it on and off at will? Did she feel guilty about using it? Contemptuous of the man in her thrall? Because it was spider and fly.

"If you're sure it isn't any trouble."

"Absolutely not. Twist or olive?"

*What key?*


The martini took forty minutes to arrive, during which time the drinks wench avoided eye contact. As a result, we lacked even the thawing power of alcohol as we ate the beef and chicken and their accompaniments of Olde English cabbage, carrots, and mashed potatoes.

Within the limits on communication imposed by Henry's performance, we managed to exchange some of the basic information that people usually share before sex and the first date. Or the first date and sex. We were working in reverse. Which is to say slowly, awkwardly, and at risk of running into things.

"What do you do?" she said. "I'm guessing you're not traveling the world to play piano. Sorry, I didn't mean . . ."

"No offense taken. Hard to make a living when the going rate is fifty cents a song."

Clever, pointed, and utterly stupid. The petty tip had not been her fault, and I didn't want to force her into defending Richard. She let it go.

"What do you think I do?" I asked.

"Computers?"

Her expression said: *Please tell me I've guessed wrong and you're an*

*Amway distributor or a tobacco lobbyist or a door-to-door missionary who's murdered his buddy. Anything but computers.*

"I'm an architect." I took a sip of water before continuing. "A database architect."

Did her expression lift briefly, when she thought for a moment that I might be interesting? I switched the conversation back to her and the job that everybody finds fascinating.

"Have you always wanted to be an actress?"

"Since I was five. I did acting classes and a few ads. I didn't get a big role until I was nineteen. A woman came to the Law Revue to see her son, and she was the casting agent for *Mornington Police*."

"The Law Revue?"

"I was finishing my first year of law at Melbourne Uni. I was in the revue, Susie saw me and offered me the part, and I said yes straightaway, and my mother was—"

"—no doubt delighted at the career move." I knew what my own mother would have thought about trading a professional career for the vagaries of the performing arts.

"She wasn't. We're a law family. My father, one of my sisters, my brother. But acting is what I've wanted to do all my life." As she had already told me, possibly with the implication that she would have preferred me not to side with her mother in devaluing it.

My hole-digging was interrupted by the arrival of the martini, in the hands of the manager himself. Despite it being garnished with a black olive, and perhaps not the ideal accompaniment to syllabub, Angelina thanked him profusely and apologized again for the trouble. He had half turned away before he remembered a minor oversight.

"And would the gentleman like something to drink as well?"

It took no small amount of self-control to give a straight answer. "Just a beer, thanks."

I spent a few minutes pretending to listen to Henry ("I says, 'ow about giving me some 'ead, darling, and she says to me, 'en-er-ry, I'd rather just 'ave it off'") while I absorbed the fact that Angelina had been smart enough to get into law school and gutsy enough to leave it for a shot at her dream.

I should not have been surprised at the former. She did not have any of the flakiness or verbal tics that I associated with stereotypical young actresses or models. To beautiful, sharp, and sexy, I could add intelligent and strong-willed. To her assessment of me, she could add sarcastic, belittling, and not very funny. I'd had my chance and not been up to it.

I headed for the pay phone in the entrance foyer, between the cigarette machine and the cardboard cutout of Henry VIII pointing the way to the bathrooms, to call a taxi. No point prolonging things, not with a long trip home ahead of us. The manager intercepted me on my way back.

"Was the martini all right? Sorry about the olives—we ran out of green."

The bar ran out of green olives? But had black?

"You had to go out for the olives, didn't you?" I said.

"And the Cinzano. Bloody girl came back with black olives. In oil. Bugger me."

We both laughed.

"She's on TV, isn't she? In that cop show? Your wife."

She was wearing her rings.

"Yep."

"The missus'll be sorry she wasn't here. But good luck to you."

I returned to the dining room to find Henry VIII dragging— literally, by the hand—Angelina onto the stage. There were five women up there already and Henry was riding roughshod over the first lesson of performance: if they don't want you, get off.

It was apparent that the group was supposed to represent Henry's six wives. Two were old enough to be his mother and the sexual innuendo did not play well. Maybe that was why, when he directed his schtick to the beautiful woman who was young enough to be his daughter, he supplemented it by grabbing her bum. Through the slit in her dress, though that aspect of it looked to be an accident. We were in a restaurant that had no pretensions of class, in eighties suburban Australia. The comedian was acting the part of a roué. The grab was so short as to be almost a pat, a gesture.

None of that mattered. Angelina turned and swung with the full force of her arm. Henry's lapel microphone broadcast the crack as her hand smacked into the side of his face. There was a moment of collective shock and silence, then the entire audience burst into applause. For a moment I thought Henry was going to hit her back and I stood up, but he composed himself and walked off.

Then someone called out: "Sergeant Kerrie!"

I suppose it was inevitable. Another round of applause.

There was an upright piano at the back of the stage and a re-engaged audience. All I had to do was fit the pieces together.

I was still working it out as I climbed the stairs onto the stage and signaled Catherine of Aragon et al. back to their seats.

"Do you know 'Greensleeves'?" I said to Angelina.

"You sure?" she said. She was shaking.

"I'm sure. He's okay. They love you."

I am at heart an introvert, happy with my own company and not uncommonly lost for something to say at a party, or indeed a theater restaurant. But performing for an audience does not bother me in the least.

I took the wenches' mike off the stand and stepped back. I hoped that the bonding I had done with the manager would buy me a little time.

"Let's have another round of applause for Angelina Brown: Sergeant Kerrie from *Mornington Police*. Lesson for us all here—never mess with a cop. Or a woman." Laughter and applause. "Angelina's kindly offered to do a song for us while Henry gets his syphilis treated." More laughter. The manager had appeared below the stage and gave me a signal that I interpreted as *Okay, but don't push it.*

I passed the mike to Angelina, walked to the piano, and played the first verse of "I'm Henry VIII, I Am," in C. The instrument was in woeful shape, not just out of tune but worn out. I tried an F sharp chord—all black keys—and it was better.

My dad told me—only about a hundred times—about a Peter Cook and Dudley Moore sketch where Dud is the piano teacher and Pete insists that the black keys play louder. Eventually Dud agrees, forced into it by Pete thrusting money at him. But there was a kernel of truth in the story, which my dad also pointed out. The black keys on old pianos are often in better condition as a result of being used less.

In the absence of a microphone, which Angelina was now holding, I shouted: "This is a song written by Henry the Eighth for Anne Boleyn after she told him to keep his hands to himself."

I played "Greensleeves," and Angelina sang beautifully in B flat minor. We did "I Am Woman"—her choice—as an encore and left them wanting more.

In the taxi, Angelina took the middle seatbelt, up against me. I put my arm around her and she leaned in.

"I'm amazed you knew how to play 'I Am Woman,'" she said.

"Not the first time I've been asked. There aren't too many feminist anthems."

"There should be. So we don't have to destroy our credibility by singing songs from the seventies."

"Golden era of popular music. Right up to about 1971."

"You must be older than you look."

"And you? 'Both Sides Now'? 'Daydream Believer'?"

"I'm not that into music. I mean, I like singing, but I don't spend my life listening to the radio. My dad was into music, so I grew up listening to his stuff."

"We have that in common." One small step in the direction of soul mates.

"I was a prima donna about the martini, wasn't I?" she said.

"Only a bit."

"Don't let me do it. It's an acting thing. We ask for Perrier water and stuff that doesn't cost anything but makes us feel respected. Because most of us get paid basically nothing. I'm incredibly lucky to have a regular role. Do you know why I slapped him?"

"Because you could?"

I hadn't intended any sort of psychological insight. I was simply observing that she had the audience on her side.

"How did you know that? When you're an actress, you have to put up with so much and you can't do anything. Part of me wishes I could have come up with some cutting remark, but he did something physical to me, so I gave him a physical response."

"You were brilliant."

She kissed me, and, given her example, I responded in kind.


I had no problem with it being a long drive back to civilization, and apparently nor did Angelina, telling me she'd had the best time in ages, even without the singing. Which was good, as I was beginning to feel that our relationship might not be sustainable without a piano. Her determination to make the date a success had been real, and the awkwardness had been largely in my own head. "Come on," she said, "you were funnier than the professional comedian."

I dropped her at her parents' house in the leafy suburb of Kew, after asking the taxi driver to take us around the block a couple of times while I kissed her goodnight.

For the record, there is no historical evidence to support the popular attribution of "Greensleeves" to Henry VIII. The earliest reference to the tune appeared thirty-three years after he died.

And two months after I'd come to Australia for some space to sort myself out, I was having an affair with a married woman.

# 6

It was a bit dramatic to call it an affair. Angelina and Richard may still
have been legally married, but—despite her occasional use of the present tense in talking about their relationship—there were no signs of
them reuniting. That said, we still had to deal with the basic problem
of an affair, albeit with her parents taking the place of the spouse. She
did not want them to know that she was dating so soon after the
breakup.

"They'll think that's why I left him."

"So? You're an adult. Let them think what they want to think."

"It's not that easy. They're really straight, and I'm living in their
house."

On top of that, Angelina had a busy schedule of acting and singing classes, as well as shoots in the evening and a growing involve-
ment in Actors' Equity. I had my day job.

When we did find time, there was the question of how to spend it.
For me, it was simple. I wanted Angelina all to myself, across a table
in a restaurant or in my bed.

If I could relive one moment of my life, it would be an evening in
the courtyard of Jim's Greek Tavern, a ten-minute walk from my
apartment, drinking BYO cabernet sauvignon out of glasses that might
once have been Vegemite jars, and eating barbecued octopus and lamb
kebabs and the best whiting I have ever had. With the big mustachioed

guy who welcomed us as a couple and, of course, Angelina, dressed down in jeans, relaxed and laughing with me as I believed she did with no one else, under the blue Australian sky. And a walk back to my apartment in lieu of dessert.

Angelina loved those evenings, too, but she also wanted to *do* things: see and discuss a film or play, go to a wine tasting, hear a public lecture. Time with Angelina was precious and I did not want to spend too much of it listening to the Socialist Alliance debating the role of women in the Marxist utopia.

One day in late October, when we had been seeing each other for about six weeks, she arrived at my flat unexpectedly, carrying an oversized handbag that she proceeded to unload on the kitchen bench. Pasta, vegetables, bread, cheese, and a bottle of red.

"Singing teacher canceled. I'm going to cook dinner for us." As I uncorked the wine, she added, "I hope you realize how special this is."

I had cooked meals a couple of times after we were famished from spending all day in bed but not in the mood to go out. It was not as if this was the first occasion that we had dined in.

She elaborated. "I never, I mean *never*, did this for Richard."

"He did the cooking?"

"The first time I made dinner, the very first time, right after we got back from our honeymoon, I screwed it up totally. My mum did all the cooking at home and I had a big sister. I'd never lived by myself. I know—spoiled brat."

"Your mother didn't work?"

"Not after she had children. I rang her up and asked her how to get the peel out of the mashed potatoes. The *pureed* potatoes."

"You're kidding me." We were both laughing.

"Richard didn't think it was funny. He thought I was unbelievably stupid. Which I was. I really can't believe I did that. But I was trying to cook three different vegetables at once and not overcook the meat, which happened anyway while I rang Mum. So I said to Richard, 'Your turn tomorrow, then,' and he said, 'No, I've got to study for my bar exams; I earn more than you; you do the cooking.' And I said, basically, 'No. I'm working and studying too, and I earn just about as much as you do. Which is only true as long as I've got a job on *Mornington Police*, which I won't have if I'm trying to work a second job as your servant.'"

"So who ended up cooking?"

"Neither of us. We got takeaway or frozen dinners, or ate out. I didn't clean, either. We ate off paper plates. Plastic cutlery. Until Richard caved in and we got a cleaning lady. That's what it's like being married to me."

As she put a full packet of spaghetti into cold water, she added, "Funny—back when I first got together with Richard, I was really looking forward to doing this."

It may have been the worst pasta I had ever eaten, but it was followed by some of the best sex I could have imagined.

I was in a fortunate position in that arena, thanks to Richard being Angelina's reference point. I had the experience of being in a long-term relationship and a couple of girlfriends before that. I was no sexual athlete, but I did know that the idea was for the other party to enjoy it, too.

It still took a while to get sorted. I was not surprised: Angelina had had more than a year of being told she was no good. The effort I put into making it better probably did more for our relationship—the relationship we weren't supposed to be having—than instant success would have.

In the end, it was Angelina who found the metaphorical key. I had the literal key. It was after midnight. We had seen a play in Carlton and were walking back through the Exhibition Gardens. Angelina was analyzing the performance, as she always did.

"We call it the fourth wall, and when the playwright chooses to break it, and acknowledge the presence of the audience, as voyeurs . . ."

She broke off to watch a possum scaling a tree, then spoke into the darkness.

"Remember the night you asked me out? When Shanksy had gone home and it was just us in the bar?"

"Vaguely."

"Do you ever think about what almost happened? Before you went all noble on me?"

I didn't. There was no need to fantasize about what I already had in the real world. "Do you?" I asked.

"Well, you asked me to tell you what got me . . . twitchy . . . and . . ."

I had a key to the bar in my pocket. Shanksy had given it to me for morning practice in case the cleaners hadn't opened up. Fifteen minutes later, we were on one of the leather sofas, lights still off, clothes on the floor, making up for what we had missed a few weeks earlier. Angelina had definitely tapped into something, but just when it seemed we might be getting there, I had the familiar feeling of it slipping away.

Angelina broke the kiss. "What if someone comes in?" she said.

So that was the problem. Then I realized it wasn't. It was the opposite.

"And catches you?" I said. It could have been "catches us," but instinct told me it was about her.

That did it. I picked her up and carried her to the door to block anyone who might have forced an entrance from a main street, climbed two flights of stairs, and knocked down a second locked door, and took us both back to the night in the North Balwyn bedroom that started it all.

Happily for both of our spines, it took only a few sessions to get past the need for a door as a prop, but the fantasy of being caught was a constant. Over the life of our relationship, I must have delivered a dozen variants of the landlord-comes-to-collect-the-rent / producer-barges-into-your-dressing-room / astronaut-returns-early-from-his-spacewalk fantasy—all in the "Daydream Believer" accent.

Of course we talked about it. Did she subconsciously want Richard to catch her? I guess it was possible, but it was hard to see how that would translate into a sexual fantasy. Had she been caught masturbating? Not that she could recall, though it led to a stimulating discussion. Was it tied to the actress's need for dramatic tension?

"Stick to your day job, Dooglas."

As for me, I got no direct excitement from the threat of being caught. But I was happy to enjoy its effect on Angelina, not only in the moment, but as a growing confidence in her own sexuality—and a recognition that she was not solely responsible for the breakdown of her marriage.

We managed a few day trips on weekends when Angelina was not filming. She had a little red Ford Laser and we went sightseeing around Victoria, wine-tasting in the Yarra Valley, strawberry-picking somewhere, browsing in country antique shops: all the things that new lovers do.

People recognized Angelina quite often, but they seldom did more than smile and wave, adding to the general feeling that all was wonderful with the world. There were no photos in gossip columns. Australia at that time seemed to be more civilized than the UK about those things, or maybe she was not famous enough.

My memories of that period are not linked to songs. Music had brought us together but it was not a significant part of what followed. I didn't need to listen to songs to remind me of our relationship when I was busy living it. We were also blissfully, stupidly happy, and my musical taste runs more to the melancholy. It would have been a good time to be a Beach Boys fan. We visited the bar a few times together, and I always played, but Angelina only sang once or twice.

We caught the occasional live band, and I have fond memories of a night at a pub listening to a blues combo that she had wanted to see, more because it was an all-female lineup than because of any taste for the genre. I had a brilliant time and would have done more of it, but she preferred movies and theater.

There was just one song that I remember, because I made a deliberate effort to do so: "Walking on Sunshine," playing on the radio as we drove down the Great Ocean Road, the two of us singing our heads off, and Angelina radiating happiness and youth and freedom. And I thought, bottle this moment, Adam. You will not see its like again.

It was 10:45 P.M. in Norwich, 9:45 A.M. in Melbourne. The little window popped up again.

*Wassup?*

# 7

*Wassup,* "Sent from my phone," gave me no sense of connection with the twenty-three-year-old Australian I had fallen in love with, or with the forty-five-year-old she must now be.

She had been more formal when she last wrote to me, twenty years earlier.

> *Dear Adam,*
>
> *Charlie and I are getting married in three months. For what it's worth, I still love you and probably always will, but it seems we are not meant to be together. You will be forever my soul mate.*
>
> *Love,*
>
> *Angelina*

*Charlie.* She had mentioned him once, barely, in an earlier letter. No details, beyond the predictable profession. And *getting married.* Not living together, not hanging out for a bit to see how it went. Out of the frying pan.

The letter was handwritten, on proper stationery. To Adam, not Dooglas. From Angelina, not Angel, which had been her signature on the notes she would slip under my door. I wondered how long it had taken her to write it. Songwriters don't know what they put into songs, and perhaps Angelina did not know what she had put into that note.

When I read it the first time, I saw the declaration of eternal love as a sop, an apology, a consolation prize.

I replied, I hoped not with any bitterness. It was a long letter, saying that I would never forget our time together, wishing them nothing but the best, telling her that I was okay in my life.

As time passed, I came to see Angelina's words as an expression of pain, a wish that things had been otherwise. But it was years before I understood her letter for what it was, consciously or not. *Please Adam, come and save me. Save us.*

Now, unless we wanted to play a game of one-word e-mails, it was time to be a bit more expansive. What did I want to tell her?

This is what I wanted to tell her:

*Since we parted, my career has gone from strength to strength and, as you would expect from someone who was an expert in his field at twenty-six, I am now at the peak of my profession and in charge of the European operations of a major software house.*

*Thanks to the company share scheme and a well-judged investment in a lottery syndicate, Claire and I are comfortably off, and I work primarily for the intellectual stimulation. I have taken my piano playing to the next level and am in demand as a session musician as well as having a regular gig with a local band.*

*We have two children at secondary school. Dylan is a talented singer-songwriter and Hillary is prominent in student politics. I keep fit and recently ran the London Marathon.*

What I actually wrote, after sleeping on it, then spending most of the day thinking about it, was:

*Not much. Still contracting. Living in Norwich. Still with Claire. No kids. You?*

Even that was a bit of a stretch, as I was between contracts—the one that had finished four months ago and the one that did not yet exist. At least I'd managed to suppress the sarcasm:

*Not much since you last wrote. Besides the Internet. And German reunification. Sad about Princess Di.*

After I hit Send, I found myself reflecting on the twelve-word summary of my current circumstances. It was not the gap between what might have been and the way things had turned out. Half the men of my age once imagined themselves scoring the winning goal for England or headlining Glastonbury.

My problem was that I was, in fact, living the dream. Eighteen months earlier, in the dying throes of a demanding contract, I had asked myself what I wanted from life, what sort of *lifestyle*. The answer was: work part-time, play pub quiz, listen to music, be supportive of my mum, and spend time with Claire. With the exception of the last item, which had been circumscribed by Claire's job, it was exactly what I was doing. Why should I want to create a different dream for Angelina?

It was the middle of the night in Melbourne, so I was not going to get a reply for a while. And I was now running late for the pub quiz.

Claire was driving up as I walked out. I waved and she waved back.

Our glory days were behind us. There were only half a dozen pubs running regular quizzes in Norwich, and several teams took it more seriously than we did.

I had started playing after work a few years earlier, when I was doing some local contracting and Claire had started coming home late. Two colleagues of about my age, Stuart and Chad, had invited me along, and my knowledge of music had helped carry us to some memorable wins. I kept it up after the contract finished. Chad had recently stopped coming, but his partner, Sheilagh, was a regular.

It was more a social thing, particularly for Stuart's and Sheilagh's workmates who made up the numbers when they were inclined. On this winter's evening, only Stuart's colleague Derek had been inclined. Derek was a sports fan, which was useful, but what we really needed was someone under forty-five with a passing knowledge of twenty-first-century popular culture. Pokémon? *Grey's Anatomy?* Justin Bieber? Pass, pass, *pass.*

Tonight's quizmaster was a man of mature age and conventional tastes, aside from a penchant for multi-part questions.

*"Part One: The horse race that stops a nation is . . ."*

Stuart gave Derek a look that said, *Let Sheilagh have a shot first.* It was technically a sports question, but it touched on history and geography, and our expert in that area needed a confidence boost, or at least a bit of cheering up.

"Melbourne Cup," she said.

Derek nodded: *Write it down.*

*"Part Two: When is it held?"*

The first Tuesday in November is a public holiday in Melbourne. The horse race may stop the nation for a few minutes, but it stops the host city for the whole day.

My colleagues were not going to accept any excuses for missing the department's chicken and champagne breakfast at the Flemington Racecourse. Nor, to my surprise, was Angelina going to accept being left out of it.

"I thought you had a commitment," I said.

"I told you: I had about five invitations and I said no to all of them. I'm an actor, not some sort of . . . decoration for a bunch of middle-aged businessmen to ogle."

"Not sure my lot will be any more civilized."

"We'll find out, won't we?"

It was a bit of a lark: formal dress for some, fancy dress for others, plastic champagne flutes, takeaway chicken, and all of it in the car park.

It took us a while to locate our group among the similarly attired racegoers with their coolers—*eskies*—and folding tables. Angelina was wearing a knee-length black dress with a black-and-red sash, black stockings, heels, and the most elaborate hat I had ever seen, at least until that morning. Technically, it was not a hat but a fascinator, featuring a stiff net that floated to one side of her face. A racegoer dressed as a beer can recognized her and the two of them narrowly avoided knocking each other over.

Booze on a warm spring morning, high heels on asphalt and grass, fragile headgear: it was a recipe for sprained ankles and perhaps worse. There were signs of overindulgence around us, but my colleagues behaved themselves and made Angelina welcome, after admonishing me for not sharing my personal life with them.

Angelina was more surprised than they were. "You haven't told anyone you were seeing me?"

"They're my clients. For two more months, then I'm gone. I wouldn't expect my doctor to tell me who he was dating."

"I get that, but . . ."

"You're Angelina Brown."

She laughed. "I don't know whether to be insulted or flattered."

Apparently she decided that restricting my showing off to databases and piano playing was a positive, because she reached up and kissed me. In front of my workmates, one of whom decided it was an opportunity to introduce herself. Tina—on wobbly heels, with an entourage of admin staff.

I hardly saw her at work and had put our awkward half-date out of my mind. She had not.

"Oh my God, everyone, this is Angelina Brown. Angelina, this is everyone. You're not going to believe this, but I basically introduced them. I took Seagull to this bar. . . ."

Angelina burst out laughing. "Seagull?"

Tina helpfully explained the joke, which fitted nicely with her story: "Because, no offense, Adam, I got nominated to tell you, basically on behalf of everyone, to pull your head in a bit, which to be fair you have done, and she—Angelina—was there, in the bar, having a drink, and Sea . . . Adam . . . was like a rabbit in the headlights, so I said, 'Play something on the piano.' I mean, he wasn't going to impress her by sounding off about databases."

"Good advice," said Angelina.

"Then, after you'd gone, I had to tell him who you were."

"*You* told him who I was? He said he'd never heard of me."

History was already being rewritten.

"Not until I told him. Of course, he was gobsmacked. Anyway, I could see where it was going. I walked out and, well, here you are."

"Thank you," said Angelina. "You were right: without the piano, I wouldn't have been interested." She smiled. "And that might have been a mistake."

"Not bad for computer nerds and insurance clerks?" I said as we joined the throng heading into the racecourse proper.

"They were great. Especially Tina. Considering you dumped her for me. Seagull."

"I suppose lawyers would be doing something a bit more salubrious."

Angelina pulled an envelope from her handbag—red and black to match her dress—and passed it to me.

"We're about to find out."

"I thought you said no to the corporate events."

"Dad gave me these. He can't go—conflict of interest. It's one of the big law firms. Law's different."

I opened the envelope. Angelina apparently had not done so. Because with the tickets was a note. *Tony: If you can't make it, feel free to give these to your famous daughter. She'll be a lot more decorative than you.*

We were in one of the corporate marquees, in what was called the Birdcage, with no view of the actual races. It was all about the drinking and socializing, and I was grateful that I had gone easy on the bubbly at breakfast. Though Angelina knew only a couple of the guests, and then only vaguely, she still had plenty of attention.

The lawyers were predominantly male, from sharp-suited thirty-somethings to overweight barristers with double-breasted jackets unbuttoned in the heat. They were louder and more intoxicated than our morning group. Even with me at Angelina's side, and the presence of wives and colleagues, a few were a bit boorish.

The women were dressed to the nines in hats and high heels, perhaps more expensively than the car park crowd, but no less flamboyantly.

My accent led me into a conversation with one of them who was considering a move to the UK. Angelina excused herself to circulate, and the woman and I were well into the London housing market by the time she returned.

"I'm going to put a bet on," she said. "Are you coming?"

"I'm not a gambler."

"Come on—what about the roses you sent me?"

"Seemed like a sure thing to me."

"Lucky you don't gamble, then. But you have to have a bet on the Cup. Pick a horse."

I scanned the whiteboard with its list of the twenty-three starters.

"Empire Rose."

Angelina held out her hand and I gave her ten dollars.

"Each-way bet. Five for a win, five for a place."

"Wimp."

The woman's husband—a nice enough bloke who worked in patent law—had joined the real estate conversation by the time Angelina returned with my ticket.

"Who'd you back?" I asked.

"Hidden Rhythm. For a win."

We watched the race on a TV screen mounted high in the air, in the sunshine, with delayed sound from all around the course and the cheering of the crowd making the commentary unintelligible. I had no idea which horse was winning or where mine was.

Near the finish, a jockey in a red cap streaked to the lead, the shouting and commentary rose to a crescendo, and a few moments later the place-getters were posted on the screen. Empire Rose was not among them, nor Hidden Rhythm. Nobody seemed to have backed the winner, an outsider named Tawrrific.

Angelina grabbed my arm. "Watch the tall guy."

A big chap, probably mid-thirties, had turned away from his companion, a shortish, dark-haired woman of about the same age, and was shuffling through a bunch of betting tickets. He found the one he was looking for, tapped his lady, and gave it to her. Her expression lit up, and for the next few minutes we all shared in the glory: twenty dollars on the winner at 30-to-1. Six hundred dollars—more than enough to buy champagne all round.

As the winning lady toured the tent pouring the spoils, my patent attorney friend filled us in.

"Eloise Ditta. Divorce lawyer. Supposed to be a ball-breaker. If you're bitter, get Ditta."

Angelina smiled. "Who's the husband?"

"No idea," said the patent attorney. "Why?"

"I was behind him in the bookie's queue. He put twenty dollars on every horse in the race."

I did a quick calculation. "Bloody hell—four hundred and sixty dollars. Not great odds."

"I suppose not."

Later, Angelina joined a bunch of other celebrities to judge Fashions on the Field and I had time to reflect. What sort of life did Angelina want? The car park or the members' enclosure? Would she rather be the hard-nosed divorce lawyer or the celebrity fashion judge? I had not sensed any envy toward Eloise: her win, her job, even being the center of attention. There was just that moment of admiration for the guy who had backed every horse in the Melbourne Cup to ensure his wife would win.

"*Part Three: Name one winner of the Melbourne Cup.*"

"Phar Lap," said Derek.

"Hang on," I said. "Do you know what year? Because that'll be Part Four. That's how this guy works."

"Correct," said Sheilagh.

"Jeez. Nineteen thirty something?"

"Tawrrific, 1989," I said. "At thirty to one."

"What do you need me for?" said Derek.

"There must be a song about it," said Stuart. "But I sense a disturbance in the Force."

# 8

A week or so after the Melbourne Cup, Shanksy buttonholed me between sets.

"Still seeing the actress?"

I smiled a big, happy smile.

"Remember the joke about the nine-inch pianist?" said Shanksy.

"I'm being nice to her."

"Pleased to hear it. I've got another one about a genie."

Shanksy helped himself to a drink. "Bloke walks into a bar, and
he's got this tiny head. He's a pinhead. Barman says, 'What happened?'
Bloke says, 'This genie appeared, stark naked, long legs, big tits, and
offered me a wish. I say, 'How about a little head?' and . . .'"

I laughed. I hadn't heard it.

Shanksy took a slug of his soda water. "So the moral is?"

"Don't look a gift horse in the mouth?"

He nodded. "And don't get a big head."

I wasn't. On the contrary, I was painfully aware that the relationship was temporary, and not just because I had a flight booked for the
end of December, only six weeks away. Angelina could do better than
me. I was trying to keep my expectations in line with reality, which is
to say I was trying not to fall in love with her. Or at least I was trying
to deny that I had already done so.

We had finished dinner at Jim's Greek Tavern on a warm evening in the courtyard. It had been several days since we had seen each other and I was mentally halfway to the upstairs loft in my apartment when she said, "Let's have a drink at the bar."

We walked to Victoria Parade and I ordered two glasses of sparkling wine while Angelina found a table.

Shanksy pulled a bottle of real champagne from the fridge. "On me," he said. "As long as you don't play."

I gave him a look of mock offense.

He uncorked the bottle. "If I had a lady like that at my table, I wouldn't be playing the piano."

When I had poured our drinks, we clinked glasses and Angelina said, "So why? Why me?"

I could have laughed at the ridiculousness of the question. But apparently it was not obvious to her that a database architect and jobbing piano player of average looks would think that only a cosmic error could have delivered this beautiful, intelligent, and ambitious television star into his arms.

I told her all that. I added that I saw something of myself in her. We were both performers. Even at work, I wanted to show my client that I was worth what they were paying me.

She laughed. "You're such a know-it-all. Patti Smith *and* Bruce Springsteen. 'Root i' togevver, din' vey?'"

"You know why I'm a show-off?" I said, compelled to prove that I knew the answer to that too. "When I was a kid, I had to play for my dad every day. I'd come home from school, and he'd say, 'What've you got for me today, lad?'"

Angelina smiled at the hammed-up version of my dad's accent, but didn't laugh. "And?"

"At first, I'd just do an exercise better than I'd done it before, but later it was always a proper song. I'd pick something he liked—from his records. Now you understand why I know all that sixties and seventies stuff."

Angelina refilled our glasses.

"My parents' marriage was pretty screwed," I said. "I felt I was doing my bit to keep my dad from leaving."

Then I told her the part I had not told anyone else.

"When I was fourteen, I stopped practicing. I was a stroppy teenager and I was stuffed if I was going to practice piano twenty minutes every day so I could play for my fucking father who was never home and who I knew even back then was cheating on my mum." I emptied my glass, again, and put it down. "So he left. Never came back."

Some adolescent part of me was waiting for Angelina to draw away in horror. Of course she didn't. Her eyes filled with tears and she took my hand.

"Don't say anything," I said. "I've never said that out loud before, and I know you're about to say, 'No, no, don't blame yourself'—but you weren't there. They made a bad decision getting married in the first place. Then they had to live with it because of me. And if I feel like being kinder to myself, and to him, I'd say he left when he decided he wasn't needed anymore."

"But he was, wasn't he?"

"Probably," I said. "But I've got some okay memories. If he'd stayed, all the bad stuff would have buried them."

"Did you miss him?"

"I think I missed the good parts. A fantasy, not the reality of what he'd have been if he actually stayed. If that makes sense."

"It makes loads of sense. My mum and dad: I can't imagine them without each other. But I can relate to what you're saying. About letting them down, driving them away, which is part of why . . . Then there's me and Richard. I so much wanted it to work."

"And we both blame ourselves."

"You said not to say it wasn't your fault—" she began.

"If you want to make me feel better, tell me why you chose me. Because this is the best thing that's ever happened to me."

Angelina looked away for a few moments. "On the night you played for me, you were probably the only person in the bar who didn't know who I was. And you liked me anyway. With the panda eyes and everything. Just for whatever was happening right then. Richard had been in a shit all night, and everyone was tiptoeing around him, and you saw it and made a joke of it. I thought, there's someone who's prepared to take a risk, do something for me, and he doesn't even know who I am . . . And now you do."

It was true. She had been more open than me in sharing her background, her uncertainty about her marriage, her plans and dreams. I knew who she was.

We looked at each other for a while, holding hands across the table.

"One of us has to say this first," she said. "It doesn't mean that there's anything after December or that I've given up on my marriage, or that if I did . . ."

She was speaking slowly and that gave me time to go first.

"I love you," I said. "It doesn't mean I'm going to throw in my contract and run away with you and live happily ever after, but I love you."

"I love you, too," she said. "With all that stuff."

If there was one conversation in my life that I could have over again, to keep the feelings but change the words, it would be that one. Because, at the same time that we declared our love for each other, we ensured it was doomed.

# 9

There was no e-mail from Angelina in the morning, and by four P.M. I had to concede that she was not going to reply to me that night—or, perhaps, ever.

There was an obvious explanation. A few years earlier, I had registered on a school reunion Web site and was inundated with e-mails—all right, six or seven, but it felt like a flood—from girls I had known at school, a couple of whom had been well beyond my reach in the popularity stakes.

They were all divorced. Without exception, one word put an end to the correspondence. *Claire*. To their credit, they were only interested if I was single. If Angelina and Charlie had parted, why would she not put out a feeler to see what I was up to and withdraw it just as quickly when I told her?

I opened "Sent Items" and looked at my message again. It was innocuous enough. I started browsing Wikipedia, but could not concentrate, and finally I did something I had not done for two years. I dug out my trainers and went for a jog.

It was a short one. Up to Eaton Park and back, about a mile and a half in all. I could not believe how unfit I was.

In the bathroom, I took a hard look at myself in the mirror. I was no longer the lean, lightly tanned young man I had been in 1989. My beard needed a trim and so did my waist. I had been wearing tracksuit pants instead of jeans for the last couple of months, and there was a reason for that.

I wondered what Angelina looked like now. It wouldn't be like her to let herself go, but she might have said the same about me. What had twenty-two years done to the rest of the cast of my Melbourne sojourn? What had happened to Shanksy, to Tina, to the actress I remembered as Jayne Mansfield? And Richard?

Angelina had met Richard during the year she studied law. He had given a guest lecture and afterward she had approached him with a question that led to a drink and . . . nothing. *She* fancied *him*, but he did not contact her until she was established in her *Mornington Police* role.

I assumed that Richard's diminutive-movie-star looks had been part of the attraction. Angelina denied it.

"He's smart. When you spend most of your time with actors, you realize that looks aren't everything."

"When you spend most of your time with computer people, you realize that being smart isn't everything either," I said. "But we still end up being attracted to smart people."

"I'm not apologizing for being attracted to good-looking men."

"Compliment accepted."

"He chose me, too. I was young and I took a risk, but he was ambitious, and I thought he saw me the same way. I thought we'd have this big life."

"And?"

"It wasn't as awful as you keep implying. You met him on two bad nights. I was interested in what he did. We had lots of things to talk about."

"You lay in bed discussing corporate law?"

"Law in general. And politics. Like whether employers should have to offer paid maternity leave."

Law in bed. That might have been one reason for the problems in their sex life.

"Let me guess. You said yes, and he said no."

"Right. But he had good arguments. Things I hadn't thought of."

"So he won?"

"If that's the way you want to look at it."

"Hardly surprising, seeing it's what he does for a job," I said. "What about acting? Did you talk about that?"

"Not the theory. It doesn't interest him."

It wouldn't have, since Angelina knew more about it than he did and he couldn't use it to put her down. There were doubtless deep psychological reasons for his behavior, but my mother, sight unseen, would have diagnosed short man's syndrome.

One night, quite late, after we had spent the earlier part of the evening in my loft, Angelina took me to a Chinese restaurant upstairs in one of the city's laneways. It was an institution, a dive, crowded and noisy and about as far away as possible from the white-tableclothed is-the-blackened-lobster-to-sir's-liking places I imagined her going with Richard.

We had a table by the door and the waiter had just poured our wine into teacups when a blond woman and her besuited escort, brown paper BYO bag in hand, arrived at the top of the staircase.

I saw him before Angelina did and automatically stood up, so quickly that I knocked the table over. Teacups and wine hit the floor, and the restaurant went quiet.

We were only a few yards apart. I was looking at Richard and he was looking at Angelina. No more than a couple of seconds passed before he spun on his heel and dragged his lady out with him. I had met her before, though it took a moment to see past the comfortable jeans and loose long-sleeved T-shirt: Angelina's colleague at *Mornington Police*, Constable Danni. Jayne Mansfield.

Angelina looked as if she had been hit. The color had gone from her face. She half stood, then sat back again as a waitress pushed past to deal with the spill.

"Can we go? Please."

"Wait a minute or two. Let them clean up."

I persuaded her to stay and we talked it through. The problem was not about us being seen together, nor even about her having to deal with Jayne Mansfield at work, but Richard being out with someone else, anyone else.

"It's my problem, not yours," she said. "I told you at the beginning, I haven't given up on trying to make my marriage—our marriage—work. I knew he was probably seeing someone. It's just being hit in the face with it . . . Them out together, like a couple. And here I am, with someone who says he loves me and it's going nowhere. I'm wasting my time. I'm wasting your time."

From the start we had agreed that our relationship would end with my departure from Australia. Without that guarantee of an ending, I doubt that Angelina would have been prepared to embark on an affair at all. I think she saw it as a process of sorting herself out, doing the things she should have done before she got married, and then picking up again, with Richard or someone else. But now something had shifted, even more so than on the night we admitted we were in love.

Did our relationship have to be going nowhere?

Putting aside my difficulty in believing that Angelina was in my life, let alone in love with me, the problem was a practical one. I had signed up for a fifteen-month job that plenty of contractors would have killed for. My reputation would be mud and the project set back if I pulled out after the Australian leg, taking the experience with me. I had nine months of country-hopping before I could see Angelina again.

Angelina was tied to *Mornington Police*. Walking away would be fatal to her budding career. Her dream was to become a leading actress—a Judi Dench or Meryl Streep or Lauren Bacall. It was a stretch from an Australian soap opera, even if she'd had a prodigious talent. Sergeant Kerrie was not Lady Macbeth. Angelina was working hard at it, taking classes in acting and singing and even doing some teaching herself. But there were no guarantees and she could not afford a false step.

I was familiar with the territory. I played piano better than plenty of rock stars. It didn't matter. Nobody criticizes John Lennon's piano playing on "Imagine." Or, to take an extreme example, Al Kooper's organ on "Like a Rolling Stone," the Greatest Rock Song of All Time. The punters would not know Al Kooper from J. S. Bach.

After a certain point, it's not about the last ten percent of technique but whether you answer a casting call for a madcap TV show or marry Paul McCartney. There is only so much of that sort of luck to share around. I'm not saying I didn't dream of stardom, but I planned for a career in computing.

Angelina was making no backup plans, professionally or personally. She would continue with her acting and singing studies, try to keep in work, and wait for the break.

It was late November. We had been seeing each other for less than three months since the rainy night excursion to the Mock Tudor. We may have been in love, but we had never spent a night together, never met each other's families, never been out with any of her friends. It had made sense when there was a looming end date.

"Would you wait for me?" I asked.

She took a few moments to answer. "What does that mean? Not see anyone else for nine months?"

I had not thought it through, but that seemed to be the spirit of it. I nodded.

"What would I be waiting for?"

"This." I waved my hand to indicate us, the room, everything. The hordes wolfing down congee at the long table detracted somewhat from the gesture.

"Seeing each other, like this?" she said.

"Being together again. Seeing how it goes. Nothing to get in our way."

"I suppose that's right. Nine months would be just about the time I'd need to sort out the divorce, find somewhere to live, have everything ready for you."

I caught the edge in her voice in time to avoid digging a deeper hole for myself. She got up and went to the bathroom.

When she came back, she said, "I don't know. Let's see how it goes."


In the last few weeks, the sense of time running out was inescapable. Angelina made more of an effort to be with me, even skipping singing classes to lie on the grass in the Exhibition Gardens with her head on my chest. Despite my best efforts to live in the moment, to take everything I could from the time left, I was becoming like the Japanese tourists posing for group photos, gathering memories.

In early December, I organized a day trip to Mount Arapiles, about two hundred miles northwest of Melbourne, and booked a beginners' rock-climbing lesson. It seemed like a fun thing to do together, and concentrating on something physical would give us a break from the ticking clock.

The day started well, driving to breakfast with the sun rising behind us. Angelina had warned me that she was afraid of heights, but I didn't expect it to be a real problem.

It was. She refused to do the climbing lesson and wouldn't even walk to the edge of the path to take in the view. It was a full-blown pathological fear: her father and sisters freaked out looking over balconies. I had my lesson, and Angelina managed to take a few pictures, but I couldn't help feeling it was symptomatic of what was happening to our relationship.

On the return journey, I played psychiatrist. What did her fear of heights signify? Was she afraid of being at the top?

It prompted our only real fight. *She* had no fear of failure. *She* was the one taking the risks, working in the most insecure of professions, while *I* was able to walk into a well-paid job anywhere in the world. When was I going to take some risks?

"Hey, I was the one who went rock climbing."

"With an instructor and a load of safety equipment. You know that's not what I'm talking about."

"I don't want to be a full-time musician. I get to play piano all I want. If I played piano all the time, I'd probably get bored with it. The way it is now, I love it. Is there a problem with that?"

Apparently there was. Angelina was silent for the rest of the trip, but left a note under my door the next day.

*Sorry. Thank you for trying to make the most of the time we have left. I'm just sad there's so little.*

# 10

It took a week, exactly a week, from Angelina's first e-mail. Wednesday morning, 9:30 A.M. in Norwich, 8:30 P.M. Melbourne time. I had resolved to put the whole thing out of my mind, and then up popped the window.

> *Hi*
> *Still married to Charlie. Three kids. Working full time.*
> *Angelina*
> *xxx*

*I have a husband. I have children. And I have a job in Australia. Do not entertain any thoughts inconsistent with those facts.*

Except for two things.

The first was the *xxx*. It's not as though three kisses at the bottom of an e-mail meant *I'm still in love with you*, or even *I want to kiss you three times*, but they suggested that something remained from our past. The second thing was that she was writing at all, and apparently not to ask about holiday options. What had prompted it?

I composed my reply with some care. Angelina might have initiated the exchange, but her replies had reflected mine in the amount they disclosed. It seemed it was up to me to decide if and how it escalated.

*Very belated congratulations. A lot happens in twenty-two years.*
*Happy?*

The reply took less than fifteen seconds.

*Thanks. A quarter of a lifetime. Kids are great. Work challenging,*
*but I love it.*

I noted the omission of the marriage and went back to her previous e-mail. *Still married to Charlie.* Still. Was there a suggestion that this was a temporary state of affairs? How would I have written it?

I scrolled down and saw that I had written *Still with Claire.* If anything, that reinforced my interpretation that things might be shaky for her, or at least a bit dull. But how else would she say it? *Everything wonderful with Charlie?*

Before I could reply, there was another message from Angelina.

*Charlie's out tasting wine. It's his regular Wednesday thing.*

And two Wednesdays in a row you've e-mailed your old lover. Because you're lonely—or bored—without Charlie, or because he's not watching?

We were at a turning point. I could ask the names of her kids, what sort of work she was doing, where they lived. I sensed that if I did, I would slowly dismantle my fantasy of her. I was being offered the pill that would make me hate the taste of alcohol. It was too big a decision to take without more information.

I wrote:

*I'm e-mailing my lover from twenty years ago. It's in danger of*
*becoming my regular Wednesday thing.*
*xxx Dooglas*

Not as witty as I'd have liked, but it would have to do. She had left me hanging the previous week and I would return the favor. I shut down the computer and went for a run.

The shot of adrenaline from upping the ante carried me to an extra circuit of the park before I changed and walked into town where, along with doing the week's shopping, I introduced myself at the piano shop and spent an enjoyable couple of hours chatting and trying out keyboards. Back home, I managed to restrain myself from checking my e-mail and headed for the pub.

I was on fire all evening, and my resolution to stick to a single pint in the interests of weight loss only added to my edge. *Phil Upchurch's big hit of 1961?* "Oop Poop Ah Doo." *Roy Orbison song covered by Creedence Clearwater Revival?* "Ooby Dooby." *Capital of Burkina Faso?* Ouagadougou. Sheilagh barely got a look-in.

"You're looking fantastic," she said. "Have you got a job or something?"

"Started running again." A week ago, but I *was* feeling a difference.

"Well, keep it up."

We nailed second place, beaten only by the pub champions. Stuart waited until Sheilagh went outside to make a call before offering his take on my reinvigoration.

"Are you having an affair, mate?"

"What? No." And then, because I knew I should share it with someone and that person was not going to be Claire, I added, "Someone I used to know got back in touch."

"Old geezer, happily married, wanted to talk databases, right?"

"One out of three. She's married, she lives in Australia, and we've exchanged about a dozen words on e-mail. No big deal."

"Except for the new personality. So you've told Claire and she's good with it, right? Copying her in, maybe the four of you can have a holiday together. And since it's no big deal, you can stop now."

"It's only a few e-mails. Just woke me up a bit."

"I'm not complaining about that. I suppose it was the only way you were going to get out of the funk. Other than getting a job, which, of course, is out of the question. I keep thinking one day I'll pick up the

*Telegraph* and there'll be a picture of you holding a blanket over your head, and I'll find I've been playing the pub quiz with the bloody Unabomber."

"Come on, I've been fine. I'm out three nights a week."

"True, but with what sort of people? Seriously, I know your mum's been sick, I know you and Claire are struggling a bit, but you've been flat as a tack since before Christmas. Maybe you need some sort of distraction, but these things turn dangerous quicker than you think."

On the bus home, I checked my e-mail. Four messages from Angelina.

*Do you want to live dangerously?*

Stuart had been prescient. There's a lot of time to get to know people between pub quiz rounds, and I had two circles of friends as a result. Sheilagh and Stuart were in the center, with Derek and the other once-a-weekers around them. I counted myself lucky. Short-term work assignments are not a good way to build long-term relationships, and I had lost touch with the friends of my early adulthood as they retreated into family life.

Claire's friends were scattered around the country. She and I went out together on the weekends, but we had not been out with another couple for a long time. And none of my conversations with anybody involved flirting, innuendo, and double entendres.

The next message just said,

*Well?*

She had waited three minutes.
Then:

*Hey, I asked you a question.*

Eight minutes. And, finally,

*Wimp.*

She would be asleep now. I e-mailed her something to wake up to.

*I was in a meeting. Feeling dangerous now.*

I was feeling extremely dangerous. Claire was still up, working at her computer. When I kissed her good night, I tilted her head and kissed her lips instead of her cheek, and she gave me a smile back.

I slept till eight A.M., went for a jog, stole some of Claire's muesli and yogurt for breakfast in place of my usual fry-up, and checked my inbox. There was a message.

*xxx*

That was it. But it lifted me for the rest of the day, so high I couldn't concentrate on anything. For the first time in living memory I felt switched on, in that driven, edgy way that affects your whole body. Wired. The way I used to feel before a big date.

They say your libido hits the downward slope hard at forty-five, and I was staring down the barrel of fifty. In less than a year, my friends would gather in some typically English pub, drink pints, and wish me happy birthday. After that, Claire and I would go home, she might feel obliged to offer me some sexual favor that I would feel embarrassed about accepting, and later I would go to sleep in my single bed without ever feeling what I felt when those three kisses appeared on my screen.

It was odd, in a way. Sex had been an important part of my relationship with Angelina. But my memories of her were romantic, nostalgic, downbeat. She had not featured in my erotic fantasies. I could see that changing.

I walked around the house like a caged lion, making coffee just for something to do, which made the problem worse. I was going to go crazy without some sort of distraction. Stuart had had a point.

I e-mailed my contracting agency in London. Distraction or not, I was due to do some honest work.

I only needed to work six months a year to match Claire's income. Although I had lost interest in the progress of database technology, there were plenty of legacy systems needing maintenance and enhancement. Veterans prepared to forgo the excitement of the new were rewarded with premium rates.

On the other side of the equation, Claire had thrown in her project management job to join a start-up software company that was doing better at building a brilliant child-support payments system for one government client than at making a profit. Three months ago, an American company had offered to buy them out and they had been in negotiation since then. As one of the principals, Claire could be coming home at some time in the future with a big check and no job. Or a transfer to run the new owner's Ouagadougou office.

I had no plan for dealing with that, let alone next Wednesday.

# 11

Back in 1989, I did not have a plan, either. Just a hope—a fantasy—of how events might play out.

The Australian leg of my contract was due to finish on the Friday before Christmas and I was booked to fly to New Zealand on December 28. Six weeks there, then a further seven months on the road, including the final stint at home.

If Angelina truly loved me, she would wait. I would return to Australia and we would pick up where we had left off, our love for each other only strengthened by the separation. She could continue her career and I would find a local contract.

Angelina's position was less certain. Yes, she loved me; yes, she hoped it would work out—but she couldn't promise. She never said it as clearly as that, and I never asked her to. I didn't want to push her into defending her not-completely-abandoned marriage. Better to let it fade than try to argue it down.

My last day at work coincided with the Christmas parties for both our department and the studio where Angelina studied acting. Partners were not invited to either event, but Tina made an exception.

"It's your farewell. We'd have done something separate, but it's like having a birthday at Christmas. You have to double up. But we decided you should invite Angelina. If you're still seeing her."

I explained that Angelina had another commitment, but she turned up at the function room venue at 10:30 P.M. with everyone three sheets to the wind. She had barely walked in when our project manager, an older guy named Pete, got behind the piano and announced that I would be sent off in a manner befitting my extracurricular interests.

He launched into a parody of Tom Waits's "Mr. Siegel." I saw it coming—"Mr. Seagull"—but by the end of it I had tears running down my face: of laughter, of sadness that I was leaving, and of something else. I had no idea Pete could play, let alone that he was at least as good as I was—and a better singer. He had been there that first night at the bar celebrating our colleague's new baby and had let me have my moment. If he had taken the piano stool himself, Angelina would not have been holding my hand now.

Pete put the point beyond doubt by following up with a spare and beautiful version of "Walk Away Renée," while Angelina squeezed my hand harder and harder, and we both looked straight ahead.

"You two are so cute together." Tina had appeared on cue. "I was going to ask you guys what you're going to do when Adam goes away, but it's obvious, isn't it?"

Was it obvious to Angelina what was going to happen? All that was obvious to me was that I didn't want to go.


The following Sunday was Christmas Eve. Angelina met me at my flat and we took a tram to the Myer Music Bowl for Carols by Candlelight, a Melbourne tradition. At seven P.M. there was already a big crowd on the lawns in the natural amphitheater behind the fixed seating.

We shuffled around until a group with the full picnic paraphernalia laid out on a rug recognized Angelina and made room. She pulled a parcel from her bag.

"Don't lose our spot. Here's something to keep you occupied."

There is a famous Bob Dylan song in which the narrator's lover hands him a book of poetry and he sees his own feelings reflected on the page. The gift-wrapped anthology that Angelina gave me was bookmarked at a sonnet by Elizabeth Barrett Browning.

*Go from me. Yet I feel that I shall stand*
*Henceforward in thy shadow. Nevermore*
*Alone upon the threshold of my door*
*Of individual life, I shall command*
*The uses of my soul, nor lift my hand*
*Serenely in the sunshine as before,*
*Without the sense of that which I forbore,*
*Thy touch upon the palm. The widest land*
*Doom takes to part us, leaves thy heart in mine*
*With pulses that beat double . . .*

Her hand on my shoulder in the Victoria Parade bar, that first night, counting the beat.

*. . . What I do*
*And what I dream include thee, as the wine*
*Must taste of its own grapes. And when I sue*
*God for myself, He hears that name of thine,*
*And sees within my eyes, the tears of two.*

I read it over and over while I waited for her and, as in the Dylan song, the words rang true. His lyrics did not include a summer evening and a crowded hill and a Sonnet from the Portuguese, but they would now be as much a part of it for me as if he had sung "Henceforth in Thy Shadow" instead of "Tangled Up in Blue."

I assumed Angelina had headed for the ladies', but she did not come back. It would be easy to lose someone in that sea of rugs. I sat while the celebrities and the choir and the whole audience sang in unison the songs of my childhood Christmases when my mum and dad were together in a place where the snow really did lay round about, deep and crisp and even. I sang, too. And then I couldn't. I wasn't sob-bing, just a bit moved, but enough to get in the way of singing.

There was a family sitting on the rug next to me, and the father lit a candle and gave it to his daughter, who must have been six or seven. She was already holding her own candle, and she passed the newly lit one to me. It was a moment from a movie: close-up on the little girl's face; big close-up of tear rolling down the guy's cheek; cut to the father, smiling that he's managed to avoid the embarrassment of confronting the choked-up guy but has still done his bit in spreading the goodwill. Mid-shot of the guy waving his candle. Shot from the stage of the crowd all waving candles together. We are surely entitled to one cin-ematic moment in our lives.

I wondered where Angelina was. I wanted to share this with her.

Cut to the stage.

"The next song is by the late John Lennon," said the compere. "And some very special friends are going to sing it for us."

The cast of *Mornington Police* walked on. And instead of the ex-pected "Merry Christmas (War Is Over)," they sang "Imagine." With the choir behind them and Angelina in front, carrying everyone else.

Unlike most of the audience, I was a performer. I wasn't just watch-ing her; I was in her head, knowing how she would feel with the en-tire audience singing and waving candles in the night. To be the very heart, the *pulse*, of a city of three million for four minutes, doing it all with the noise your breath makes as it runs over your vocal cords.

In that moment I knew that I wanted to spend the rest of my life with Angelina, have kids like the little girl who gave me the candle, grow old together. I would do whatever it took to make that happen.

I blew out the candle and put it in my pocket. I still have it. I should have held on to the thought as tightly.


That night, for the first time, Angelina stayed over. On Christmas morning we slept in, had coffee for breakfast, and exchanged presents. I gave her a locket that opened to reveal a photo of the two of us at the piano. Shanksy had taken it with high-speed film to avoid alerting Angelina with the flash. It was grainy but caught the moment.

I had bought the locket in an antique shop on Gertrude Street, and the proprietor, an older woman, spent a good hour helping me choose it while teasing out my story. After I had paid, she offered the final judgment on the piece—and on my relationship.

"If you expect her to wait for you, you'll have to offer to marry her."

I took the locket, but not her advice, which I knew, with the wisdom of a twenty-six-year-old, belonged to another era.

Angelina put the locket around her neck and left it on. Later, I saw that she had removed her wedding and engagement rings.

Her present to me was a cassette recording of the previous night's performance.

"It's a bootleg," she said. "The soundboard guy would lose his job over it."

She had written on it, *Imagine: just imagine. Merry Christmas and all my love, always, forever, Angelina 25/12/89.*

Then she did the thing that I would come to realize, beyond all she had said and done before, meant that she wanted to make a future with me after all. She invited me to her parents' home for Christmas dinner.

# 12

Angelina was nervous about introducing me to her family, and for once I felt older than her, not least because her younger sister and brother were also living at home.

Apparently, Richard had been an admired member of the clan. Angelina had told her parents nothing substantial about me and didn't want me to be smartarse or sarcastic or make jokes about being a real architect. Or about politics. Stay right away from politics. Best not to make jokes at all. But otherwise I should just relax and be myself. As long as I didn't . . .

And so it went on the drive to Kew, where I had dropped her off after our date at the Mock Tudor.

I knew her family history, as Angelina knew mine. No skeletons of note, beyond the younger sister, Jacinta, being "troubled," which in the Brown family could mean not studying law.

Angelina's father, Tony, met us at the car, and I warmed to him immediately. He was a big, bluff, balding guy, not at all what my mind had conjured up from Angelina's description. A Family Court judge, but very much the antipodean version, in tailored shorts and white knee socks.

"We saw you on the box last night," he said to Angelina. "Those singing lessons weren't such a waste after all, eh? Your mother and I have been getting calls all morning."

Mother was a different story. Tall, thin, a passing resemblance to Princess Margaret, and introduced by Tony as "Angelina's mother." She did not invite me to call her anything else.

Nor did she waste time getting to the point. "How's Richard?"

"He's gone to Sydney, to see his parents," Angelina said.

"You told me you were staying with him. Where have you been?"

Mrs. Brown's glance at me suggested she had jumped to the right conclusion.

"I told you I was staying at the house. To water the plants and feed the cat."

"You should have gone with him."

"Mum? We're not together."

"People should be able to put aside their differences at Christmas. I honestly can't—"

"Mum. Remember? Carols by Candlelight."

"Did you really have to be there? There must have been twenty of you. I'm sure if you'd told them you needed to be with your husband . . ."

We had ten minutes or so more of Richard—his family, his bar exams, his need for a supportive wife—before Mrs. Brown returned to Carols by Candlelight.

"Did you have to sing that awful song? So many beautiful Christmas carols and they have to sing pop music, I don't know why—"

"I think it's one of Richard's favorites," I said, deadpan.

Angelina's expression said *Careful*, but Mrs. Brown turned her attention to the turkey with a parting "You need to put a cardigan on over that frock."

Dinner itself was a strange experience, and not just because of the roast turkey and plum pudding at the height of summer. My presence threw an extra factor into the family mix. I was officially the visitor from England, the traveler separated from his family. The absence of Angelina's recently-ex-husband and the lack of any credible reason for her to know me undermined that innocent explanation. Grandma, Mrs. Brown's mother, didn't bother trying to make sense of it and called me Richard.

There was no beer or wine. I am not much of a lunchtime drinker, but this was one occasion where a pint would have been welcome. Jacinta, whom I recalled was an apprentice hairdresser, poured me a glass of lemonade and passed it down the table. I sipped it and was rewarded with the unmistakable warmth of alcohol.

Angelina's older sister, Meredith, "worked in policy" and was occupied with a baby. She had her mother's looks and already something of her personality. Her husband was a dork of the first order, right down to the heavy-framed glasses and surreptitious glances at Angelina, who had not put on a cardigan. His surname, White, tied neatly to his profession as a dentist, so much so that I cannot recall his first name.

The brother, Edwin, between Angelina and Jacinta in age, had deferred legal studies to pursue his cricketing ambitions. He seemed uninterested in discussing anything else, so I suppose he deserved credit for focus. He made a few jokes about the English team, but fewer than my workmates had. Allan Border's Australians had recently given England a drubbing at home, after being the underdogs. Possibly Edwin was just being tactful. If he was, he had not got it from his mother.

"Do you have brothers and sisters?" she asked me.

"No, I think I put my parents off the idea."

"That's a shame. Children without brothers and sisters turn out so selfish."

"Mum!" said Angelina.

"Moom? My godfather, you're picking up that accent. It's sounding like *Coronation Street*." She turned back to me. "But you don't need four, either. We're not Catholic. Two would have been plenty, but Tony wanted a boy, and then Jacinta was an accident. Before you know it, you've got four."

She surveyed the table. The accident, who had been popping up and down from the table to her mother's undisguised irritation, walked behind me and performed a sleight of hand to replace my empty glass with a full one. I liked her a lot.

Mrs. Brown had not finished. "Four children. One more and we'd have needed a van. We could have used one on the night—"

"Mum! No. Everyone's heard the story." This was Jacinta.

"I'm sure they haven't. Alan certainly hasn't."

"Adam," said Angelina.

"I haven't heard it," said the dentist.

I was happy to hear the story, especially if Angelina was a part of it. I did not expect Mrs. Brown would hold back on the details out of respect to anyone's sensitivities.

"Meredith was doing her moot—"

"Mock court," said Tony, presumably for the benefit of visitors unfamiliar with longstanding English tradition but also clarifying that Meredith had studied law. In case there had been any doubt.

"We know what a moot is, dear. On the same night as Edwin's speech night. And Angelina was in the school play at MLC."

"My school. Methodist Ladies' College," said Angelina. "I was the understudy for the lead. It was the one night I was down to do it myself."

Mrs. Brown laughed. "I always forget that bit and Angelina always reminds me. Anyway . . ."

I lost track of who needed to be where and when, but essentially Tony and Mrs. Brown had divided the duties. They had left thirteen-year-old Jacinta at home, not alone as it transpired because she had invited a few friends around—for drinks. There followed a farce of phone calls from concerned parents, detours, and an outbreak of alcohol-induced vomiting in the car. Angelina found her own way to the school play, and somehow her parents managed to catch the critical moments of the moot and the speech night. All good, then.

Dr. White saved me from asking.

"What about the play?"

"Oh, I should have mentioned that. That worked out, too. It was on all week, and we went the following night."

"But Angelina wasn't in it?"

"Oh yes, she was, just not in the lead role. We saw the proper lead, and she was just marvelous, wasn't she, Tony? Only a fourth former, just a little girl, but couldn't she act? If we'd gone on the other night we wouldn't have seen her."

I was watching Tony, and Tony was watching Angelina. He knew exactly what was going on but didn't say anything.

As Angelina helped clear the table, Jacinta, who had disappeared during the telling of the saga, gave me a tour of the backyard, with its cricket stumps painted on the side of the garage and stash of cannabis in the bike shed.

"Your mum and dad don't drink?" I said.

"It's Grandma. She's a Methodist. Mum drinks a bit. Dad drinks a lot."

That made sense.

She passed me the joint. "What's the deal with you and Angie?"

I took a considered toke. "We're good friends."

"She's high maintenance," said Jacinta. "I mean, she shouldn't have married Richard, he's a dick, but did she tell you she won't cook or wash the dishes? And now she's cheating on him, right?"

"They've split up."

"Having time out while Angie grows up, according to Mum. Don't get me wrong: she's my sister. My favorite sister. In case you hadn't noticed, it's not the sort of family where you want to be a black sheep. If you come back and get together with Angie, you have to let me stay any time I want."

She took a final long drag on the joint and stubbed it out on the brickwork. "Don't worry—I'm on your side."

We went back into the house and unwrapped presents. A flannel nightie for Angelina and a parcel to take to Richard.

Then Mrs. Brown started on politics. The public had seen through Mr. Hawke's socialist nonsense and the next election would sweep a new wave of young Liberals—which, in British terms, meant conservatives—into office. Had Richard thought of standing? The mention of Richard must have reminded her of me.

"What do *you* think of our prime minister, Alan?"

Angelina corrected her for the third time. "Adam, Mum."

I gave her the answer I would give a taxi driver: "I've only been here six months, so I don't know enough to comment on local politics."

"Good policy," said Tony.

Tony was a judge, a man of some experience in family dynamics, his own in particular. He had given me precious counsel that amounted to *Do not engage with Angelina's mother on this subject*. I could blame the alcohol and the joint for ignoring it, but they merely lowered my inhibitions. It wasn't the politics: Angelina's mother was no more forthright than my own, and she was entitled to her opinion. The problem was her constantly putting Angelina down.

Mrs. Brown gave me the opening, as she had been doing all day. "I'll say one thing for you English, you know what's good for you. I don't think anyone can say Mrs. Thatcher hasn't been good for England."

"Certainly not me da," I said, and Angelina flashed me a look. I ignored it. "Bein' dead 'n' all."

"I'm sorry to hear that."

"But when 'e were alive, 'e hated 'er. Stands to reason. With 'im being a miner."

"Your father was a coal miner?"

"Aye. Down pit."

"Well, with respect to your late father, I'm sure he was an honest worker, and I don't blame him personally, but the unions—Arthur Scargill, am I right? The man's a communist."

"Aye. So were me da. Then 'e got the black spot on 'is lung."

The story was spinning out of control, for the simple reason that I didn't have an ending—or even a point—in mind when I started. My father had died from lung cancer, but cigarettes had been the culprit, not coal dust. I did my best to join the dots.

"So those what says the miners didn't deserve a decent livin'—they never been down pit. They never seen me ol' da coughin' his lungs out into a dirty hanky."

"Oh my godfather—we've just eaten."


Tony walked with us to the car. It was hard to read Angelina's body language, possibly because she wasn't too sure how it had played out. Tony enlightened us both.

"You bastard," he said, and burst out laughing. "Down pit. Your dad wasn't a miner, was he?"

"He was a musician. But he wouldn't have minded."

"I'm sure he wouldn't. I hope you're not driving."

He gave Angelina a big hug, then turned back to me and put a hand on my shoulder. "You look after my girl."

Somehow I had got away with it, even earned some credit with Tony, and no doubt Jacinta. My dad might not have minded, but my mother would have been ashamed of me.

# 13

Brunswick Street was deserted on Christmas Day and Angelina parked outside my apartment.

"Is it okay if I stay again?" she said.

"Of course it's okay. I've always wanted you to stay. What about your mum?"

"I'm old enough not to let her run my life."

That was a step in the right direction. It was only a few hours since she'd spun the story about feeding the cat.

I had not noticed her putting her overnight bag into the car. Nor, apparently, had Jacinta seen her purloining the remains of the liquor, and we finished Christmas Day sitting on my bed washing down mince pies with warm vodka.

Unprompted, unless you count a lazy hand on a bare thigh as a prompt, Angelina said, "Is there anything you don't know about me, anything I haven't told you?"

"How would I know?" I said.

"I've told you everything I can think of. Is there anything that doesn't make sense?"

"Guess," I said.

"You want to know why I haven't let go of Richard?"

I nodded. My question would have been, "Why won't you promise to wait for me?" But surely part, if not all, of that answer was Richard.

He had always been in the background: today at the family home, the night I asked her out, that first evening at the piano.

"You've met my parents," she said. "You answer the question."

"Your dad's a Family Court judge. So he comes home with stories of people who've made stupid decisions, screwed up their marriages. Probably not flattering stories. You didn't want to be one of them."

"Keep going."

"And they've made their own marriage work. They're still together."

"Despite my mum having an opinion on everything and my dad having this disgusting old jumper that he won't throw out."

"Bit like my dad not coming home at night."

"Sorry. I wasn't trying to compare. I'm just saying they're role models for toughing it out, finding a way to make it work. You can never be completely sure you've found the right person, or the only person, or how you'll both change, but you make a commitment. . . ."

"And you think, since my parents didn't stay together, that I might be a bad risk?"

"I'm the one who screwed up a marriage, and did nothing to fix it except wait for Richard to apologize. I think it's the opposite. *You* don't want to screw up. So you're cautious." She lay back on the pillow. "What question do you think I'd want to ask you?"

Ah. It had been a circuitous path to the topic that only needed to be discussed if we had a future together. The one subject I had brushed aside when it came up. I had done that a few times.

"You'd say, 'You left a relationship because you didn't want to have kids. Is that going to change?' Right?"

"Not quite. I'd say, 'Why are you so worried you won't be a good father?'"

It was a better question. My own ruminations on the topic had never got beyond a gut feeling that I was not ready, notwithstanding the moment at Carols by Candlelight. But if Angelina had read me right, then it went deeper, no doubt back to my desire not to follow my own father, and perhaps a fear that I had inherited more than his ear for music.

She didn't wait for my answer. She sat up and put a hand on either side of my face.

"Adam, listen to me. I know you. I know you better than anyone else. You'd be a fantastic dad. Not just because of who you are, but because you care so much about not getting it wrong. In the same way you don't want to get marriage wrong. If I ever had kids, I'd be happy for you to be their father."

Then, as if to separate the part about herself, about us as a couple, she repeated, "You'd be a fantastic dad. One day, when you're playing with your kids, wherever it is in the world, whoever you're with, remember I was the one who told you that you could do it. That's my real Christmas present to you."

We stayed up all night. It was Angelina's idea: "We've never seen the dawn together, and I don't want to sleep tonight anyway."

My warehouse did not have a balcony, but there was an external ladder to the roof. It was warm, and we told each other the story of the four and a half months we had known each other, filling in the gaps, arguing about our already diverging memories.

"He sent one of the wenches out to get the olives? In what she was wearing? He wouldn't have."

"He did."

"Oh God, the poor girl."

"That's why you got a black olive instead of green."

"It wasn't black."

"I'm promising you it was."

She laughed. "You're probably right. I wouldn't have known what color to expect. It was my first martini."

"What? You—"

"I was trying to impress you."

"Me. *You* were—"

"You. The international consultant who just happens to play brilliant piano and has the answer to everything."

"Well, now you know I don't."

"None of us do. We just have to find a way through with what we've got."

"Like the manager. 'No trouble at all, *madame*. Oh shit, what do I do now?'"

"That poor girl."

The vodka was almost gone when the sky started to lighten and we finally went to bed.

The following evening, most of the local cafés were still closed. I made some spaghetti with a can of tomatoes and we drank a bottle of Yarra Valley cabernet, which we had bought on one of our days out. It was our last night but one before I departed, and we did not know when we would see each other again. We had made love most of the afternoon and were both restless.

Angelina looked out the window onto the almost empty street. "You want to see if the bar's open?"

Surprisingly, it was. There was no one there except Shanksy.

"I thought you'd gone back to Pommieland," he said.

"New Zealand. Day after tomorrow."

He made us eggnogs, and we sat at the bar, happy to have him there. He turned on the television, the one I had used to watch three episodes of *Mornington Police* a lifetime ago. We watched the highlights of the one-day cricket match between Australia and Sri Lanka, and drank two more eggnogs each, quietly writing ourselves off.

At 9:30 P.M., Shanksy turned off the television.

"I think it might be closing time," he said.

"I think so, too," said Angelina. "I think everything's been said that's going to be said." She turned to me and her big brown eyes looked into mine. "Do you know 'Angel of the Morning'?"

I walked to the piano, and played an A, just as I had on the night she walked into the bar and my world changed. And, like the first time, I let her sing the first line unaccompanied: there would be no strings to bind my hands, if her love couldn't bind my heart.

I continued, hitting a chord at the beginning of each line. E again. A. E. It was she who chose to start. B minor: facing the dawn, alone.

Her voice was soaring, absolutely soaring, in the empty bar. I played the piano properly as she started the chorus, and kept the accompaniment going into the next verse. I had never played with such *passion*, and our audience of one had stopped in the middle of the room, transfixed.

Angelina's voice wavered as she sang the last verse, and I was puffing my cheeks out and blowing through pursed lips like a goldfish to keep back my own tears.

At the end of the final chorus I did a reprise, because the tears and the days and the years bit works like a pre-chorus, as though the song has no ending. The traditional way to finish the song is to stretch out the last "baby"—*bay-ay-bee*—and follow with some dramatic instrumental work to bring things to a close.

Angelina didn't take that option. I was ready to go around again, but then realized she was finishing as she started, that night five months ago, a cappella.

*Then slowly turn away*
*I won't beg you to stay*
(D chord, long, *long* pause) *With me.*

Then, with an actress's sense of drama, Angelina slowly turned away and walked out of the bar. The goldfish trick stopped working, and Shanksy came over and put a clumsy arm around me.

I spent the next day packing up. Angelina had left her bag, and I put her bits and pieces from the bathroom into it. Toothbrush, contact lens case, a vial of Obsession.

It was feeling like a breakup. I was still trying to make sense of how the night had ended. You can only read so much into lyrics, especially as the song in question had other meanings for us, but the line about the strings that bound her hands had surely been directed at Richard on the first night.

I held out some hope that I would see Angelina before I left. She knew where to find me and had the excuse of the bag. At ten P.M., I walked to the bar.

The place was busy, considering the time of year.

"She hasn't been in," said Shanksy. "The boss wanted to send you a thank-you present but we didn't have your address. Anyway, be good to keep in touch."

I gave him my mother's address and my Brunswick Street one. "If he's quick, he can save on postage. I'll be there till about noon tomorrow."

That message would be passed to Angelina if she turned up. I had a couple of beers, left Angelina's bag with Shanksy, and walked home.

I had gone to bed when the doorbell rang. I pulled on my jeans and raced down the stairs. It was not Angelina but Lucy, one of the girls from the bar, out of breath and sweating. The night was still warm.

"She just came in."

I sprinted back upstairs, grabbed shoes and T-shirt, and raced ahead of Lucy. Shanksy's expression told me the bad news.

"She was only here five minutes. Didn't even have a drink. Picked up her bag, sang one song, walked out."

"Who played the piano?"

"She did. She wasn't bad."

"What did she sing?"

"One song," said Shanksy. "Brought the house down. As always. 'I Will Survive.' Gave it everything she had."

# 14

Angelina wasn't at the airport when I checked in. Elizabeth Barrett Browning and Gloria Gaynor were competing for space in my head.

*Go from me, go on, go*
*Alone upon the threshold of my door*
*Walk out that door, just walk away*

My hope that Angelina's farewell was a dramatic response to a painful but temporary separation had been overtaken by a feeling that I had screwed up, badly. I found a pay phone and rang her parents' number.

"Brown residence." Angelina's mother.

"Hello, I was wondering if I could speak with Angelina."

"That's Alan, is it? Have you tried her at home?"

Jesus. "No, I've misplaced the number."

Mrs. Brown kindly gave me Richard's number and I was pondering whether Angelina might be feeding the cat, if a cat existed, when I heard a familiar voice call my name. I turned and saw her running toward me, dodging people and bags and carts.

Not Angelina but Jacinta, her younger sister. She reached me, flushed and flustered.

"Shit, shit, shit. I couldn't find what flight you were on and then the taxi didn't come and Mum wanted to know where I was going and I said, 'I'm eighteen, it's none of your business,' and she went troppo. . . ."

I put my hands on her shoulders. "I've only got a minute before I have to go. What's happening?"

"Are you in love with Angie? Yes or no? Because if it's no, just get on the plane and I'm not telling you anything. Except that you're a shit."

"Yes."

"Okay: she loves you, too. So it should be easy. But everyone's being stupid. Including you."

They called my flight.

"Hang loose—they always call early," said Jacinta. "On Tuesday—Boxing Day—about one o'clock in the morning—the next morning—she comes into my room and says you guys broke up. And we talked all night and she told me everything. Don't worry, I don't mean *every-thing* everything, and it wasn't like I hadn't worked it out. I'm like her big sister. I don't mean like Meredith—I mean, I didn't get married to the first guy I got together with. So I'm way more experienced, but she still won't listen—"

"Simple question. Does she want to be with me?"

Jacinta looked at me, and I realized that even now, with the plane waiting at the gate, I was asking Angelina to commit first.

I took a breath and added, "Because I want to be with her." Then the word that mattered. "Forever."

I'd done it: cut the Gordian knot. Not in the way I should have, face-to-face with Angelina two days earlier, but even as I said the words to her sister I felt the doubt fall away. A door had opened, the light was streaming through, and there would be a path we could walk down. We—Angelina and I—would make it work.

That was the moment. It was also the moment that I understood what had been holding me back: a fear that I wasn't good enough. That she was too good for me. Everything that had made our relationship strong, everything I loved in Angelina, had only added to the weight of evidence.

Angelina had understood that, and what she had said on Christmas night about my dedication to making things work was meant to allay my fears. Perhaps it was that; perhaps it was the validation from Jacinta; perhaps it was simply that the reality of losing Angelina trumped everything else. The reason didn't matter now.

Then Jacinta spoke. The frustration in her voice had not gone away.

"It's not that easy. Yesterday I'm saying to her, go see him. Sort it out, tell him you'll wait for him if he . . . And then there's a knock at the door and it's him. Richard. He came back from Sydney. And he drags Angie off. Not physically—she followed him. Then I ring her and she can't talk, and when she calls me back she says things have changed and they're going to sort it out and she doesn't want to talk about you. Which is . . ."

Which is everything I should have realized would happen. I *hadn't* been good enough, not good enough to step up when she needed me to. For a moment I was angry with Jacinta, the messenger.

"What am I supposed to do?"

"I don't know. Something. If you really love her, you'll find a way. She loves you. Whatever she says. She's my sister and I want what's right for her, and I think that's you if you really love her. You do, right?"

"'Fraid so. But I'm not sure I can do anything about it at the moment."

"I'm in so much shit over this. I'm not talking to Meredith."

"Meredith?"

"She called Richard. After you came to Christmas. She swears she didn't, but it wouldn't be anyone else."

"Maybe it was your mum."

"No way. Mum wouldn't bother hiding it."

"Probably only trying to do the right thing. We're all trying to do the right thing."

All I could think of was that the right thing, the only decent thing, now, was not to get between Angelina and what she had wanted all along. And I hoped, wishing her only the best, as the man who was about to step graciously aside, that one day she'd come home and find him screwing the cleaning lady.

Final call was up for my flight.

"Give me your address," said Jacinta.

"I'm going to be traveling."

"Write to me. Tell me where you are. In case something happens."

I gave her my work address in New Zealand.

"I've got to go. Thank you for doing this."

I hugged her and she hugged me back. I held on for a bit longer, pretending for a few seconds that she was someone else.

"If I don't see you again, have a good life," she said. Then, "Have you got any Australian money left? The taxi cost me twenty-two dollars."


I finished my first week of work in Auckland by buying drinks for my new colleagues. There was a piano in the bar, an opportunity to play, and I didn't take it up. I didn't feel like it.

A few weeks later, there was a letter for me, Angelina's parents' address on the back. The good news ended there.

It was a note from Jacinta: just a scrap of paper saying, *In case you're still interested, they're still together.*

Attached was a newspaper clipping: *Judge Slams Society Lawyer,* with a photo of Richard and Angelina that looked to have been taken a couple of years earlier.

Richard had been indiscreet about a matter before the courts and, as a result, a trial involving a minor celebrity had to be abandoned. He had lost his job and was facing disciplinary action by the Law Institute.

His slip of the tongue had apparently occurred at a pre-Christmas drinks function in Sydney. He had probably known what was coming when he flew back to Angelina, who rated a brief mention in the article as a *Mornington Police* actress.

Surely this would be enough to knock him off his pedestal. I was not so naïve as to see it breaking them up, at least not immediately. On the contrary, it was probably the reason Angelina had taken him back. That, plus him saying, "I'm sorry; I've changed; the other woman didn't mean anything." As well as her being vulnerable after what had happened with us, the desire to believe in her original dreams and judgment, and perhaps some confidence that she had an answer to the sexual problems. Not to mention having her own place again. I would have moved in with Richard myself if the alternative was living with Angelina's mother.

Angelina was now presumably the breadwinner. She would see an opportunity to be supportive, perhaps in return for Richard doing the cooking and ironing. How Richard would respond to the change in roles was another matter. Regardless, Angelina had chosen to try to make a difficult situation work, and I had to respect that.

In Singapore, a couple of months into my world tour, I spent some time with an American consultant. Bob hailed from Idaho and was a technology guru of about forty with the regulation beard and Buddy Holly glasses. Over chili crab and Tiger beer, he told a story of working in Poland in the early seventies, when the Iron Curtain was firmly in place, and meeting a heart-stoppingly beautiful woman.

He had pictures, and his description was a fair one. She was also intelligent, cultured, and, for reasons he could not fathom, interested in him. He thought, Life doesn't get any better than this for a computer geek; we'll deal with any problems as they come along. After knowing her only two weeks, he asked her to marry him—and they were still together.

"How old were you?" I asked.

"Twenty-six."

Bob was giving me the same advice as the woman in the antique shop. Too late now.

That did not stop me chewing it over. And over. It was no single thing. It was my job, her job, my unwillingness to commit, her unwillingness to bury her marriage, my concerns about fatherhood.

But the nub of it was this: if Angelina had truly wanted me, she would have been willing to wait and then give us both time to let the relationship develop without the need for any bigger commitment.

At the same time, her self-esteem may have been torn down so comprehensively by Richard, with some help from her mother, that she needed that commitment to see her through. I had left it too late, not just through fear of making a wrong decision, but because I had not believed I was good enough for Angelina, a belief she had reinforced by not offering to wait for me.

I wanted Angelina to prove her love by doing it my way. She wanted the same of me. But we had each doubted ourselves too much to do what the other needed.

In Hong Kong, I read Gabriel García Márquez's *Love in the Time of Cholera*, in which the hero must wait until his seventies before being united with his beloved. In a moment of melancholy, I inscribed my copy *Angelina, I will love you always. Adam* and sent it to her, via Jacinta. It was an unhealthy book for me to have read at that time, and to have then inflicted on Angelina. Just wait long enough and somehow the right people will die, the stars will align, we'll get over ourselves, and we'll be together. And, in the meantime, what?

In Johannesburg, I had a few dates with a woman who was staying in the same block of serviced apartments—Swiss, working for a pharmaceuticals group. Brigitte was good company and we had fun, but I was not ready to take a relationship to the next stage. My heart wasn't in it.

Angelina wrote to me twice. The first time was when she and Richard finally broke up. It had taken just over a year.

> *I'm sorry I didn't write earlier. I hope you'll understand that I was trying to get on with my life and I could not do so if I stayed in touch with you. Thank you for the book. I loved you too, and if you really were going to love me forever then I made the wrong decision in not waiting for you.*

*I think so often of the time we spent together, but I have to let go of it to move on. I keep thinking we were meant to be, but I can't expect it to happen now.*

*I'm OK and have been getting a lot of support from Jacinta (you remember my crazy sister) and Charlie, who's a big bear who used to work with my father.*

*I can't change the past, but I'm so sorry that I screwed up.*

*Love*

*Angel*

I had finished my marathon contract with the insurance company and landed a new assignment in London. The letter came to my mother's address in Manchester.

My mother brought a certain amount of sanity to my life or, alternatively, she cemented in the insanity that had caused the problem and stopped me from fixing it. A married woman I'd only known for a few months—an actress, for goodness' sake—putting pressure on me to commit, and me only twenty-six.

"You're well out of it. Thank your lucky stars it wasn't a local lass. When your grandfather went to war, my mother waited for him for three years. This girl needs to get her own life sorted out before she starts messing yours up. How long did you say she'd been married? Oh, for heaven's sake, she needs to grow up."

More than anything else, I was torn, guilty that I could not get on a plane and go to Angelina. I had promised eternal love, and when she called it in I was not there.

# 15

My client in London was four years older than me, short, strawberry blond, cute in a freckly, jeans-and-sloppy-jumper sort of way, and a bit of a gym addict. She interviewed me for the job, and I liked her immediately. Her name was Claire.

We had a rapport: it often seemed that we were the only two who knew what needed to be done and wanted to get on with doing it. She enjoyed a reputation for astuteness, fairness, and absolute unflappability. Every problem could be solved; nothing that happened at work was worth losing sleep over; the past was for learning from.

Among those in need of Claire's steadying influence was a data modeler named Gérard. Out of the blue, he asked me for a drink after work—in his case a Campari and soda with a twist of orange. We chatted for a while about why the specification he had given me was an unworkable fantasy, a view that Claire had endorsed.

"We should hardly be surprised. She's putty in your hands."

Claire was putty in no one's hands.

"How do you work that out?"

"There's no other reason for her to agree to denormalizing the reference tables. Ask her out. Relieve us all of our misery. I presume the interest is mutual."

It was, but I was not going to ask my client for a date, especially on such tenuous evidence. Perhaps when the contract was over, six months or so down the track.

"If she fancies me, she can ask me out."

A couple of days later, I walked away from my terminal and came back to find someone had sent a message from my account. To Claire.

*Dinner and a movie tonight?*

I hit Recall, something you could do back then, but it was too late. The message had been read.

"Guilty as charged," said Gérard, calm in the face of my absolute bloody apoplexy. "Someone had to do it, and tragically you lacked the cojones."

"Right then, Cyrano de Bergerac. We're both going to see Claire and you can tell her what you've done. You'd better hope she can take a joke."

"Shall we see if she's replied before we get too excited?"

It was my turn to buy Gérard a drink that evening. Before going to dinner and a film with Claire.

She was great company, but we were both conscious of working together and our conversations stayed on safe territory. After two dates, I decided to push it a little and booked dinner at the River Cafe in Hammersmith.

Half a drink into the meal, she put down her fork and said, "Date number three. Friday night. Special restaurant. What should I assume?"

"You're the project manager. I wouldn't want to disappoint you by falling behind schedule."

"You've got that part of me worked out. How about I tell you something about the other part and you can decide whether you want to keep seeing me?"

"The secret life of Claire Axford?"

"Enough of it to stop you wasting your time and money. I'm not a foodie. This is nice, but so is curry, and fish and chips. If you want to impress me, you can cook me a roast dinner. My perfect night out is listening to music. And I don't want to have children."

"That's it?"

"Barely the beginning. But you needed to know that much. Especially with regard to children. No point starting out with mismatched expectations."

There was something immensely appealing about her no-nonsense façade, *because* I was sure it was a façade. There was more to her, and I wanted to be the one to see it.

It was after eleven P.M. when we finished the meal.

"Not too late to catch some music?" I said.

"Full marks for paying attention."


"I thought we agreed on music," said Claire, arms folded. I had managed to deflect her questions about venue as I let the train pass the clubs of Camden Town and alighted at Hampstead.

"We did. This is my place, and I'm going to play you some music."

"I meant live music."

"Of course."

"You play something?"

"Piano."

"All right. I let myself in for that. I'll come up for a cup of tea, but for future reference, I'm more of a rock 'n' roll person."

While Claire made herself tea ("I know how I like it"), I plugged the electronic keyboard into the stereo, cranked up the volume, then had second thoughts. An acoustic piano can make plenty of noise in a small flat, and it seemed appropriate that the Rönisch Three Crown that I had decided would accompany me through my life should be my weapon of choice.

Claire walked in with her cuppa. I ripped my right thumb down the keys and tore into Jerry Lee Lewis's "Great Balls of Fire": big chords, strong bass line, and my best Little-Richard-in-full-cry impression. Claire stopped dead, put down her teacup, watched for a few seconds, and burst out laughing. And then she was singing with me, rocking, hitting the top of the piano in time with the beat, still laughing. It was the first time I had seen her let go. And it was the first time I had played a full song since "Angel of the Morning" in Shanksy's bar, almost a year before.

I must have played for an hour and a half, Claire into it as much as I was, the barriers down. It was only rock 'n' roll, but it was a huge release after so long.

The next morning, she made coffee and I asked her about the issue with children.

"I suppose I can't object to your asking a personal question after I've spent the night with you. I'd be a terrible mother. I had a really bad role model and I don't want to pass it on to another generation."

Like me, Claire had been an only child, but in her case it was because her sister Alison had died of meningitis at the age of three, a few months before Claire was born. Her mother had never got over her grief, nor taken the risk of loving a child again. Claire's father had died of a heart attack when she was six. Claire had decided that it was better not to have children of her own and risk repeating her mother's mistakes. I could understand that.

When my lease ran out a few months later, I moved in with Claire. She got me playing again and we caught a lot of live bands. Her taste was broader than she had indicated, but she wasn't much of a lyrics person. She just wanted the pure hit of music.

It was her way of opening up emotionally. Intimacy and conversations about feelings did not come easily to her and, after a few sessions with a psychologist before she met me, she had decided that therapy created more problems than it solved. She had made a strength of her emotional detachment, built a career on it, and was not going to tamper with that foundation. Except with music, and only with me. The band would play, I would wrap my arms around her, and there would be a connection beyond anything words could achieve. And if I wanted to reach her: a song at the piano would cut straight through to a place she would never otherwise let me into.

It was a while before she shared a bit of information that I should have guessed.

"You know that message Gérard sent to me? I got him to do it."

It was almost a year before I met Claire's mother, Joy.

"Bottle of something?" I asked Claire as we packed the car for the overnight stay in Norwich. It was a Saturday, and her mother would be turning sixty-five the following week.

"She doesn't drink."

I had already been warned that we would not be sleeping together.

"Religious?"

"Hardly. That'd involve some sort of hope."

"Come on, she can't be that bad."

She was. I would have picked her for seventy-five rather than sixty-five; short like Claire, but slumped shoulders, bent and gray. No hug—not even a smile—for her daughter. I had been promised that I would hear about Alison in the first few minutes, and Joy did not disappoint.

"I'm sorry, Adam, you'll find dinner's very plain. It's hard to get enthusiastic about cooking when you've lost a child."

It was so contrived that it was almost funny. Thirty-two years had passed. Over lamb chops and mushy vegetables, Joy managed to weave Alison's death into every second sentence.

"Christ," I said, when Joy had headed to the bathroom. ("My bladder's never been the same since I had Alison; it's a price to pay for only three years of life.") "Is she like this all the time?"

Claire nodded. "I'd come home and have hurt myself or broken up with my boyfriend, and she'd say, 'Wait till you've lost a child. Then you'll know what it's like to suffer.' You see why I don't do this too often."

Even Claire's level-headedness had its limit, and it was apparent that she was approaching it as we cleared the plates.

"You all right?" I asked.

"I've been better. I'm going to need some time out very soon."

"Say you're not feeling well."

"I can't leave you with her."

"'Course you can."

Claire made her excuses and went upstairs. Joy led me to the front room, sat on the sofa, and pointed me to the armchair.

"'Can I make you a tea?" I said.

"I'm all right. Would you like a glass of brandy? I keep some for cooking."

I tried to conjure up a picture of Joy flambéing a baked Alaska.

She began to get up, then said, "It's in the sideboard in the dining room. You'd better pour me one, too."

I poured two and brought the bottle over. We talked for a couple of hours, about the work she did with the local hospital, about Claire's late father, who had been a real estate agent, and about her desire to stay where she was living until her death. She would not be led on Claire, but nor did she mention Alison except in the context of keeping the house. After the second refill, she even smiled a bit. It seemed that the depression and obsession with Alison were reserved for Claire.

Finally she got up, steadily enough considering what she had drunk. We had not discussed the sleeping arrangements.

"There's a spare bedroom?" I asked.

"Oh my God, no, you can't sleep there," said Joy. "But you should see it."

By the time I followed her upstairs, I had guessed what would be behind the door of the middle bedroom, but not the extent of the creepiness factor. Faded wallpaper with Beatrix Potter characters, a single bed with clothes laid out, a few soft toys and dolls, a big box. Just an ordinary child's room from 1958. I was happy to sleep on the couch.

Joy closed the door of Alison's room. "I haven't been much of a mother to Claire. Are you two thinking of having children?"

"Not yet."

"I hope you do. Claire's always wanted children."

Then, while I was taking that in: "You don't need to sleep on the couch."

Perhaps thinking I might misunderstand her and bunk down on the single bed with the teddy bear and dolls and little-girl's clothes, she added, "You can sleep in Claire's room. Just don't tell her I let you."


Sunday morning, driving out of Norwich, Claire was quiet and I found myself reflecting on her concerns about motherhood. I had uncritically accepted her decision not to have children because it sat well with my own, Angelina's reassurances notwithstanding. But her mother's revelation rang true.

I ran the flag up the pole. "Seeing your mum reminded me of what you said about having children."

"Well, now you know why."

"Not really. You've turned out all right."

"Glad you think so. But—"

"So, even with a mother like that, you got through. If we had children, they'd have a better start than you did."

"Adam. I don't know where you're going with this, but I thought I made it clear at the outset . . ."

"Date number three. We've come a way since then."

Claire was driving, eyes fixed on the road ahead. "You're telling me you want a family? Now? After—"

"You'd only be half the equation," I said. "I'd be there. I'd do what it took to make it work."

"You'd be there? Should I take that as some kind of promise?"

"Claire, you know I love you. I'll be here as long as you want me to be."

"But you really want children? With me?"

"Only with you."

Claire drove in silence for about ten minutes, then pulled off the motorway.

"You okay?" I said.

"I'm fine. I just thought that if we're going to make it permanent, I should meet your family as well."

Then, four hours later, parking outside my mother's house: "Adam, I'm really not sure about this."

"We've come all this way. You have to meet her now."

"You know what I'm talking about."

"I'll be there. We'll look after each other. That's what love's about. You do love me, don't you?"

"I'd have thought you'd have worked that out by now."

Over the next few weeks, Claire would bring up the topic then drop it, showing none of the certainty and confidence that characterized the rest of her life. It seemed clear enough to me that she did want children. So did I. Though neither of us expressed it with any clarity, we felt that being a mother would give Claire a chance to show the part of herself that she held back in the adult world. I wanted to see it more often, too.

But if it was going to go forward, I would have to be the driver. Without Angelina's declaration of confidence in me, I would not have been able to do it. While her words had not made a great impact at the time, lost as they were in our last-ditch efforts to save our relationship, they now gave me a semblance of confidence that it was possible to overcome a bad start.

Claire's friend Mandy, a human resources manager, and her husband, Randall, a networks guy, were also trying for a child. Despite Mandy being a tiny bit too driven, we all got on well and over time became close friends.

With their support, Claire and I worked our way through the parenthood issue to the extent that we saw our future as a family rather than a couple, with children at the center of our emotional life.

After all that, Claire didn't get pregnant. Medical intervention was a step too far for her, and because she didn't want to have any tests there was never a specific moment when we acknowledged that we were not going to have children. I had myself tested, which was pretty straightforward, and it seemed that all was well there, which, in a way, was a shame. I would have been willing to explore options on my side.

After some soul-searching, I decided not to share the result with Claire: it would only have put pressure on her to do something herself, or to take an unfair share of the blame for it not working out.

There was another thing that we had not factored in: we had agreed that we would get married when Claire got pregnant. As time passed and one didn't happen, the other got lost, too.

Somewhere along the way I stopped playing piano. I suppose I grew out of it. Plenty of people play music, join bands in their teens, but unless you're one of the few who manages to make a living at it, giving it up is part of the passage to adulthood—and parenthood.

I kept practicing, but fell into a habit of just doing exercises on the keyboard with the headphones on.

Early in our relationship, I had told Claire about Angelina, to the extent that there had been a woman in Australia, that she was an actress in a TV series whom I'd met when she sang in the bar, and that she and her husband had got back together. Claire asked me a few questions, I gave her the answers, and that was that. She was more interested in my live-in relationship with Joanna than a three-month affair in another country.

It was only with the passing of the years, as my relationship with Claire cooled, that memories of Angelina resurfaced. Should I have shared that with Claire? To what end? Surely all of us have private thoughts that would only create conflict, make laughingstocks of ourselves, or hurt others if we shared them. I was committed to Claire, and if I had the occasional moment of nostalgia, that was for me to deal with.

Long before that, the second letter from Angelina came, the one I came to interpret as *Come and rescue me*. I didn't, and she married Charlie.

Claire became my life partner and, in time, Angelina became my Great Lost Love, a poignant memory to add pathos to a sad song, with no substance in the present world. I forgot about *Love in the Time of Cholera*.

Until my inbox went *Hi* and *Do you want to live dangerously?*

# 16

On Wednesday, I was at my desk in London. Thanks to some smart work on the part of my agent, there had been a change in my lifestyle: a contract with a major oil company in the West End, daily travel covered, just six weeks, great rates, and an immediate start. It was a long train ride from Norwich, then a short hop on the Tube from Liverpool Street.

I had learned a little about the consulting game since my days of heaping advice on Tina and her Australian colleagues. The essential lesson of a further twenty years' experience was *Shut up and listen*, a mantra that sat uneasily with my undiminished need to prove I deserved the money.

On my second day of listening, I discovered that my desk had been taken from one of the field workers, who now had nowhere to put his family photos. I offered to work from home three days a week to ease the pressure on office space. Nigel got his desk back and I passed the savings in train fares back to my client.

But on Wednesday I was doing one of my two days at the London office and fitting Angelina into my lunch break.

I sent the first message, right on noon, eleven P.M. her time.

*So, what brought all this on?*

*Brought what on?* came the reply a few seconds later.

We should have been using instant messaging, but we were in our forties. E-mail was more our speed.

*Communication. It's been a little while.*

*Just feeling twitchy.*

Jesus. Twitchy had been her word for being turned on. Did Charlie see her e-mails? Did she use that word with him?

*Twitchy . . .*

*I was using the word in a broad sense.*

A broad sense.

*First time you've felt twitchy, in a broad sense, since 1989?*

*I was very twitchy in 1989.*

*I'd forgotten . . .*

We went on in that vein, saying nothing that would suggest we were intelligent adults, or indeed that we had anything of substance to say to each other after all this time, while I munched on an apple and drank a bottle of mineral water. My inquiries about why she had got in touch were deflected. I did manage to convey that I had a job.

*Have to go. Keeping lunch breaks short: long commute Norwich– London.*

*TTYL xxx.*

*Come again?*

*Talk to you later. Where have you been living?*

Under a rock, apparently.

On the Friday, working from home, I had an attack of cabin fever, which I treated by catching the bus to the supermarket and buying a Jamie Oliver shoulder of pork for dinner, skipping lunch to keep the calories under control.

By the time Claire got home, the Weber was making enticing smells, the potatoes were in the oven, and I had a bottle of Rioja open. I had not intended to set up a seduction, but that was the way she read it.

We ended up in her bed, the bed that had once been ours. It was good to put myself back in the real world, remind myself what I had. Afterward I got up to go to the bathroom and Claire said, "Hey, come over here," and patted my belly.

"We're looking distinctly trimmer," she said. "Stay."

So I stayed the night with my partner. Life was not getting any simpler. Better, but not simpler.

We slept in on Saturday morning, and I made coffee. Claire went to the gym, I went for a jog, we went to a café for lunch together, she had some work to do, I browsed the Net, made pasta for dinner, opened another bottle of red, and then it was bedtime. I looked at Claire, she looked at me, we kissed—and went to our separate beds.

I can't explain it. If I had followed her to bed, I know she would not have sent me away. I more than half wanted to. But I was drawn back to my room, where I did something I had never done before. I lit the candle that sat on my bedside table. I turned off the light and let it burn for a few minutes. Then I blew it out.

Over the next week, I was conscious that something had changed in me, beyond the reenergizing that had pushed me back into the work-force. It manifested itself as a desire to play and sing again. I had kept up the daily practice, often just swinging around in the chair to play a few exercises as a break from the Internet, but without any heart. And no voice. Singing required a different sort of effort and a certain emotional state that, until now, I had almost forgotten.

Claire caught me one evening. "Were you singing?" she said. "I haven't heard you sing for ages."

"There's a reason for that."

"You really ought to think about this six-months-on, six-months-off thing. I think work's good for you."

"Could be. I just don't want it to take over my life."

"Point taken. Sing me something."

"It was just practice."

Come Wednesday, I was back in London. No choice about that: there was a weekly team meeting that I was expected to attend, and Angelina's availability seemed tied to Charlie's wine-tasting night. I had spent quite a bit of time thinking about our next exchange.

Between *Hi Dooglas* and her *TTYL xxx*, I managed to establish that she did not want to talk about her current life, but that reminiscences were fine, even when they slipped into flirtations.

*Do you still have the dress you wore to the Mock Tudor?*

*Which one?*

*Blue, split down the middle. Of the top.*

*Believe it or not, I've still got it somewhere. Not sure I'd be brave enough to wear it now. I know why you remember it.*

*Why?*

*You were all over me in the taxi. It didn't offer a lot of protection.*

*Lucky the driver didn't throw us out.*

*You wear a dress like that, you've got to expect that response.*

*Expect but not deserve.*

*That's what I said. I seem to recall you didn't mind.*

And so it went. Harmless fun.

# 17

I settled into a new routine, or at least managed to assemble the components of my life into a workable shape.

My contract was extended indefinitely, and I was able to organize my London travel to accommodate the pub quiz three nights a week.

My relationship with Claire had taken a turn for the better. On Friday nights we would eat together, open a bottle of wine, and sleep in her room. We never discussed it; it just happened. It was not about Claire substituting for Angelina. I had no image of what Angelina looked or sounded like now. It was just a flow-on from feeling alive again.

I was making good progress with the jogging, and with the diet. I was playing real music and singing, often well beyond my regulation twenty minutes. My voice was coming back.

The exchanges with Angelina were the most routine thing of all: a quarter of an hour of online flirting from my desk, once a week, at noon to begin with, then later as winter turned to spring in England and the clocks changed on both sides of the world. I learned nothing about the present-day Angelina beyond the fact that her sexual proclivities had not changed.

*Been caught recently?*

*In your dreams.*

*I think that one's yours.*

*Possibly.*

*We're applying for a home loan, and the bank manager steps out for a few minutes . . .*

*Behave.*

I would sometimes go over the e-mail threads again, and it's fair to say they occupied more than fifteen minutes in my thoughts each week, but I did not let my imagination take me further. As for Angelina's motivation: I assumed that she wanted a little of the risqué fun that you can't expect in a long-established marriage, and had chosen a collaborator who was at a safe distance, shared some history and, thanks to the passing of time, had no emotional attachment.

When Claire reminded me that she would be spending a three-day weekend with her walking club in the Lake District, I found myself feeling edgy at the prospect of being alone. My busy life was working well; I didn't need any unstructured time. A trip away with Claire seemed like a good idea.

"I don't suppose partners are invited on these drinking fests," I said on the Monday morning, as Claire woke me with coffee.

"Everyone's welcome. But this one's a point-to-point—we end up somewhere different from where we start, so you can't stop behind and do barbecue duty."

Claire was referring to holidays from more than ten years earlier. Randall and Mandy, still without children themselves, had moved to Silicon Valley for weather, money, and adventure, and pushed us to do the same. Claire might have gone, too, if I had been willing.

After they moved, we got into a routine of joint holidays (which Randall, in due course, called vacations), alternating between the U.S.

and the UK (which Randall had stopped calling home). Mandy was a hiker, and she pulled Claire into it. It worked for everyone: Randall and I would spend the day in scenic surroundings drinking and preparing a barbecue for our partners to eat on their return. If a walk were particularly famous or promising, we might even join them.

Mandy and Randall continued their efforts to start a family. Where Claire had drawn the line at medical intervention, they tried all the options and, after four years of the best that California clinics could offer, produced a pair of British-American twins.

We were envious, of course, but the IVF and then the kids took a bigger toll on their relationship than the failure to have children had taken on ours. A major screw-up on Randall's part was the last straw and there was a horrible custody battle before Mandy won the right to return to the UK with the children.

As happens with divorces, we ended up on one side: in this case, Mandy's. Claire had not pushed it, but she did not have a big social circle outside work and Mandy was her closest friend. She was also the one living in the UK, so there was a practical aspect to it. Randall and I exchanged e-mails for a while, but it fell away. Mandy now lived in Liverpool and Claire had joined her walking club.

"I can walk," I said. I was regularly *running* six miles.


I bought some decent walking kit from a London outdoors shop. Technology had moved on since I had last used a rucksack: the one I bought sat clear of my back and had a built-in rain cover. I took the salesman's advice that leather boots belonged to the Middle Ages—or the middle-aged—and chose a pair of blue Gore-Tex shoes that would not have been out of place in a skate park. A lightweight jacket, neat trousers in matching blue rather than khaki, and waterproof overpants completed the ensemble.

We took the Friday off and made it a leisurely drive. I sensed that Claire had been in two minds about having me along, but there was no tension. Whatever our sleeping arrangements, we were still a couple.

About an hour into the drive she punched the Stop button on Elton John's "Skyline Pigeon."

"If I can interrupt your dreams of flying off to distant lands," she said, "I can give you an update on real life. Distant lands might be part of it."

"I gather you're getting closer to a deal."

"It's looking like I'll have the deciding vote. VJ wants to take the money and run. Tim still thinks we can do better growing the business ourselves. But he's not going to stop us if we both want to sell."

"You think they might have set it up that way? Split the vote so you have to make the decision?"

She laughed. "You may be right."

"So?" I said. "What do you want to do?"

"I want to do what's right for the product. I don't know if you've noticed, but it's been my baby for the past four years."

"I have noticed."

"I know it's been tough on you. But we're almost there. They're offering distribution in the U.S. The Americans administer child support at the state level—so we're talking potentially fifty state governments. Plus D.C. and all of Canada."

"You can't market it yourselves? From here?"

"Not to government clients. You have to have the infrastructure. Offices, sales reps, contacts. That's what they're offering. But they're going to need someone who knows the product inside out. Which means me. It's possible the sale won't go ahead unless I'm prepared to go to the States and kick it off for them."

She turned from the wheel and looked at me.

"For how long?" I said, glancing out my window at England's green and pleasant land.

"A year. Maybe longer. That's what I wanted to talk about."

"We talked about going to the U.S. when Randall and Mandy went."

"That was permanent. This would only be for a while. You worked overseas."

"In my twenties."

"I'm serious about this. It's really important to me."

"I'm taking you seriously. But the deal's not done yet. Let's jump it when we come to it."

Claire waited a few moments, then pushed the Play button.

We were staying at a pub in Ennerdale Bridge, where our walk was to start. Another couple of about our age turned up while we were having a drink in the bar. Claire introduced them as Kate and Liz, members of the walking club, and they joined us for dinner.

"How's the big deal going?" Kate asked Claire. Claire saw her maybe once every six weeks, and she knew about it.

"Painfully," said Claire. "No guarantees it'll go ahead."

"If they don't buy it, someone will," I said. "It's a great product."

And hopefully, if someone else bought it, they would have their own experts and not need Claire to relocate.

I had cut short our conversation in the car for the simple reason that I did not want to move to the U.S., away from my friends, my mother, and a local job network. Or, for that matter, from England, my home. But I was beginning to realize that if Claire needed to go she would do so, with or without me.

Her job had become a bigger part of her life than I was, and that would surely continue to be the case if she was running all over America. My own unwillingness to move must have been sending an equivalent message to Claire: living in England was more important than our being together. If the deal went ahead, our relationship would quietly come to a close. It would be sad, and I had not started imagining a life alone, but nor was I contemplating any action to prevent it.

We went up to our hotel room, to a bed with those crisp clean sheets that you never get out of the dryer at home. It was a Friday night, but I sensed Claire was not in the mood to follow recent tradition.

---

We met the other dozen walkers in our group the next morning. The rain had been coming down all night and was showing no signs of stopping. I stood out like Boy George at an AC/DC concert. Everyone else, Claire included, was wearing shorts. Heavy leather boots, checked flannel shirts, oilskin jackets: this was old-school hiking. I had my rucksack's rain cover on and my high-tech gear was keeping me dry, but I was glad I had resisted buying the carbon fiber walking poles.

The walkers were mainly women, and they made me welcome. If they thought my attire was out of place, they kept their opinions to themselves. The surprise was Mandy. She had changed a lot. It had only been ten years—eleven, she reminded me. She was . . . *middle-aged*.

Claire had never seemed middle-aged to me, though she was now fifty-two. Was it the gym and the absence of kids, or had the change been so gradual that I still saw her as she was when I met her? We were both old enough to be grandparents, but I did not feel it. Years ago, I had groaned when my father said he still felt twenty-five inside.

Mandy had not only put on weight and wrinkles: there was something matronly about her bearing and her personality, too. She had not had an easy time, and it was showing.

The walk was tougher than I had expected. The North was having a wet year and the streams—the *gills*—had turned into rivers. I managed to keep up, as there were a few in our group who were quite a bit older, though they had an advantage in experience and sure-footedness. I shared the hand-holding and catching duties with Kate as we negotiated the crossings. Unexpectedly, I found myself enjoying it.

There was a point when I was standing, hand outstretched to catch my fellow adventurers as they made the last rock-hop, when it came to Claire's turn and she lost her balance just as our hands connected. But I had a grip, she held on, and I pulled her up to the bank and a brief hug. It was a nice moment that probably would not have been so noticeable if our relationship had been on firmer ground.

It was not all Chris Bonington and the North Face of the Eiger. I had a chance to talk with Mandy, and found that we had little to say to each other. It was polite but stilted. *Are you working? Who looks after the kids? Of course I'd ask that if you were a man.*

Toward the end of the day, I caught up with her again and dipped my toe in the metaphorical water.

"Are you still in touch with Randall?"

"I don't have any choice. He's legally entitled to speak to my children."

Ouch. Biologically speaking, "my children" was correct, as there had been a problem with Randall's sperm. But it set the tone. And set her off.

"You know the grief process model? Elizabeth Kübler-Ross. DABDA. Denial, Anger, Bargaining, Depression, Acceptance. A divorce is like a death. So the model applies. I looked at it and I thought, bugger this, I don't want to end up at Acceptance. I'm never going to accept what he did. And I don't want to end up depressed. You can see what I'm doing, can't you? I'm working back through the stages."

"And obviously you weren't going to end up bargaining endlessly."

"I didn't bargain at all. I spent five minutes in Denial, got to Anger, and decided there was no place from there that I wanted to go."

"So you're still angry?"

"You can't tell?"

By the time we reached our lodgings, checked in, and hung our wet gear in the drying room, I was exhausted and fell on the bed while Claire showered. The intimacy of a hotel room is different from that of a three-bedroom house. Claire was walking around naked sorting out her clothes, whereas at home she would have traveled from the bathroom to her bedroom wrapped in a towel. What would it take to make this a part of my life again?

Dinner was a big affair, with wooden tables pushed together to form a single long one. The inn had a good feel about it—low ceilings, not too many right angles, and an open fire. The rain was bucketing down outside.

We had joined with the other half of the club, who were walking in the opposite direction. Car keys were exchanged according to a scheme that ensured both groups would have transport at the end of their walks before returning the cars to their owners at prearranged locations. It was all quite clever and we were left in no doubt about who the clever person was.

I put Ray in his early to mid-sixties. He was shortish, bearded, a bit of a garden gnome.

Tap on cider glass: "Good evening, ladies and gentlemen, and welcome. First, if I might, a few formalities."

Apologies were tabled, the new walker was welcomed, and tomorrow's weather forecast (rain) was presented. Rules for completing the car swap, sharing the bill, and finding the toilets were elucidated before Ray returned to his seat at the head of the table.

He stood again as the dinner plates were being cleared and pulled out a concertina. He must have carried it all day on his back, an option not available to a pianist.

He played a few folk tunes and, to give him his due, he was all right. He knew what he was doing and had an enthusiastic audience, not least Claire.

"Enough of my amateur noodling," he said after a bow and round of applause. "I shall relinquish the spotlight to Amanda, queen of the Johanna."

There was a piano. Mandy was a competent player, at least with a sheet of music in front of her. But her response was predictable. "Oh, no, Adam's much better than me."

Mandy was sitting beside me. I realized later that Ray must have assumed I was her new man.

Claire, on the other side, squeezed my hand. "Sorry. You don't have to."

I shook my head at Ray, but it was only a formality.

I sang "Walking in Memphis" and found I was enjoying myself. I had forgotten how much I loved performing. The opening line about putting on blue suede shoes earned a round of laughter and applause—

they *had* noticed my kit—as did the reference to the pouring rain. The lyrics were not without resonance for me, either. The piano player asks the singer if he's a Christian. I was tonight, in the sense of being part of something beyond my usual world. With my partner. Feeling the afterglow of hard exercise. And a pint of good ale on the table beside me. What was I missing out on in life? What was holding me back?

I did the Dylan–Springs obscurity "Walk Out in the Rain" and got another cheer for the line about sore feet.

Then a familiar scene began to play out. A punter gets up, walks self-consciously to the piano, and asks for a song. Said punter is usually male, and the song is of deep emotional significance to him.

Once I was included in a team-building retreat, despite not being on permanent staff, probably because I was a contributor to the team's dysfunction. It might well have been my last chance: when there are problems with teamwork, it's easier to offload the contractor than fire the permanent staff. After dinner, we gathered around the piano and the boss, who had my contract in his gift, asked me to play Bob Seger's "Against the Wind."

By the time we had put aside commitments and deadlines, and finished running against the wind with people from long ago who were not our current partners, there were tears in his eyes, and possibly mine, and I got two renewals of that contract before the love ran out.

One day, somewhere in the world, someone was going to request "Delilah" or "I Did What I Did for Maria," and a pianist would have to decide whether to call the cops.

What was Concertina Ray going to ask for? Most of the time, requests are about love: unrequited love, lost love, and, occasionally, love being experienced right now—"You Are So Beautiful." Then there are songs of angst, of loneliness and alienation: Jon Voight walking New York to the accompaniment of "Everybody's Talking." And the unadulterated ego songs: I had Ray picked for "My Way."

"D'you know any Gilbert and Sullivan?" he said.

All right: that was not what I was expecting. I could name the operettas, but my repertoire was limited. I played a couple of chords, found the tune, and sang:

*I am the very model of a modern major-general.*

Would that do? It would not.

"Gilbert *O*'Sullivan."

"Alone Again, Naturally." Not the first time I had been asked for that one. Despite myself, I felt a twinge for this guy and his concertina and his once-a-month social circle, using a song to send a desperate message that he couldn't bring himself to say in his own words.

I played the introduction, and again he stopped me—and spelled out what he wanted.

I had never been asked to play the song he requested, but I knew it. The lyrics have not traveled well. There may have been a time when an uncle's love for his niece, with explicit reference to age difference and marriage, was seen as innocuous, but that time has passed. I doubted Concertina Ray wanted to confess an interest in little girls. Too late, anyway: I was already feeling my way through the intro.

Let me be fair to Ray. People take what they need from a song and ignore the rest. "Walk Out in the Rain" is not about hiking. "Walking on Sunshine," the chorus of which brought back happy memories of driving down the Great Ocean Road with Angelina, has lines about waiting for the loved one to write, to return, which passed me by at the time.

Ray probably had not thought much past the title of his selection and the general romantic feeling of the tune. As I sang it, he turned from me and looked out into the audience. At Claire.

*Clair.* That's the title and the first word. It only took me a few moments to realize what was going on, but by then I was committed. Ray was channeling the song I was singing, projecting it at my partner, apparently in ignorance of our relationship.

I played it straight, sang *da-da-da* over the dodgy bits, and made it a proper love song, as though I was singing it directly for her. Ray played some nice fills on the concertina, and when I nailed the key change from A to B flat in the instrumental break, he followed without missing a beat. After thanking me, he took the vacant seat beside Claire—*my* seat—while I sang "Goodnight Irene" and tried to gauge what was going on between them. I got no sense that she was telling him that he'd made a fool of himself.

I left it to Claire with an *e* to raise the subject. I had just been playing requests.

Upstairs, she was almost embarrassingly positive about my turn on the piano.

"Are you okay? I know you don't like to play, but you looked like you were enjoying yourself. Anyway, thank you. You were great. I love you playing."

It had been a long time since either of us had said those words, even with the qualification. Then she added, "I don't know what's changed lately, but keep doing it."

I had walked twelve miles up and down hills in the rain and drunk several pints, but we managed to make up for missing Friday night.

Before we fell asleep, she gave me a nonanswer to the question that was still in my mind.

"Don't worry about Ray. He's a sweetie."

# 18

I was relieved that the hike was only two days. I had woken to discover that hiking used different muscles from jogging, and the second day was tougher than the first. I had a fuzzy head from drinking, though the rain set that right, and I found myself walking with Mandy again.

"How are things with you and Claire?" she asked.

"Not too bad. Actually, pretty good."

"That's the way it looked last night. I must say it's a relief. I'd got the impression you two were having problems. Claire's needed a bit of support with all the stress she's going through at work."

"We've both been pretty flat out. What's the story with Ray?"

"You noticed. He's a bit funny, at first, but he's all right. He lost his wife a couple of years ago. You've nothing to fear. As long as you take care of Claire."

I wanted to press her, confirm that there definitely was nothing to fear from an unattached man who had declared an interest in my attractive partner who was feeling unsupported at home, but we had apparently talked enough about me.

Mandy launched into the divorce story without prompting—a long tirade about the custody dispute. The problem, to my simple way of thinking, seemed to be that they wanted to live in different countries, but the story she told was a litany of complaints about someone I had once counted as my best friend. I interrupted as the muddy track up the hill robbed her of breath.

"You know, as a friend, someone who likes both of you, it's pretty sad to see it come to this. If you add up all the good things—"

"You're a T, aren't you? A Myers-Briggs Thinking type? Am I right?"

We did not spend all the time at those team-building retreats singing around the piano.

"INTP," I said. I remembered the result of the personality test but not what all the letters stood for.

I for introvert, of course—a surprise for those who confuse a love of performance with a desire for intimacy with strangers.

And there was the tolerance for uncertainty. P for perceiving rather than J for judging. That one had stuck for obvious reasons: "Ps often don't understand that Js need to get closure, to have a decision: Js would prefer the wrong decision to no decision at all," the facilitator had said. Was that all it was? Had one different letter determined the course of my life?

"Right," said Mandy. "T. So you make decisions based on cold, hard facts. You and Claire. I'm an F. Feelings. I make decisions based on values."

I remembered this one now. "And emotions." Ha. That didn't sound so superior.

"Whatever. Randall violated my values."

I waited.

"We went to a marriage counselor and he asked us to rate our marriage on four dimensions."

"Sounds like he knew his audience."

"Sorry?"

"Models. Grids. Speaking your language. A two-by-two matrix, right?"

"No, it wasn't. If I'd meant a matrix I would have said two orthogonal dimensions. And he uses it with everyone. The four dimensions were Emotional, Practical, Intellectual, and Physical—meaning sexual. And what do you think he rated me as sexually?"

"The therapist?"

"Yes, the therapist. I slept with the therapist so he could score me."

Ha-ha. Except someone once had sex with me to find out if she was any good.

"No," said Mandy. "Randall. We had to rate each other."

"Out of what—a seven-point Likert scale? Somewhat satisfied? Neither satisfied nor dissatisfied?"

"Out of ten. What do you think he said? I suppose you guys talked about that sort of thing while you were doing the barbecue. What did he say to you?"

Women will never believe that men don't spend a lot of time talking about their partners, and that when they do it's seldom in a negative way. In all the hours I had spent drinking Coors and marinating ribs with Randall, neither of us had ever asked the other: "What's the missus like in the sack?" Randall was the only person I had shared the Angelina story with, but I had never mentioned her sexual journey, which had been an important part of it, let alone any of the details.

I knew more about the San Francisco Giants than I did about Mandy's performance in bed. I was happy for things to stay that way. I made an attempt to convey that sentiment without appearing uncaring. She ignored it.

"I'm not trying to say I'm something special. I'm just normal. I mean, I don't think most women want to—"

"Too much information. What did he score you?"

"Seven. He gave me a bloody seven."

"Better than zero. Or six. I'd have thought that was all right. Leaves room for improvement."

She wasn't smiling. "You know, on the NPS, a seven isn't even a recommendation."

"What's the NPS?"

"Net Promoter Score. Rating whether customers will recommend you."

"Right."

"The point is, there I was trying to look after twins who took turns in staying awake. I didn't have *time* for sex, and then he criticizes me for it."

"I suppose if you're not having it at all . . ."

"That's the bloody point, isn't it? He was rating me on how I was before it stopped. Explains everything. I felt like asking how he rated *her*."

"Her?"

"Her."

"You're talking about . . ."

"There's only one person I'd be talking about, unless you know about others."

"From what he told me, it was pretty awful."

It had certainly been awful after Randall had confessed. If he had been in England, he might have talked to me instead of a therapist about his guilt over a drunken one-night stand. And I might have told him about a recording my dad had of a Lenny Bruce performance from about 1960—a triple album on vinyl. I used to play it from time to time, partly to wind up my mother with the bad language. There was one routine that stayed with me, about a guy in an ambulance who has lost his foot in a multi-fatality road accident, and he's coming on to the nurse. She can't understand how he can be interested in sex at a time like this. "I got horny," he says pathetically.

It was probably a better explanation of what Randall did than anything his therapist came up with. Lenny Bruce laid some further advice on my twelve-year-old self: *Never confess.* Even if your wife catches you *in flagrante*, deny everything. That, he implies, is the social contract.

Things have changed since then, and Randall's therapist helped him reach a point where he could share his story with Mandy, explain that it was impulsive and meaningless and that he was terribly, terribly sorry, so the marriage could continue on a basis of openness and trust. And the rest is history. When it comes to infidelity, every partner becomes a Myers-Briggs F-for-Feelings with their values violated.

"How did you rate him?" I asked.

"How do you think? After what he'd done and then having the

hide—the sheer bloody hide—to compare me to her on sexual performance, I rated us *emotionally* as zero. So everything else was zero, too. If you've got no relationship, the rest doesn't matter."

Message conveyed, Mandy strode ahead, the rain came down again, and I was left inside my hooded jacket with my thoughts. How would I rate my own life at the moment?

Practical was a nine, only missing a perfect score because of the commute to London. That wasn't such a bad thing. Best of both worlds. Call it ten. Claire and I had the domestic arrangements down pat. The absence of children might have been a problem in some other dimension, but not here.

Intellectual: the job was keeping me sharp and I had a mind-exercising pastime with the pub quiz. Claire was a smart, rational, and pragmatic partner. The issue of moving overseas was a case in point. She had taken my request for time to think about it at face value, rather than making an argument of it. Couldn't do much better: another ten.

Sexual: better than it had been for years. Did it matter that some of the stimulation might have been coming from outside? It was fantasy—any sex therapist would acknowledge the role of fantasy in spicing up the routine of a long-term relationship. I might well be doing the same thing for Angelina and Charlie.

Emotional: Claire and I had a connection, but most of it was under Practical. I could not deny that the emotional side had faded with the years and our failure to have a family. Surely that happens to everyone, but for us it had never been easy, because of Claire's background. I had filled the gap in my own life with music, but doing so involved memories of a past that had come alive again. If the wall between fantasy and reality broke down—if I became romantically involved with the present-day Angelina—I would be in the same position as Randall and Mandy, with all the rest counting for naught.

# 19

The first crack in the wall dividing fantasy from reality appeared an hour after we got home on the Sunday night. I checked my e-mail and there was a message from Angelina, sent the previous day. All of her earlier messages, bar that one *wassup?* from her phone, had been sent on Wednesday evenings.

*Have you got Skype?*

I e-mailed back:

*Yes, but I can't use it at work.*

I thought that would be the end of it, but the next morning there was a reply.

*Doesn't have to be in working hours. I'm by myself this week. What's your user name? Mine's The-Angelina-Brown.*

Cop that, Equal Opportunity Commissioner Brown and Newspaper Columnist Brown and all the other Angelina Browns around the world. The former actress from *Mornington Police* is *The* Angelina Brown. I e-mailed back.

*Mine's Nine-Inch-Pianist*

*I hope you don't use it for work*

*It's my hand span*

*I'm sure it's that too. Seriously, people get fired for less. Rightly so*

*I'm having you on. It's Bee-Flat*

*Later this morning your time? Or now?*

*At work in London. But home tomorrow. 10 p.m. your time OK?*

*Perfect. xxx*

Tuesday at one P.M. in Norwich, I logged on to Skype. My location was still registered as the Netherlands from a trip to The Hague for work a few years earlier. I had not bothered with an avatar.

Angelina had a photo—a glamorous professional head shot. It would be ludicrous to say she had not changed, but she was immediately recognizable. I had only two pictures of her. One was the shot with Richard in the long-faded newspaper clipping that Jacinta had sent me. The other was Shanksy's photo of her singing by the piano, his gift to me on the December morning when I caught the plane home. They had become so familiar that they no longer spoke to me.

Now I saw her again. She was older, but that made the image more compelling. I was looking at the real person that I was about to speak to, not some fantasy from the distant past. She had cut her long hair and her face had lost some of its youthful plumpness, if that's the right word, but it was by no means sharp. It just made her eyes bigger.

The Skype photo marked the beginning of the ghost behind the e-mail messages taking on flesh and becoming not only a real person but the person I had known two decades earlier.

I went for a jog—out to eight miles now—and took a hard look at myself after the shower. My plan was not to show myself on Skype, but if the offer was *You show me you and I'll show you me*, I wanted to take it up. It was only my face, I reminded myself, which looked like that of a forty-nine-year-old contract database architect. At least I did not need my glasses to read the screen. But there was one easy improvement I could make.

Scissors. Razor.

My chin looked a bit weak, as it does when you shave your beard after becoming accustomed to it. On the positive side, my face looked clean, professional, and distinctly younger. Straight nose, clear complexion, clear eyes. A full head of hair, with not a lot of gray amid the black.

At 10:40 P.M. Melbourne time, I gave up waiting for Angelina to call and hit the Voice Call button. No video. One thing at a time.

She answered, also without video. There was a short pause, then her voice in the speakers, clearer than a phone. She could have been in the room with me.

"Do you know 'Because the Night' by Patti Smith?"

Her voice was perhaps a little deeper, but it was unmistakably hers. It took me a moment to realize she was repeating the first words she had ever spoken to me, words that I had responded to in the accent that had given her reason to invent the Bring a Brit invitation and . . .

"And Bruce Springsteen," I said. "They wrote it together."

"Oh God," she said. "You sound so . . . unchanged."

"So do you."

I wanted time to slow down, slow right down and stop. This could never happen again, this reconnection after so long. It was a huge step forward from messaging, a completely different experience. Perhaps she felt the same way, because the link went silent.

I turned my back to the computer, switched my keyboard on, and unplugged the headphones. I had not planned this, but it felt right. Though I was not going to attempt "Because the Night."

I played Van Morrison's "Brown Eyed Girl," the song I was playing when she walked up to the piano that first night in the bar. I sang the opening words, asking where we had gone, what had happened to us when the rain came, and was overcome with a flood of nostalgia—

for her, for Shanksy pulling me a beer, for the version of me that sang at a piano. It was a million miles away from the flirtation of our earlier exchanges.

I had to stop singing for a few bars to pull myself together. When I picked up again, my voice was shaky.

I finished the song and half expected to find she had hung up, but the connection was still open. She spoke first.

"Oh my God—it just takes me right back. Do you remember the day we drove to the beach at Point Addis and walked all that way with the picnic basket?"

"And it rained."

"That's what the song reminded me of. And we were huddled under that overhang of rock . . ."

We went on for an hour and a half, revisiting the things we had done, things I had not thought about for years. We were talking about events rather than feelings, but memories of how we felt, how we had been, sat behind all of them. There was just one reference to current times, or at least post-Australian times.

"You didn't have children," she said.

"Not through lack of trying."

"I'm sorry. When you said 'no children' in your e-mail, I thought . . ."

"No. But I'm not sure we would even have tried if it hadn't been for what you said to me that Christmas. So thank you."

"Except—"

"No. Thank you. It was better to have tried."

I realized it was true only as I said it. I had long acknowledged that Claire's and my focus on a family had been at the expense of our own relationship. But if I had never stepped up and tried, encouraged Claire, our relationship would have suffered in a different way. And we would have been the less for not facing our fears.

Finally, she said, "Remember the night at the bar? When Shanksy bought us a bottle of champagne?"

The night I told her I loved her. And she told me she loved me.

I said, "Like it was yesterday."

A long pause and then: "We were so young."

The two of us said nothing for about a minute, and it seemed the right time to hang up. I went to click on the red button and saw that she had already gone.

# 20

The next day, I was back in London and Angelina's e-mail was waiting for me when I knocked off for lunch.

*I'd had a couple of drinks last night. Hope I didn't sound too sloshed.*

I e-mailed back: *That'll explain the story about the pool cleaner.*

*I told you that one? He was very cute.*

Then: *Pleased to see you haven't lost the accent.*

*Does it still have the same effect?*

*What effect ;-)*

It was the same sort of banter as a week earlier, but it didn't feel the same. I could hear and see the woman behind the words. The genie was out of the bottle.

Whether or not it had been true before, I now had to acknowledge that I was having an affair, with a flesh-and-blood person in the present time. There was a simple test that Stuart had alluded to, and which had applied from the start: I was being as secretive about it as if we had been renting a hotel room.

I suppose there are people who could go on indefinitely deceiving their partner and themselves, but I was not one of them. I had to make a choice. The choice was between a bit of transgressive fun that had little prospect of becoming anything more, and a twenty-year relationship, a twenty-year *life*, with a house and friends and coffee in bed in the morning, the life that I had recently rated as traveling well in at least three out of four dimensions.

It took me longer to sort it out than it should have. Our e-mail exchanges were giving me the mojo for everything else and I did not want to lose them. I could give up any time I wanted: just not this week.

The resolution came from an unexpected quarter. My recent pub quiz performances had been stellar, despite work getting in the way of research.

We were running neck and neck with the pub champions, and the guest emcee had loaded up the rock 'n' roll questions. I was carrying the team. Sheilagh had been doing it hard for the past couple of weeks, but she seemed brighter on this night.

I had kept us in the race with a challenge on wine bottle sizes: a Bordeaux jeroboam is different from a champagne jeroboam.

Last question, scores tied. This one's for you, Adam.

*Bob Dylan has written the same woman's name into two different songs at least once. What is the name?*

No idea. I don't know many Dylan songs after the 1970s, and the man is still churning out albums. The way the question was framed suggested that there might be more than one possibility and that Dylan may not have recorded the songs himself. I dug into my memory as the discussion went around the table. Sara, his first wife, subject of the eponymous song, was the favorite.

"'Sad-Eyed Lady of the Lowlands' is about her, too," said Stuart.

"The question says *name*. Her name's not in the song."

We did a rapid dump: Ramona, Johanna, Louise, Maggie, Lucy,

Nellie, Ruth from Duluth, Jeannie, Rosie, Hazel, Ophelia, Claudette, Marie, Patty Valentine from "Hurricane," Valerie and Vivienne (T. S. Eliot's two wives), Mary-Jane, Queen Jane, Queen Anne, Lily, Rosemary, Cinderella . . . No duplicates.

"Angelina," I added.

"Farewell Angelina" was a sixties song. It was pretty enough, but not romantic, except for the name. Dylan had written it for Joan Baez to sing.

We were in trouble. "Sara" was the obvious choice, so avoid that. Surely not Ophelia or Hazel or Claudette. It was up to me. I went with the idea that he had written at least one of the songs for someone else. And a bit of nostalgia.

Nobody knew that the name meant anything to me, so there were no guffaws or snide remarks. And "Angelina" it was—subject and title of a song recorded in 1981 but not released until 1991.

I was wrong about Dylan not recording "Farewell Angelina": his version had been included on the same compilation of rarities. Details, details. We had the point.

The champions had gone for Rosemary, but an appeal to the official Dylan Web site established that the Rosemary of "Lily, Rosemary and the Jack of Hearts" was spelled differently from the Rose-Marie of "Going to Acapulco."

Our win was brilliant but inconvenient, as the prize was free drinks. I had promised to be home for dinner. Since the Lake District hike, Claire and I had been eating together, even when one of us was late. But I had to share the celebration and sink a pint of the winnings. Fifteen minutes wouldn't matter.

When it turned to thirty, and the house band was tuning up, I said, "Have to dash," and walked out with Sheilagh, who put her arms around me when she kissed me good night, then started crying. Her marriage was over. I held her for a while and kissed her again on the forehead. When I let go Claire was parked next to us in the car.

I climbed in and didn't say anything.

Claire—logical, pragmatic, and a good judge of behavior—won most of our arguments and I took some pleasure in turning the tables occasionally. There had been a kitchen cupboard door with a broken hinge that could only be closed by a complex sequence involving another cupboard and an up-down-up manipulation. Claire was constantly on my case to fix it, and eventually she blew up and told me she was going to call in a handyman. At which point I demonstrated that the door could be closed in the conventional way, having fixed it some weeks earlier. It was my *Ye of little faith* metaphor. *Remember the hinge?*

I was waiting for Claire to bite, so I could proffer my innocent explanation. And in future, I could say *Remember the affair with Sheilagh?* and we would laugh. At least, one of us would.

Except Claire stayed quiet. I thought at first that she must have decided there was nothing to it. Then the silence dragged on, and I realized that she was thinking about it, putting the pieces together and deciding how to respond.

If I was ever going to come clean with Claire about Angelina, now was the time. The reality fell short of what Claire might be imagining with Sheilagh: three-times-a-week clandestine meetings covered by a farrago of lies.

The unvarnished truth: *A girlfriend from twenty years ago in Australia got in touch, and we exchanged a few e-mails and had a chat on Skype. I've decided it's not a good idea, and I won't be doing it again. I should have told you earlier, but I'm telling you now. Sorry. But it's not nearly as bad as what you were thinking.*

In the unlikely event that Claire wanted to know how I *felt* about it all . . . Well, that would not be a bad thing. We could do with more conversations of that kind.

"Claire . . ."

"Adam, if you're going to promise there's absolutely nothing going on, then say it. If not, I don't want to discuss anything until we get home."

I could have given her a flat-out denial, but it would have been disingenuous. There *was* something going on, and it was time to clear the air. When Claire was ready.

Claire parked the car, made herself a cup of tea, and sat at the dining table. I opened a beer, just to have something in my hand, and sat opposite.

"I gather you've been seeing someone. No?"

She had given me my chance in the car and now did not wait for an answer. And it seemed she had not recognized Sheilagh.

"All right then," she said. "You know I've been looking at moving to the States. I'm assuming that if I do, you won't follow me. Which would mean the end of us as a couple. I think we both understood that, but I'm making it explicit."

I just nodded. This wasn't about Sheilagh or Angelina anymore.

"And we've both been letting it sit, letting our relationship hang on whether or not a business deal goes through. Is that fair—what I'm saying?"

"It's fair," I said. "And you haven't been taking our relationship into account in deciding whether to sell the company. Is that fair?"

She thought for a few moments before replying. "No, it's not. You don't know because we've never discussed it properly. It might have been true a few months ago, but what I haven't understood is why things have changed lately. I thought it must have been the job, but now you've given me the answer." She looked hard at me. "Are you hearing me?"

"You're saying it's over?" I said.

She wasn't, but it was where the conversation was heading, and it was there already in her tone.

"I think you're the one who's made that choice," she said.

"It seems you'd made the decision already."

"I think *we* had. But you could have had the decency to . . ." She sighed. "It doesn't matter."

She was right. It didn't matter. Explaining about Sheilagh and Angelina at this point would not solve the deeper problem that was now out in the open. And I could tell, despite her appearance of control, that Claire had exhausted her capacity for discussion. We put dinner in the fridge.

In my room, I lay on the bed in the dark. Despite what we had said, the situation was not beyond saving, if we both cared enough. If either of us cared enough. Claire only had to say, "You're more important than the deal, so we'll stay in the UK." Or I could say, "I'll go to the States." But why would I say that if Claire didn't value our relationship enough to make the equivalent offer?

Rather than turn on the light, I lit the candle. Then I switched on my computer and downloaded the Dylan song that had given me my moment of glory.

I know lots of songs. I don't just know their names so I can score points in quizzes, I know the songs *themselves*. The likelihood of me being blown away by one I have not heard before is extremely low.

That said, I was in an emotionally receptive mood. The candle that had burned as a young Angelina's voice filled the Myer Music Bowl more than twenty-two years earlier lit my room. I had drunk an extra pint after being on a reduced-alcohol regime for the past few weeks. Not to mention that I was on the verge of splitting with my partner of twenty years, in part because of a woman whose name was the title of the song.

There was all that.

Finally, there was the possibility that my brain had been turned to mush by listening to popular music for so long. They used to talk about rock 'n' roll damaging the mind, and it turns out there may have been some truth to it. If pornography can change the physical structure of the brain, why not music? I had spent months—years—in my room with my playlist going nonstop. Most of those songs were three- to four-minute paeans to love: love experienced, love lost, and love remembered. Candles burning, candles in the wind and rain, candles sat before.

My brain had been well and truly washed when it came to love.

I had the headphones on. Dylan plays an intro, a little noodling on the piano. Then he sings, the voice familiar but more emotional than I was accustomed to, declaring that it's in his nature to take chances, submitting to the pull of the past, committing to the journey, all in a torrent of passion and imagery.

By the end of the second verse, I was completely undone. I could say I was moved, shaken, overcome, but that would not do justice to how I was feeling. "Undone" was the perfect word. What had I been doing for twenty years? What did I do now?

I e-mailed Angelina and told her it was over with Claire.

# 21

As a database designer whose daily work relies on making objective decisions, as a pianist who understands both the power and limits of music, and as a certified Myers-Briggs T-for-Thinking personality, I need to make it clear that I did not leave a twenty-year relationship because of a song.

Yes, listening to "Angelina" for the first time was a profound experience, but you should not rush to download it in the hope of having the same response. Once, I asked a bunch of friends and colleagues to nominate their favorite songs, and I put together a mix tape of their selections. It was utterly pedestrian, and not because I had more sophisticated taste. I was not making the connections that they were and the songs didn't resonate.

*American Songwriter* magazine rates "Angelina" No. 28 in Dylan's extensive oeuvre, so I can at least claim it as a songwriters' song. But he left it off a mediocre album in 1981 and, though he's toured almost nonstop since that time, he has never performed it live. I would like to think it's because the song is too personal but my head tells me the opposite. Wikipedia opines that it "makes for a pleasant listen."

That was broadly what I thought in the light of the morning, with the candle out and my rational hat on. The music did not make the decision for me, but it took me to a place where I could access the emotional dimension that Mandy's shrink had talked about.

My emotional life was all about Angelina, and had been for a while, certainly since the Skype call, and arguably as long as I had been listening to music with her in my mind. I was letting both Claire and myself down by continuing the relationship. It might still be within my power to save it, but there was not enough left to save.

I probably should not have sent the e-mail to Angelina. It was more about locking in my decision than asking anything of her, and she could well feel that I had transgressed the boundaries that we had set for ourselves. I was not setting off in pursuit of her, but of what she represented. At forty-nine, I was looking to live the part of my life that currently existed only in song.

I moved out, which is to say I packed a bag, worked a half day in London, and took the train to Manchester. There was no question about who should stay and who should go. The house had been left to Claire by her mother. Perhaps, after the time we had been together, I had some legal claim, but I would not be pursuing it. The piano could wait. Elvis would have to hang on a bit longer for his evening meals.

I was on a mutual two-week-notice arrangement at work and I let them know that I would be finishing up. I was not going to commute from my mother's place outside Manchester, even a couple of days a week. It really didn't matter anymore.

Before leaving the house, I spent a long time writing Claire a note in my rusty handwriting.

*Dear Claire*

*I really am sorry. There's nothing between me and Sheilagh— that's who you saw me with; she and Chad have broken up—but everything you said was fair. We've been drifting apart for a while, and I was holding on to the idea that you might stay in the UK. It seems that last night just brought forward something that we were heading for anyway.*

*You've been busy with work, but I haven't stepped up, and you must have interpreted my unwillingness to move to the US as a lack of support. Fairly so. You deserve more than I've been giving.*

I spent a while thinking about whether I should say more. I did not want to hurt Claire for no reason, but I also didn't want her to assume an unfair share of the blame. She deserved to know what had been going on, to make sense of what she had been seeing.

> *There is something else. A couple of months ago I reconnected with someone from the (distant) past, and it brought up a lot of stuff that I didn't resolve properly at the time. So, even at this advanced age, I need to sort myself out.*
>
> *Thanks for everything you've done for me and us. We had a lot of good times and I will remember all of them. And good luck with the sale.*
>
> *I hope we can stay friends and in touch—just call if you need help with anything. We can sort the practicalities out once the pressure's off with the company sale.*
>
> *Love,*
>
> *Adam*

I read it through again and saw what was missing. "Friends," I'd written. No mention of love, past or present, except in the valediction. When had I last told her I loved her? Writing "I love you" now would feel forced and disingenuous, and she would read it that way. I could hardly write "I once loved you."

I left the letter and my keys on top of the piano, our place for message exchange. There was something there already. Not a note but a business card, from a piano tuner.

I played an F sharp and felt the chord go through me. Keyboards are all right, but there is something special about a good acoustic piano, and it had been a long time since this one had sounded right. I sat on the stool and played the first two lines of "Angelina." It was an easy tune, but I could not remember the words.

Trains are one of the great symbols of popular song, but there was no romance on the 9:30 A.M. to Liverpool Street or, later that day, the commuter-packed 6:30 P.M. to Manchester. It was on the trip to my mother's that what I had done began to sink in, bringing with it an overwhelming feeling of emptiness.

I had walked away from my best friend, my home, my *life*, and surely hurt Claire in the process—Claire, who must have taken time out from her job, presumably while I was working in London or visiting my mother, to get the piano tuner in. It was something I could easily have done while I was between contracts or working from home if I had not wanted an excuse to avoid playing it for her. She had been making an effort, thinking things were changing for the better, and I had let her down. For what? A romantic daydream that had no roots in anything or anyone.

Angelina was a fantasy, given substance only in our puerile once-a-week exchanges that she had probably initiated to fill a small hole in an otherwise happy marriage. I had no way of translating my longing for something more into anything concrete, like a plan for the next day or next week or the rest of my suddenly barren life.

# 22

My mother was, as always, pleased to see me. The feeling was not entirely reciprocated.

The modern (and when I say "modern," I mean post-1900) approach to counseling is based on listening and occasional interpretations and suggestions, allowing the patient, over an extended period, to gain an understanding of his problems and to devise ways of dealing with them. My mother came from an older tradition of personal observations and advice, repeated until the patient conceded defeat. In my mother's case, the beating over the head was combined with razor-sharp insight.

"You never did get over that married woman in Australia, did you?"

"Potatoes are good. How do you get them so brown?"

"Kylie. That was her name, wasn't it?"

The misunderstanding was the result of a flippant remark back in 1990. Kylie was then the archetypal Australian name, and I had never bothered to correct my mother. Her lectures were easier to take with Angelina's name left out of them.

She didn't wait for confirmation. "She's done you a lot of harm. She should have been ashamed of herself, carrying on with a young man. An innocent traveler."

"Mum, I was twenty-six. I was older than she was."

"She was married. When my mother married my father, she knew he was off to the war, and let me tell you those American servicemen would have been all over her. She was a very attractive woman when she was young. You've seen the photos?"

"No," I lied.

"Of course you have."

"Don't know, Mum—it's been a long time."

My mother went to get the photos. Whenever she needed an exemplar of marriage, she cited her parents. She and Dad had not done so well. Dad had an ego the size of a baby grand. He was a natty dresser, a lover of music of all kinds, and a womanizer. He knew everyone in the Manchester music scene—the Bee Gees, the Hollies, the Smiths in their early days—and had a million stories. I would wager he went to the Judas concert at the Free Trade Hall, whatever he told my mother.

Even as a teenager I knew he was playing around. He drank, too, another habit I inherited. I managed to avoid the smoking that gave him lung cancer, but my mother can take the credit for that. My father was only a peripheral part of my life by the time he checked out.

I had three definitive moments with him, all tied to the piano. It was hard to imagine how a definitive moment with my dad could be tied to anything else.

When I was a kid, learning the instrument the old, hard, classical way, he came up while I was practicing.

"Not much fun, is it?" he said.

"You're the one making me do it."

"Tell me a song you like. 'Teddy Bears' Picnic'?"

"Dad! I'm seven."

"It's a good tune at any age. But you choose."

"The cherry cola song." It was playing constantly on the radio at the time.

He shook his head. "Don't know it."

"Yes, you do." I hummed a few bars.

"You want to learn 'Lola'? It's a lot harder than 'Teddy Bears' Picnic.'"

I nodded.

"Your mam won't thank me for this." Dad played the first notes of the chorus with his right hand. "Now you do it."

"I can't."

"Start anywhere you like. Play any note."

I played an A sharp, of course. In our family the B flat was always referred to by its alternative name, and sometimes as the Adam. Mum and Dad had their notes too, though it was of no interest to my mother.

At Freddie Sharp's funeral, I played "No Regrets," the song he had requested, in F sharp. Loudly, on the black keys. He had surely expected the recorded version, rather than the irony of his deserted son singing it. I did it in the original French—"Non, Je Ne Regrette Rien"—which hardly anyone there would have understood. That was the night I decided to go to Australia.

Dad sang *Lo*. And then *La*. "Play the second note."

"I don't know which one it is."

"You've only eighty-eight choices, lad. It won't be far away. Seldom is."

It took me two or three tries to find that it was the A sharp again, and then I found the third note. It got easier quickly and gave me a satisfying sense of achievement.

"You can do that instead of lessons, if you want. I'll show you what to do with your left hand once you get the hang of it. Starting on any key I choose."

"I don't have to do lessons?"

"It'll save your mam and me wasting our money. But you don't get owt for nowt."

I knew that good things came with conditions.

"You have to practice every day. Twenty minutes. That's all. If you can't find a piano, you can sing."

"For how long?"

"I told you. Twenty minutes. It'll go as slow as a wet weekend some days; other times it'll fly and you'll want to do more. And you'd be silly not to."

"I meant, when can I stop?"

"Never. Never ever. But no lessons. That's the deal."

That deal would ensure that I got plenty of practice and developed a good ear, but never learned to read music. If you can't play the dots, you can forget about being a professional pianist.

A few days later, Dad bought me the single of "Lola," my first record.

It must have taken me two or three months to learn to play—and sing—the Kinks' ode to gender ambiguity in eleven keys. Twenty or more minutes a day that my mother had to listen to her seven-year-old son singing about being picked up in a Soho club by a woman who talked like a man. She kept her thoughts to herself, or at least from me.

When I had it down, Dad showed me the chords to play with my left hand—to begin with, just once at the beginning of each phrase, as I would do twenty years later to accompany Angelina singing "Angel of the Morning."

"Feel good?" he said.

It did. I was just listening to a basic harmony, but the sound of a note against a chord touches something fundamental in us, more so when you play it yourself. My dad had chosen his words well. It didn't just sound good, it felt good.

"That's why you want to play music," he said. "That's the thing to remember."

I remembered it. Some musicians lose their love of music, particularly popular music, or it loses its power to move them. They are like comedians who understand how jokes are constructed or magicians who know, literally, how the trick is done. Music never lost its power for me, though I moved from playing to listening.

The third moment with Dad was when I was twenty-five, a few months before he joined the heavenly choir. I was playing in a bar in London—Soho, in fact. He walked up to the piano and it took me a moment to realize who he was. He had lost a lot of weight and his face was gray. He was still impeccably dressed.

He smiled and said, as though he didn't know me, "Can you play 'For Once in My Life' for me?"

I was more than familiar with this song, a favorite of his that I liked to think had a connection to better times with my mother. I just played it, without singing, concentrating on getting it right. I had always been in awe of my father's musicianship.

When I had finished, Dad said, "Play the first few bars again."

There is an augmented fifth on "life": a four-note chord if you add the seventh. An easy piano or guitar book would write it as a straight G major. But the melody note is a B, a third, and the sharp note in the accompaniment adds a bit of contrast and edge. It was a touch that probably only the singer would notice in a noisy bar.

I played it again, with the seventh, and Dad watched and said, "Bugger me, lad, you've listened. You played it properly. I've always faked it."

He put a twenty in my tips jar and said, "You'll be all right." Then he moved so he was standing behind me and said, "Do you remember 'Lola'?"

I sang "Lola," and by the time I was finished, he had gone. That was the last time I saw him.


A day that had started with moving out of a twenty-year relationship continued with quitting my job, and ended with moving in with my mother was always going to be tough. Claire had left a message on my phone: I wasn't asking you to leave; I'm sorry I misjudged the situation with Sheilagh and didn't give you a chance to speak; call me when you're ready to talk. It was kind, but it changed nothing.

Angelina had also replied, and gave no indication that I had been out of line with my message about leaving Claire. How was I feeling? Did I have somewhere to live? If our recent contact had anything to do with the breakup, she would swear there had been nothing of substance. It had never been her intention to come between Claire and me, just as she hoped I did not want to disrupt her marriage.

I sent a brief and rather formal reply, thanking her for the concern and assuring her that she was not responsible for my actions, that Claire and I had been contemplating going our separate ways for some time, and that I had never harbored any illusions about a relationship with her.

I had cause to revise my thinking after my mother went to bed. An e-mail from Angelina, sent just after seven A.M. her time.

> To: bee.flat@zznet.co.uk
> CC: charles.acheson@mandapartners.com.au
>
> Hi Adam
>
> I don't know what your work and accommodation situation is, but Charlie and I are heading off on Friday to our place in France (Burgundy), arriving Saturday. We'll be there for a week then going on to Milano. It would be great to see you after all these years, and you'd be welcome to stay for the full week and beyond if you wanted to. If you can get to Lyon or Macon we can pick you up from Sunday morning onwards.
>
> Hope things are working out for you.
>
> Kind regards
> Angelina

*Milano*, not Milan. And Charlie Acheson not Charlie Brown. What did he think, or know? Not everything, because he was not copied in on the second e-mail.

> Dooglas
>
> PLEASE come. I'd love to see you.
>
> Love
> Angel

I slept on it, but in the morning I had a decision to make. There was the practical problem of work: I was still committed to two weeks on the London job. Whether or not I accepted Angelina's invitation,

I needed to put in some face time, so I took the bus to the station and boarded the early express to London. It was midafternoon in Melbourne. I e-mailed Angelina from my phone:

*Do you have a broadband Internet connection in France?*

I thought it unlikely, but decided that if the answer was yes, I would go.

*It's France, not Albania. Are you really coming?*

*Looking forward to it. xxx*

In my London lunch hour, I booked tickets on the Eurostar to Paris and the TGV to Mâcon with a stopover in Paris on the Saturday night. It would have been possible to do the full journey in a single day, but I hadn't seen Paris for a long time. I e-mailed the arrival time to Angelina, copying in Charlie.

I got an e-mail straight back—from Charlie.

*Got it. Thanks. All good. What's your mobile number? Mine below. Will meet you at Macon TGV station. You'll probably recognize my wife . . . Any probs, just call. Any food prefs? Looking forward to meeting you. Charlie.*

I was going to be living with this guy for a week. Did he know I was Angelina's former lover? I was not going to take anything for granted. Claire knew about Angelina, but only in concept. I had not mentioned her in living memory. I doubted she would remember her name.

I texted Charlie my mobile number and did a quick Internet search, turning up two Australian Charles Achesons. "Director—Mergers and Acquisitions Partners" looked a better bet than "Legendary Try Against All Blacks."

Late Thursday night, at my mother's insistence, I e-mailed Angelina again: *Anything I can bring?* There was no reply—they were probably on the plane.

My mother was supportive of me taking time out with Australian friends. Small doses of each other went a long way and "It'll give you both a chance to think about things."

To confuse the situation further, Claire texted me.

*Sheilagh came over totally distraught. Thought it was her fault. I set her straight, but you should contact her. Stay safe. We should talk. Call me when you're ready. Elvis missing you. Love, Claire.*

I had texted Stuart with the news the previous day, and he would have told Sheilagh. It had not occurred to me that she would put herself in Claire's shoes—or, more likely, imagine herself catching Chad in the same circumstances. A hug is just a hug, unless you're looking for an explanation for your partner's changed behavior. And "I was comforting a friend whose marriage had broken up" is a perfectly good explanation unless you already suspect there's something going on.

I texted Sheilagh:

*Claire and I have split up. As you know, we have been doing our separate things for a while now. Absolutely nothing to do with you. I'm OK. Kill em on Tuesday. Beatles first single was My Bonnie.*

Then I texted Claire to tell her I had contacted Sheilagh and would be spending a week or so in France with friends from Australia. I signed off *Love, Adam.* If my mother had been monitoring our messages, she would have wondered—aloud—what on earth the problem was.

Friday morning I did some shopping for her, packed my kit, and took the train to London, where I put in a half day with the client and checked into a hotel in the West End. Sunday and Angelina, not to mention Charlie, did not seem far away. There were so many unknowns. But what did I *want*?

Once, a long time ago, I had asked Claire for her project-manager take on why my client was ignoring sound advice that he had paid good money for.

"You need to know where he's coming from," she said. "Think about what he might be trying to achieve by rejecting your input. Make a list of all the possibilities."

"It could be anything. He doesn't want to lose face; he wants to get rid of me; he actually believes I'm wrong. . . ."

"Write them all down and I'll tell you which it is."

In the end there were six items, after I'd resisted the urge to include the facetious ones.

Claire didn't look at the list. "Number them *a* to *f*. And your answer is *g*: *All of the above*. People are complex. They're never just pursuing one thing. Sometimes even contradictory things. So if one thing doesn't work out, they've got something else."

My list of goals for the visit to France would have included a reality check so I could ground myself before moving on with my life. Plus the chance to reestablish an old friendship. And, if I was honest with myself, I was hoping that there might be a terminal problem with her marriage that had led to her contacting me. In which case, the scenario that a day ago I had dismissed as an impossible fantasy might become reality: I might have another chance.

All of the above.

On the morning of my departure for France, it was raining. I gave up on trying to hail a taxi and caught the Tube. It was my forty-ninth summer in England. One word, one simple promise back in 1989, and at this moment I could have been riding home from the Australian Rules football on a Melbourne tram to the loving arms of Angelina and our three children. I could not imagine it. Too much time had passed.

There was, of all things, a piano at St Pancras station, an August Förster upright that had been painted a bluish green. It looked the worse for wear, and I would have assumed it was only for decoration had there not been an Eastern European–looking guy in his mid-twenties playing "C Jam Blues" and sounding good with it. He finished, earned a round of applause from the half a dozen travelers standing around, then picked up his backpack and walked off.

It was less than four months since I had listened to the girl at Manchester station singing "Someone Like You" and thought that I would never again feel alive enough to step up and play, but today I almost reflexively slipped onto the stool and did a big intro to "For Once in My Life."

I sang my heart out and sensed a crowd building, responding to the volume and perhaps my enthusiasm.

The player who had preceded me reappeared. He gave me a grinning thumbs-up before rummaging in his backpack to produce a harmonica, a chromatic, the authentic Stevie Wonder instrument. I nodded back and he played a solo, giving it as much as I had been giving, the two of us owning St. Pancras station at eight A.M. on a wet Saturday morning.

I was swept up in the euphoria of playing, of being free, and of limitless possibility. More than that, I felt a change, perhaps one that had already happened but was only now announcing itself, a rising sense of confidence, of self-worth. I was twenty-two years older and wiser than when I last saw Angelina. If I had another chance to touch what my heart had been dreaming of, I was going to take it.

# Part 2

# 23

As I was waiting for the train, browsing the WHSmith, a slim blond woman of about forty in black jeans and high heels came up beside me.

"Excuse me, but I just wanted to say you were great. I was feeling flat and you've made my day. So thank you."

She gave me a smile that invited a longer conversation.

"My pleasure. Thank you."

"Going to Paris?"

"Just for tonight. Visiting friends near Mâcon."

"Do you know Paris well?"

"Not that well, but I'm only in transit."

"It's home for me. I commute to London."

"Well, safe journey. Thanks for taking the trouble to say you liked the playing. Makes it worthwhile."

She hesitated for a moment before walking off.

On the train, I indulged a brief fantasy about waiting for her at the Gare du Nord in Paris. It gave me a clearer idea of what I wanted. Which wasn't a casual encounter or even a new relationship. Not a completely new one.


I dined alone in Paris at the French version of McDonald's. I had thought about visiting the Buddha Bar at the Hotel de Crillon, but did not feel like fancy food by myself. Eating my McChicken Burger I wondered why we—Claire and I—had not done this more often. A couple of hours on the train reading or listening to music; a chance to refresh the French; expenses covered by a day or two of work that I enjoyed doing.

It had been fourteen years since we spent an impulsive weekend in a hotel on the Île St-Louis. We had been renting in London and decided to buy our own place. This was long before I downshifted to working part-time, and we were getting close to having a viable deposit. We were beginning to accept that there would not be kids, and that the romantic stage of our relationship had passed. The house gave us something else to focus on.

Then, one of the guys I had worked with in Australia got in touch about a scheme he had bought into. A mathematician had come up with a way to make a killing on the lottery—the *lotto*. We just had to cover all the numbers and pay a lot of entry fees.

The proposition made sense, it was legal, and the logistics appealed to my technical mind. I put in some money. We took out a U.S. state lottery outright, and after covering the overheads we put what was left of the winnings back in the kitty for the next strike.

I bought some more units and eventually lost the lot. There may have been fraud on the part of the organizers, and there was some talk of the investors suing them, but there came a point where I had to accept that I would not be seeing my contribution to the house deposit again.

I had not told Claire about the plan or the ongoing saga. I confessed over dinner at home. God knows how she must have felt: I had broken her trust as well as her dream. She just got up and walked out the front door. Did not even slam it.

An hour later she came back, wet from the rain. Her composure had not extended to taking an umbrella.

"We should go to Paris," she said. "We haven't been anywhere except Randall and Mandy's because of the house. Now it's gone, there's nothing to stop us."

I was lost for words. It was in character for Claire to put mistakes behind her, to forgive and look ahead, but this was almost beyond belief. I deserved at least to be berated and screamed at. But Claire didn't do screaming and abuse.

Dining at the Buddha Bar, where Claire—Claire who didn't like fancy food and wine—made a mistake with the conversion rate and ordered a £300 bottle of Burgundy, I began to understand. My gamble had been a bet each way. If I won, we would have been able to buy a house immediately. If I lost, our relationship would be over. I had left it up to the lottery, but Claire had taken back control.

A year later, Claire's mother died and left her the house in Norwich.

I nearly missed my train at the Gare de Lyon, having forgotten to put my watch forward an hour, then spent the two-hour journey to Macon trying to decide what to wear. By the time I had settled on a gray T-shirt and suit jacket with my jeans, and made a dash to the bathroom to change, the train was pulling into the station.

The platform was crowded with passengers waiting to board. I caught the perfume first, the fragrance I could recognize at twenty paces, then the guy in front of me stepped aside and she was there.

She *was* different. Her lips were less full, her cheekbones more pronounced, and she was slimmer, more elegant. Her hair, the same dark brown, was shorter—as I'd seen in her Skype avatar. She was wearing sunglasses, a white top with an abstract design, a short jacket, light blue jeans, and high-heeled shoes. Rings with big stones on her middle and index fingers, which were wirier than I remembered.

We stood still, silently appraising each other. Neither of us spoke. The crowd dispersed and the train pulled out, leaving us alone, and I knew, absolutely *knew*, two things. The first was that, whatever the cost and whatever might happen, I had made the right decision in seeing her again. I was back in Shanksy's bar, the night I played "I Hope That I Don't Fall in Love with You," and saw her waiting for me, holding a Fallen Angel and trying to hide her nervousness.

The second thing I knew, without anything to justify it except whatever was wordlessly passing between us, was that she felt the same way—and had not expected to.

"Say something," she said.

It took me a few moments. "You are so beautiful. Still."

It sounded just as sappy as when I had sung it for her to get a message past Tina.

She smiled broadly, then kissed me on each cheek. Her hands were on my shoulders and mine lightly on her back, and suddenly we pulled ourselves into each other, as though it was Melbourne airport in 1989 and she rather than Jacinta had come running to make it right. I held her for a few seconds, then we both let go, not awkward or embarrassed, just accepting that we had to rejoin the real world, where she lived with her husband who was waiting in the car for us.

As she stepped back, I registered what she was wearing around her neck. It was the locket I had given her for Christmas in 1989. Did it still have our photo in it?

"Are you okay, I mean with what's happened with Claire?" she said as we walked the length of the platform to the exit.

"It's been coming for a while. I think we'll stay friends. Which was the problem, in some ways."

"What about our being in touch?"

"There were other things."

Charlie was waiting in the drop zone, arms crossed on the roof of a little Renault. He was a big guy, about six foot five, mid-fifties, brown hair turning gray, neatly trimmed beard, carrying quite a bit of weight over a well-muscled frame.

He shook my hand and was friendly in that instant Australian way.

"You okay in the backseat? We don't have far to go."

He squeezed himself into the driver's seat and I was reminded of Mr. Incredible, the cartoon superhero, in his too-small car. I got in behind Angelina.

"Sorry about the smell," said Charlie. "It's our caretaker's car—he smokes like a chimney. Still raining in England? You didn't tell me, any food preferences?"

"Happy to go with the flow," I said. "If you're planning steak tar-tare, I might give it a turn in the pan."

"You okay with offal?"

"Lamb's fry and kidneys for breakfast."

In line with my healthy-eating program, I had been starting my day with muesli and yogurt until the breakup with Claire, but my mother was not for turning from the full English catastrophe.

"Oh yuck," said Angelina. "I'm going to be sick."

"Good man," said Charlie. "We're going to eat well."

It was apparent he was a keen chef, and it was equally apparent that he saw me as an audience for his cooking. There were worse ways for my ex-lover's husband to see me.

We stopped at a bar in Cluny and sat at a table on the street, Angelina beside me and Charlie opposite. It was a sunny day, I had a *salade niçoise*, we shared some fries, a double line of little kids walked by hand in hand, and that is about all I can recall. The town is, by all accounts, quaint and full of history.

Charlie was studiedly relaxed, leaning back in his chair, ordering a small carafe of red wine, a salad for Angelina, and a steak for himself in bad but confident French. He was wearing a dark blue sports jacket, blue open-neck shirt, neutral slacks, and a plain but large-faced gold watch.

There was something familiar about him, though I had not seen any images when I Googled him. Possibly he just resembled someone I had worked with or a public figure: a touch of Peter Ustinov, perhaps.

And Angelina. I was trying to join the dots between the young woman who had said "I love you," the older, sophisticated woman next to me sipping wine and delivering a history lesson on the abbey, and the disembodied source of flirtatious e-mails.

She did not stop talking.

"It's warm, isn't it? I don't want to drink too much. Charlie will have a bottle open as soon as we're in the door. . . ."

She picked at her salad, made a trip to the bar for a soda water, then excused herself to go to the bathroom.

Charlie smiled a smile that said: *She isn't always like this. As we both know.*

It suited me. *Shut up and listen* would be a good principle until I worked out what was going on.

"How's the red?" said Charlie.

"Good, ta."

"Local plonk. Gamay."

He mopped up the last of the pepper sauce that had accompanied his steak and washed it down with the remains of the red. As Angelina walked back to the table, he raised his eyebrows and pursed his lips. It was the look of approval that Stuart would give if a fetching young woman passed our table at the pub—a look that I would endeavor to ignore.

Angelina would have earned the nod from Stuart, but Charlie was her husband. On my part, the frisson I had felt on the platform was morphing into desire. The glass of wine hadn't helped.

Whatever the marital or political correctness of drawing attention to his wife's attractiveness, Charlie was no Richard. He may have been a lawyer, but that was all they seemed to have in common. Physically he was the antithesis: Richard had been neat and compact. Charlie exuded bonhomie, whereas my impressions of Richard had been of meanness and a controlling, sniping possessiveness. He would have either ordered with a Parisian accent or expected the waiter to understand English.

Angelina may have been precipitous in jumping from one marriage to another, but she had not married the same man twice. Charlie was punching his PIN into the waiter's machine before I had a chance to offer.

"Since you didn't tell me what you eat," said Charlie, as we drove home, "I thought I'd wait till I had the picture."

The village was small, but it had the basics: post office, hairdresser, a huge pharmacy with a condom dispenser outside, a couple of bars, and a tourist office that Charlie informed me was closed on weekends, in line with French traditions of service.

He stopped at the small supermarket, jumped out of the car, and signaled for Angelina to take his place behind the wheel.

"I'll walk home," he said.

It was about half a mile up a hill to the stone house, far enough from the *centre commercial* to be pretty much in the countryside. I had joined Angelina in the front of the car.

"Is this how you imagined me when we were e-mailing?" she said. "Or were you thinking about big breasts and flawless skin?"

"I was imagining Jessica Rabbit. While I was eating my lunch at work. Where were you?"

"In bed."

"So what were you imagining? A twenty-six-year-old with a beard?"

"How was the Lake District?"

She had not had to imagine. She had only to search for my image on the Web, where one of the walking group must have posted photos. The fit outdoorsman, impeccably kitted out, surrounded by friends. Not a bad image.

"Stalker," I said.

"Alcoholic. You looked plastered. I preferred the accordion player." She laughed. "I didn't have to imagine anything. I heard your accent."

I gave her a sample. "Bruce Springsteen and Patti Smith. They wrote it together. It's about two ex-lovers left alone in a French cottage, with the husband only half a mile away."

"That's not helping."

The house stood some distance from its neighbors, with a garage, a long balcony, and a garden of flowers and fruit trees. The courtyard between the garage and main building was dominated by a blue spruce, with rosebushes in flower, a substantial herb garden, and wisteria climbing the walls. Angelina's e-mail had implied that they owned the place. Charlie's lawyering—or whatever Angelina was now doing—must pay well. Or they didn't invest in lotto syndicates.

I did not get a chance to explore the interior of the house. The moment we were through the front door, Angelina tossed her bag and sunglasses onto a side table and put her arms around my neck. I had just a few moments to study her face at close quarters, to notice that the makeup covered some fine lines around her eyes, before touch took over from sight.

I don't think either of us intended more than a kiss, but things escalated. I slid my hands down and she pushed into me. It was the scenario that had fueled a hundred fantasies, but none of them had featured skin-tight jeans and strappy shoes.

"I'll get them," she said as I bent down to undo the buckles.

"It's okay, I've got this one."

"No, it's easier for me. Just steady me."

"Try the chair."

"I know how to take my shoes off."

Then the jeans: Angelina sitting in the middle of the floor, pulling on one leg, until my efforts with the other leg unbalanced her so she fell back with both legs in the air and jeans around her knees. Finally, walking backward, and ignoring her protestations, I managed to get them off—and burst out laughing.

It was not so much the physical comedy as the sense of familiarity. I could see the same scene playing out twenty-two years earlier, with Angelina behaving exactly the same way. Against all reasonable expectations, I had her back.

She sat up, still wearing her top. "What are you laughing at?"

It might have been a circuit breaker, but the buildup to this moment had gone on half the afternoon, or for three months. It was not the smoothest segue, but neither of us cared. I kissed her, and a few seconds later was backing her against the front door.

She broke our kiss to let out something between a moan and a scream, surely as much a release of tension as anything. In response, there was a loud knock at the door, which was being held closed by our bodies.

Panic and farce: Angelina on the floor again pulling her jeans back on and me trying to perform the same maneuver while leaning hard against the door. When I stepped back, decent but mentally disheveled, the door stayed closed but the knock was repeated.

Angelina pushed past me and opened the door. It was not Charlie but Gilles, the caretaker, who had seen us arrive. He was about sixty-five, short, with a neat gray mustache and a smile that suggested he had worked out the reason for the delay. Angelina's shoes were on their sides, several feet apart.

She did introductions and listened while he explained, slowly in French, that he was sorry to disturb us but wanted to check that the heating had been working the previous night and that it was not too warm, but cooler weather was forecast and a number of steps were necessary to activate the system, and it was better to be prepared but with the thermostat—did Angelina understand "thermostat"?—set to a low temperature until such time as the weather actually cooled.

By the time Angelina had sent him on his way, the moment had gone. We were in no state to seize it anyway.

Angelina looked around the room. "Oh my God. Are you okay? Do you think Gilles . . . ?"

"Probably. Will he say anything?"

"I don't think so. Not in his interests to cause trouble. I'll see if the woman at the supermarket looks at me differently next time I see her."

She was talking herself through it, but she looked shaken.

"Your room's at the end of the hall. Are you okay if I go upstairs? Tell Charlie I'm having a shower if he asks." She took a deep breath and exhaled. "Oh. My. God."

Then she picked up her shoes and headed upstairs.

The hallway passed the kitchen and bathroom before leading into a large and bright bedroom. It had a double bed and simple wooden furniture, including a bookcase stocked with contemporary fiction and popular science. The floor was tiled, with a modern rug, and Georgian-style windows looked onto the garden on one side and the courtyard on the other. There was a vanity unit, but no shower.

I sat on the bed and tried to compose myself. Everything was okay. We had just had a close shave. Gilles hadn't seen anything.

It seemed that the reality of our reunion—the intensity of it—had caught Angelina by surprise, as it had me. The encounter against the door might have been a one-off, an unconsidered moment of reckless-ness in response to that feeling. If not, was she looking for an affair, if only for a week? Or was I witnessing the end of a marriage, possibly unbeknownst to Charlie?

And what about Charlie, my host, who had been shopping for my dinner while I was tearing his wife's clothes off?

There was not much I could do now, beyond being an appreciative guest and going with the flow. Anything out of order would raise sus-picions, which would have greater consequences for Angelina than for me.

I gave myself a quick splash and a blast of deodorant, composed myself in the mirror, and walked back to the living room. This time I had a chance to look around.

Two sofas, a couple of armchairs, dining table and eight chairs, sideboard, a fireplace, and framed menus on the wall. A stereo but no television. No family pictures, perhaps because they rented it out. At one end was an upright piano, a Yamaha that I had not noticed while I was busy with other things. I remembered Shanksy telling me that Angelina had accompanied herself when she sang "I Will Survive" on that last night.

Charlie came in carrying two full shopping bags.

"Need a hand?" I asked.

"Help me unpack, if you like," he said, and I followed him to the kitchen.

"Nice place," I said.

It had a good dose of rustic charm, in keeping with the age of the building, but things seemed square and solid, and the kitchen was kit-ted out with the sort of appliances that Randall and Mandy might have bought in their California foodie heyday.

"Somewhere back in time there were plans to run it as a bed-and-breakfast," said Charlie. "The bedrooms have vanity units, but there's only one shower, upstairs, so we'll be a bit chummy."

I had surely exceeded the bounds of chumminess with the hostess already.

Around 6:30 P.M., bag unpacked, Internet connection established, and mind as straight as it could be under the circumstances, I emerged from my room to find Charlie still at work in the kitchen.

"What do you drink?" he asked.

"Not fussy."

"Beer?"

"Sounds perfect."

"Happy to have it cold?"

"However it comes."

Charlie opened two bottles of Heineken—little European quarter-liters. He raised his and we clinked them in a toast. We could have drunk to all sorts of things, but not many that were in our mutual interest.

"*Santé*. Good health," he said, then put his beer down and began zesting lemons.

# 2 4

Charlie told me a bit about the recent history of the house (bought six years ago, the kitchen since refurbished), its maintenance (Gilles was retired and living in the apartment above the garage), and business in Australia and around the world (keeping him busy).

As he spoke, he emptied lemon juice into a cocktail shaker, poured slugs of Cointreau and tequila from bottles in the freezer, added ice cubes, salted the rim of a pink-stemmed cocktail glass, then shook and upended the shaker to deliver a frothing margarita that exactly filled the glass.

"Back in a minute," he said, and disappeared upstairs. He had not touched his beer.

I went to my room and grabbed the premium gin that I had brought as a gift. No point bringing wine to France.

Angelina joined us for predinner snacks in white jeans, white singlet, and silver coils for earrings. Bare feet. Glasses, which she had not worn in her twenties. The locket was gone, replaced by an enamel medallion with browns and reds on a white background. The perfume was different, too, though only subtly so.

The evening was warm and we sat on the *galerie Mâconnaise*, the long balcony on the upper level. It was too narrow for us to face each other, so we were lined up looking out over rolling green and brown fields dotted with white cattle. Angelina sat in the middle, her knee

bumping mine from time to time. There was no traffic beyond a trac-
tor pulling haymaking equipment and an elderly woman walking her
bicycle.

Charlie opened a bottle of champagne, and passed around a plate
of lobster medallions topped with guacamole. It was a step up from
the packet of crisps I would have eaten at home if I couldn't hold out
for dinner.

"Not quite French," he said, "but I made them to go with the margarita."

He looked pointedly at Angelina, who had finished her cocktail before joining us. The lobster was followed by a selection of charcuterie
as the light began to fade.

"You're being excessive, Charlie," said Angelina. She was not touching the pig snouts and ears, which were actually pretty good.

The champagne disappeared and Charlie opened a bottle of red.
"I know I'm taking a risk, serving Beaujolais to an Englishman, but
this is something different."

I have swilled my share of Beaujolais Nouveau, but even my un-
educated palate could tell that Charlie's wine was in another class.

"You're kidding me. This is Beaujolais?" I said.

Charlie smiled and topped up my glass. I was wondering if I would
have room for the main course, but he had prepared a light meal of
spaghetti with black olives, prosciutto, olive oil, the lemon zest, and
heaps of thyme from the garden, with a green salad on the side.

We talked a bit about the house and its history. All of the windows
were barred, creating an effect that I had romantically interpreted as
Georgian. The rooms had individual locks and they had found a cache
of old video recording and editing equipment—worth nothing today
but a fortune in its time.

Angelina's theory was that a previous owner had been a pornogra-
pher. My bedroom, with light from all sides, including a frosted glass
door, had surely been the studio. It was fanciful stuff with no connection to our own present and past lives, except perhaps Angelina's ex-
hibitionist fantasies.

The wine was helping me slip into the setting and hospitality and easy conversation. As for the rest of it, there was not much I could do until Angelina and I had a chance to talk. But something had connected regarding Charlie.

"Ever played rugby?" I asked him.

"What makes you think that?"

We all laughed. I was thinking about the Charles Acheson on the Internet who scored a legendary try against the All Blacks. Charlie was of a size to do it.

"I hope you didn't play against our guys," I said.

"Never got past the state team. Too much like hard work. Not to mention lack of talent."

"Go on, tell him," said Angelina. She turned to me. "You're not going to leave here without hearing the story, so let's get it over with."

"We can go the whole week without telling the story if you don't mention it," said Charlie.

"Hey," said Angelina. "Don't get tetchy. It's a good story. Charlie scored a try against New Zealand."

This was, by any measure, pretty impressive, the more so as he would have been playing out of his league, in a state team against the finest Test team in the world.

Charlie laughed. "You have to get it in perspective. I was playing for Tasmania and we got a fixture against the touring All Blacks. They fielded their fifth-string lineup, gave everyone except the water boy a run, and beat us by about seventy points. But they got a bit careless in defense and I picked up the loose ball and fell over the line."

"Right," said Angelina. "You just *fell* across the line with it."

"I had to brush off a couple of little Kiwis," he said. "Missed the conversion too, I was so amazed at myself. Very unprofessional."

Despite the self-deprecation, it was obvious that he loved the story. This might be the moment that defined the man, the big guy grabbing the chance and not worrying about the reputation of the opposition, just doing it—only to be overcome with awe at what he had pulled off.

"Bloody fantastic," I said. "Great story."

"Tell us about the walk," said Angelina. "Adam went walking in the Lake District a few weeks ago."

"Just a couple of days in the rain," I said.

"Better than us," she said. "We haven't been walking since the Overland Track in Tasmania. Tell Adam the story."

They told the story together, in married-couple fashion, complete with arguments about the details. With a couple of other hikers—*bushwalkers*—they had carried out a teenager who had become ill. One bloke on each of the front stretcher handles, Charlie holding both rear handles. Snow coming in.

Angelina: "So this girl is dry retching constantly, and the ranger meets us—he's walked in with this enormous pack and coffee and a medical kit, and the girlfriend of one of the guys carrying the stretcher is a nurse. She tells Charlie that the girl should have some injection—"

Charlie: "Maxolon—had to inject it or she'd throw it up."

Angelina: "But the ranger won't let her do it because he needs a doctor's authorization."

Charlie: "We'd worked that out already."

Angelina: "So Charlie says he's a doctor, signs all the forms. As Dr. Charlie."

Charlie: "Dr. Charles."

Angelina: "And gives the syringe to the nurse to inject. Like, you do this—it's beneath me."

Charlie: "They were never going to check."

Angelina: "You were a lawyer. It was misrepresentation."

And so on. Were these stories intended to remind me that they had a shared history, or to remind themselves? Charlie had been the hero on both occasions.

We finished the wine with cheese and then put a dent in a bottle of Sauternes, which Angelina did not touch. Charlie reminded me that the only white wines Angelina drank were Chablis and champagne. It was news to me. She and I had drunk all sorts.

He opened another red for her, and poured a small quantity into her big glass. There was a bit of nonverbal communication (surely only nonverbal because of my presence) about the size of the serve that resulted in him pouring her about a third of the bottle.

I had never thought of drinking Sauternes with cheese. In fact, I

had never thought of drinking Sauternes, but Charlie was right. It went well with the Roquefort.

"Château Rieussec, 1983," said Charlie. "It's nice to have someone to share it with."

"You're throwing me in the deep end with the wine," I said. "Don't waste anything too good on me." I took another sip. "But thank you."

"You can thank Charlie's ex," said Angelina.

I waited for her to say, "Tell Adam the story."

"Tell Adam the story."

"We've told enough stories."

"I'll tell the story. It's okay, I'll tell it nicely."

"*I'll* tell it. You ever been divorced, Adam?" said Charlie. "Angelina and I have that in common."

"No," I said, before remembering that I was facing my own in all but name. "My parents were divorced. Does that count?"

"Ugly? Sorry, none of my business. Let me just assume it was. It always is, and all we can do is try to be as civilized as we can and not give everything to the lawyers."

I nodded. No argument there. I was getting a long way ahead of myself, but Charlie having a noncombative approach to divorce could only be a good thing.

"We were both lawyers. She'd decided she was going to live in Italy. Don't bother asking. I put all our stuff into two piles: tokens for the house, the two cars, the wine, the mortgage, and other bits and pieces. Used the Monopoly set. And I said, 'You pick which pile you want.' My sister and I used to do it as kids: I'll cut the cake, you choose the piece."

"Nice technique," I said. "If you can get the other party to cooperate." My mother would have had none of this tricksy stuff.

"Well, she'd agreed to it, and she swept one of the piles toward her. The one with the wine in it, incidentally. Then she pulled out a photo of our daughter and put it on top."

"Shit."

"Obviously that wasn't part of the deal. We were only supposed to be settling the property. First rule of decent behavior: leave children out of your games."

And conversation, apparently. Over three hours, they had said nothing about the children they had had together.

"So what did you do?" I asked.

"I took back the wine bottle that represented my collection, put it in my pile, and said, 'If you're happy with that, we have an agreement.' So I got the wine and she took my daughter, who I only see when I come over here."

"Jesus."

What would he have said to Randall and Mandy? Take a twin each and get over yourselves?

"Before you say, 'He swapped his daughter for a wine cellar,' think what other outcome there could have been. None. Or none better. Eloise was set on going to Italy."

Eloise.

I *had* seen Charlie before, slimmer, with a full head of brown hair, sorting through a bunch of betting slips to find the one that would make his wife the star of the marquee at the Melbourne Cup. Eloise Ditta, the divorce lawyer: *If you're bitter, get Ditta.* Charlie couldn't be accused of taking advantage of a weak opponent.

I looked at Angelina for a reaction but she did not seem to have twigged that I would remember. The name had only stuck because of the eponymous song. In Angelina's mind, Eloise would be connected with a lot more than Barry Ryan's 1968 hit and a day at the races.

I forced my attention back to Charlie's summing up.

"Grace was going to be separated from one of us. We could have fought for years and it would probably have still gone the way it went, with God knows how much psychological and financial damage. This way we got it sorted quickly, and Angelina and I were able to get on with our lives." He looked at Angelina. "So that's the story."

Charlie drained his glass. Angelina took another slug from hers.

"Plenty of time to finish these," Charlie said, indicating the open bottles. "Sorry to bore you with our reminiscences. And my heartless pragmatism. It must be your turn, but you're probably knackered."

I was certainly feeling the effects of alcohol. I got up, and Angelina gave me a hug and a kiss on the cheek. "Sleep well."

The house at night was dead quiet, so I heard the footsteps before the light went on in the hallway. I briefly made out a shape through the frosted glass door before it opened to reveal Angelina wearing a transparent red negligee that was as short as it could be without being pointless. She was holding two brandy balloons and a bottle. If this was her idea of a middle-aged man's erotic fantasy, she had got it pretty right.

I sat up against the bedhead, speechless. The clock showed just after midnight. Angelina hesitated for a moment, looking, I guessed, for my reaction, then walked over to me, poured two glasses, and put the bottle on the bedside cabinet. Just what I needed—another drink. But the cognac—not to mention the costume, which was a long way from what she had worn in her twenties, or what the average married woman might wear to bed in her forties—seemed to be more for theatrical effect.

The choreographed performance was the opposite of the afternoon's impulsiveness, but the slight pause to summon her nerve took me straight back to the bar in 1989 and her taking on "Because the Night." This was the woman I had fallen in love with, standing beside the bed, taking a risk, waiting for my approval—and for me to make the next move.

I was torn. I wanted to pull her into me and finish what we had started. The desire was almost overwhelming. Presidents have risked impeachment for less.

But there was Charlie. If he saw me as a threat, then he had played me masterfully. I would hate myself in the morning. And, practically, the consequences of him not being asleep, or waking and finding his wife missing, were too horrible to contemplate.

"Charlie's asleep," she said in response to the unasked question. "He's jet-lagged."

"Are you sure you know what you're doing?"

"I'm very sure. When you see St. Peter, and he knows everything, he's going to let you in. I promise."

"I thought there was a commandment specifically about this."

"I wasn't being literal. I'm thinking of a secular St. Peter."

"Right."

She leaned over and kissed me, softly. "Relax."

I couldn't, but in the spirit of the game I slipped my hands under her top, and her argument began to feel remarkably persuasive. Then there was a creak, possibly from upstairs. We both froze, then Angelina pulled away. She must have decided that discretion was the better part of infidelity, especially after the scare earlier in the day.

She took a few more moments to kiss me several times on the lips. "Night, Dooglas."

I would not be getting any answers to my questions tonight.

# 2 5

I woke to light filtering through my window and Charlie knocking on the door.

"Tea or coffee, mate?"

"Thanks, I'll have a shower first."

"Can I come in?"

Why not? Everybody else does. "Yeah. I'm still in bed."

Charlie opened the door, wearing slacks and an untucked shirt, and I enjoyed a moment of relief that circumstances, if not self-control, had kept me from having sex with his wife. He gave me a quick rundown on the bathroom protocol—plenty of hot water for ordinary mortals, but get in before The Princess uses it all.

It was strange, and intimate, sharing a bathroom with Angelina again. I could not help myself—I browsed the cabinet, and found nothing surprising. They let the house out to others, so this was a communal cupboard, but there were a couple of hair ties on the vanity unit. I picked one up and twirled it between my fingers. I had almost taken Angelina against the door the previous day, kissed her virtually naked that night, and here I was fetishising a bobble. I was careful to go easy on the hot water.

When I joined Charlie in the kitchen, he was working the espresso machine.

"Have to bring the beans from Melbourne," he said. "Local stuff's crap."

He fashioned a Starbucks-style confection with frothed milk, cinnamon, and a sprinkling of chocolate and took it upstairs.

"Got time for a stroll to the village?" he asked when he returned.

There were advantages in saying no. Angelina seemed intent on consummating our cyber relationship, and I guessed that the previous evening's visit was to have been the moment, until Charlie's detour to the shops had presented an earlier opportunity. After two near misses, I had little doubt about what would happen if I passed up the walk.

But I wanted to make my own decision and Charlie was part of that. I needed to know what was happening between him and Angelina. It was one thing to rescue her from a broken marriage, as I had failed to do before. It was another to be the cause of it.

It was a pleasant downhill walk along the narrow road in the early-morning sunshine, past concrete water troughs, freshly mown fields with hay bales scattered around, and a couple of donkeys sticking their heads over the rock wall. The village was less prissily perfect than its English counterpart would have been: a few houses in ruins; blackberry vines tangled over rock walls; shutters painted in loud pinks, purples, and greens.

Charlie filled the time with a story about tenants who had incurred the wrath of the locals through various transgressions, the most serious of which was not that they had put glass in the general waste bin but that the bottles were from Bordeaux.

On a Monday in rural France, only the supermarket was open. Charlie bought croissants, a baguette, and a small wooden box of oysters, using rudimentary French. I had done an exchange program at school, and my French was stronger, but the middle-aged woman behind the counter, who gave me a careful appraisal before attending to Charlie, seemed to be able to follow what he was saying.

"Gilles's girlfriend," said Charlie when we were out the door.

He puffed a bit going up the hill. He was carrying a lot of weight, and apparently had no intention of losing it. He had bought five "pure butter" croissants, each as big as a woman's size-six shoe, for three people.

"I always walk to the village unless it's raining," he said. "Sometimes even then. Got to keep in shape." He laughed.


I spent a quiet morning in my bedroom setting up a database restructure via an adequate Internet link, sitting against the pillows with my computer on my lap. Angelina put her head in a couple of times and made a fuss about getting me a coffee. I could hear Charlie doing the actual barista work.

When she came back with the coffee I smiled, and she said, "What?"

I let her answer her own question.

"You think I'm a prima donna because Charlie made the coffee."

"Now that you mention it . . ."

"Two things: first, I'm on holiday, and second, Charlie loves doing it. Try touching the coffee machine and you'll find out. And if he wants to show you that I expect to have everything done for me . . ." She shrugged her shoulders.

"He doesn't always do the shopping?"

She laughed. "Food only."

Then, from the doorway: "I don't want to keep going on, but . . . what I said last night. You can trust me. I mean, if that's what you want. You won't be doing anything terrible."

"It'd help if you elaborated a bit. So I could make my own decision."

"I know."

"One question. Simple question. Are you and Charlie in trouble? Your marriage?"

She hesitated before answering. "We've got some issues. I don't know what's going to happen. But I'm not looking for a new relationship."

*I just wanted someone in my corner. We're trying to work it out. No re-lationship, no falling in love, nobody getting hurt.*

Around noon, I walked to the living room to find Charlie and Ange-lina both doing what I had been doing—typing away on laptops.

"What are you working on?" I asked Angelina.

"Just work."

It seemed strange after four months of recent communication and an evening of being a guest in her house to ask, "What do you do?"

"At the moment, I'm writing an article. I do a newspaper column—mainly women's issues. I'm a human rights lawyer. For the last three years I've been an equal opportunity commissioner."

Right. Charlie Acheson is on the Internet for scoring a try against New Zealand. Angelina Brown is an equal opportunity commissioner. I could only hope that the Elephant and Castle had put up last week's win.

After lunch, a mercifully light smoked salmon omelet, I joined them in the living room, working from one of the leather armchairs as they sat at right angles to each other at the dining table. I had a pleasant and distracting view of Angelina, who was in blue jeans, a loose knitted top that fell off one shoulder, and bare feet. She caught me looking a couple of times and smiled.

The revelation of her professional persona, unexpected as it was, had only enhanced her appeal. I was enjoying the feeling: *the beauti-ful, successful woman I once knew is still a beautiful, successful woman—and she still wants me.*

Around six P.M. the legendary sportsman, barista, and occasional physician packed up his laptop and adjourned to the kitchen. I had fin-ished my own work, and as soon as Charlie left the room Angelina was over by my chair, bending down to kiss me. It was going to be hard to survive a week of this.

Charlie called from the kitchen. "What happened to the lemons?"

"Margarita," Angelina shouted back. "Remember?"

"I thought there were a couple left."

"I haven't touched them."

"No worries. I'll go out and get some."

This was going to be my last chance to say no. Angelina kissing me did nothing for rational decision-making, but my gut told me to trust her. She had given me no reason not to.

It took about fifteen seconds for the outside door to click closed, about five to run to my bedroom, and about ten for Angelina to have her jeans and top off. After two frustrated attempts in the space of twenty-four hours, desire had gone up to eleven. I pushed her back onto the unmade bed, forcefully enough to shift it a couple of feet across the floor. She was tugging at the buttons of my shirt, and I was kicking my shoes off with the laces still done up. It was going to be over in about a minute. *Awopbopaloobop alopbamboom.*

I managed to pull back. We were not in our twenties anymore, at a party in someone else's bedroom. There was no rush.

I kissed Angelina softly, on her lips and then her neck, moving down her body, taking my time as the late-afternoon sunshine bathed the room.

Long ago, I listened to Billie Holiday singing "Summertime"—not once but many times—and I thought it was as close to a perfect rendition as could be imagined: Lady Day laying out the melody in all its languid easy-living elegance, the restraint of her delivery only accentuating the feeling behind it.

Years later, I listened to Janis Joplin's live performance. It's a screaming, primal blues, the melody no more than a point of departure, but still, unmistakably, the same song. My familiarity with Billie Holiday's version only made Joplin's reinterpretation more powerful and in turn opened my mind to nuances I had missed in the original. Having experienced both versions, I knew the song in a way I could never have if I had heard only one.

Making love to Angelina felt different and familiar at the same time. Her body had changed, as had mine. She was leaner and softer and stronger—and less inhibited, turning me onto my back, then rolling us over again, urging me on, digging her fingers into me as she hovered on the brink of an orgasm she couldn't quite reach.

Finally, I picked her up, stood in the middle of the room with her legs wrapped around me, and said—in her ear but not in a whisper—"You nearly got caught yesterday. The door was unlocked and he could have opened it . . . he did open it . . . he walked in . . ." and she half moaned and half screamed, and everything fell away—the room, the fantasy, time—and it was just the two of us.

I lowered her onto the bed, both of us slippery with sweat. As we separated and I became aware of my surroundings again, there was a sound—half pop, half hiss—from behind me. I turned my head and saw Charlie, his frame filling the doorway.

How long had he been standing there? I was flooded with a feeling I had not had since I was a kid: *I've done something really stupid and I'm going to pay for it.* I thought there was a real chance he was about to kill me.

He was wearing an apron that read *Welcome to My Kitchen. Now Get the Hell Out.* But instead of a kitchen knife, he was holding an open champagne bottle in one hand and three glasses in the other.

Clearly savoring his advantage, he filled a glass, ambled over, and handed it to me. I had no choice but to take it. Naked. He poured a second and gave it to his wife, who had risen from the bed, picked up her top, and sat down again behind me.

Angelina found her voice and made a feeble attempt to wrest back the initiative. "You said you were going to get lemons."

"I did. The lemon tree's not a long walk."

Charlie poured a glass of champagne for himself.

"Drappier Grande Sendrée rosé 2002," he said, smiling. "Sendrée spelled with an *S*, an historical error that found its way into the land register. Means cinders. You probably know that. Quite distinct notes of cherry and spice. Not much made, but we know the winemaker."

It was the cheeseburger scene from *Pulp Fiction*. *When he's finished discussing the champagne, he's going to kill me.*

"So," he continued, "dinner will be at seven. We're having Belon oysters, with the essential squeeze of lemon, followed by foie gras and guinea fowl with wild mushrooms." He looked at Angelina. "And for dessert, *tarte aux pommes.*"

He took a sip of champagne, surveying the room—clothes on the floor, the bed askew, his wife and her lover.

"And now you'll both be able to concentrate on the food and wine."

He turned and walked out, leaving the door open behind him.

Angelina looked at me. I looked at Angelina, naked and holding a glass of pink champagne. As was I, though my shaking hand had spilled half of it.

Was there a trace of sadness in her eyes, an echo of that night in the upstairs bedroom almost a quarter of a century ago? If there was, it disappeared quickly.

She stood up, collected her clothes into a bundle, then clinked her glass against mine.

"See you at seven," she said.

# 26

As I sat on my bed, trying to recover enough composure to reflect on what had happened, a joke popped into my mind.

An Englishman, an Australian, and a Frenchman are discussing the meaning of sangfroid. The Englishman tells a story about a man who catches his wife in bed with her French lover. "Make yourselves decent, and I'll speak to you in the drawing room," he says. That, says the Englishman, is sangfroid.

The Australian responds with a similar story, but the antipodean husband adds, "Finish what you're doing first." That, he says, is *true* sangfroid.

"Ah," says the Frenchman, "my story ees the same, but when ze Australian husband says, 'Finish what you're doing,' the Frenchman does. That, *mon ami*, is sangfroid."

Charlie may have demonstrated the Australian version of sangfroid, but that story was a joke. Real people—even people who can make an instant decision to give up custody of their daughter and take advantage of the resulting shock to grab the wine cellar—have been known to commit homicide in such circumstances. Nobody can stumble upon their partner screwing someone else and act unsurprised. He must have known or suspected what he was going to find before he walked in.

Whether or not he had caught the whole performance, the timing suggested that he had waited until we were finished to announce his presence. There was another thing. Surely Angelina knew there was a lemon tree. Had her "trust me—it will be all right" extended to this scenario? Had she anticipated it? Or even set it up?

The one thing I did know was that Charlie—and obviously Angelina—seemed prepared to accommodate what the late Princess Diana had called a third person in the marriage. Perhaps just the once. Perhaps not.

Dinner was, unsurprisingly, excellent. Angelina was in a sleeveless short dress, a light blue one, set off by a ring with a sapphire the size of the last joint of my middle finger.

Gilles, comically small next to Charlie, joined us in the courtyard for oysters, shucked by our host at the cost of a gash between his thumb and forefinger. Gilles spoke as much English as Charlie and Angelina spoke French. I let him know that I understood him without making a show of it, and he gave me a tour of the garden on the other side of the house so we could chat.

I needed the time-out. Angelina seemed to be taking the predinner drama in her stride. On reflection, I thought it unlikely she had been party to a setup—her initial response had mirrored mine and *I knew her*—but she was better placed to make sense of her husband's response than I was. Charlie, at least, was playing some sort of game. I felt as his ex-wife must have done: What was the catch?

Gilles told me that Angelina and Charlie had installed him in the apartment above the garage in exchange for caretaking, gardening, and the occasional use of his car. He spoke well of them, as was to be expected, with just a gentle dig at their eating oysters in June and drinking wine from outside the region.

I asked him where the *citronnier* was.

"Too cold," he said. "There is no lemon tree."

Gilles returned to his apartment and Charlie led us up to the balcony for the foie gras. Angelina did not partake, and Charlie had made her a *pissaladière*, a square of pastry with anchovies and black olives.

We drank the leftover Sauternes with the foie gras. It was apparently a classic combination. Angelina stayed with the red, and Charlie's observations on food and wine matching kept us going until we moved inside for the main course.

"We'll finish Angie's Bordeaux and then try its big sister," said Charlie. "Come with me," he said, and led me downstairs to the cellar.

It could have been the moment for a man-to-man chat—or a quiet murder, the body never to be found—but he contented himself with showing me his wine collection. Was he waiting for me to ask the question? I wasn't planning to go to bed not knowing what was going on, but if I was going to start the conversation, I would do so with Angelina in the room.

Charlie selected a bottle and we returned to the dining room. The fruitwood table, uneven and with a patina of age, was set with colorful crockery, silver cutlery, and large thin-stemmed wineglasses. It hadn't taken me long to work out that Angelina and Charlie were not short of a quid, but there was nothing ostentatious about either of them, aside from Angelina's preciousness about wine.

"We'll let it settle," he said. He put the wine on the sideboard and poured us glasses from the bottle he had opened the previous night for Angelina. "Second wine of Château Margaux." He swirled his glass. "A day hasn't done it any harm at all."

I was feeling similarly relieved to have made it through the day unharmed. So far.

"Did you manage to do what you needed to get done?" I asked Charlie, making conversation. "I gather you're a lawyer, too."

"Past tense. Threw it in when we went to L.A."

This was news, though there was no reason to assume that people who had money and a house in Europe would sit around in Australia for twenty years.

Angelina finished giving her wine the swirl, sniff, sip, purse-lips-and-suck-air treatment and swallowed.

"We moved to L.A. in 1991 so I could have a chance at Hollywood," she said. "And do a bit of the tourist thing. I don't suppose you've been to Yosemite?"

Thank you, Randall and Mandy. *Thank you.*

"Couple of times," I said, with a touch of world-weariness. I could guess why she had singled out this particular tourist destination. My enduring memory of Yosemite—and the Grand Canyon—was the sheer height of the cliffs, a vertical span too great to fit in the field of vision. "How did you cope with the heights?"

"You remember." Angelina looked at Charlie—*Do you want to tell this story?*—but continued. "I freaked out. We walked up one of the tracks and that was okay, but when we got to the lookout—"

"The Upper Yosemite Fall," said Charlie, and I nodded.

"I couldn't do it. It was about ten in the morning and Charlie wouldn't let me come down until I'd gone out to the viewing area."

"You make me sound like a monster," said Charlie.

"You were. About lunchtime I just said to myself, 'Get it over with,' and then he made me stay out there for about two hours."

"Thirty minutes."

"Anyway, I still hate heights."

"But what did you learn?"

Angelina stuck her tongue out at Charlie. "You tell him."

"I said to Angelina, 'If you fall, you're no more dead than if you fell three stories.' Which is to say, you're going to have failures in life anyway, so you might as well aim high. Won't hurt any worse if you don't make it."

"L.A.'s pretty intimidating, and I was starting to think I wouldn't make it." She laughed. "I was right."

"But you didn't die wondering," said Charlie.

Once again, on the face of it, the conversation was all for my benefit, bringing me up to speed, or demonstrating the strength of what they had built together. But if their marriage was in trouble, perhaps it was about reminding themselves what they would be losing. Or were they just giving it a decent funeral?

My life did not appear to be on the agenda, and that was fine with me.

"How long were you in L.A.?" I asked.

"Eighteen months," said Charlie.

"You weren't working?"

He laughed. "One of us had to pay the bills. Angelina was studying at an acting studio, and I had a job with one of the Big Four—the Big Six back then. Got it in Australia, then organized a transfer. That said, it was a pretty junior position. I'm not licensed to practice law in the States."

"Must have been difficult, going backward," I said, earning a nod from Charlie.

"He wasn't junior for long," said Angelina. "Tell Adam the story."

"What story?"

"All right," said Angelina. "Don't complain if I get bits wrong."

Charlie went to the kitchen to check on dinner as she got started. Oddly, I was enjoying hearing how Angelina's life had panned out with another man. On the one hand, there was the reminder of what I had failed to seize, but on the other it was like being at Christmas with her family and filling the gaps in my knowledge of her life. And it was hard not to like Charlie.

He had been a member of a negotiating team for a company acquisition. There was a fault with the lifts and the two consultancy teams were stranded at street level with the directors of the buyer and seller sixty floors above them.

"Forty-three," said Charlie, returning with serving spoons.

"Whatever. So Charlie dumps his briefcase, races up the stairs, and, by the time the lifts are working again, they've got a deal."

"We had an agreement on the headline figure," said Charlie.

"The story went right up to the CEO," said Angelina. "Made him a bit of a legend."

"How did you do it?" I asked.

"I wasn't carrying so much weight back then."

"I meant—"

"I know. Wasn't rocket science. These guys knew each other. They wanted to do the deal. I just got there before the lawyers wound them up and made a meal of it. Takes one to know one."

The lawyer in the blue dress smiled. If there was some sort of put-down, she was letting it go.

"So that's what I do," said Charlie. "I'm the facilitator, the honest broker, the guy trying to find the best solution for everyone. Reassuringly expensive, but better value than paying lawyers to fight about it."

Which left one question for Angelina, although I knew the ultimate answer.

"What about the acting?"

"I wasn't good enough."

"Doesn't matter how good you are if you don't get the break," I said. "Why I'm not Billy Joel. Besides not writing 'Uptown Girl.'"

Charlie grinned at my choice of song, but Angelina just waved her empty glass.

"I'd auditioned for this role, not a big role, and one of the other women from my acting class got it. It was a level playing field: she wasn't screwing the director or anything. But she was better-looking than me, and that mattered more than how many years I'd spent studying the Stanislavski method. So I booked a nice restaurant, ordered champagne, and celebrated that we were going to go back to Australia to start a family and I was going to be a lawyer."

"Just like that," I said.

"Just like that."

Charlie decanted the red and poured a measure for Angelina. "Tell him about the waitress," he said.

"Oh, the server came over to take our order and it was the girl who'd got the part. A reminder of what I wasn't missing out on."

Charlie fetched the *plat du jour*, carved on a platter and surrounded by three kinds of mushrooms.

Angelina took only a small portion of the guinea fowl and removed the skin. She was less careful with the wine. The decanter was empty before Charlie asked her to guess what she was drinking.

"Château Margaux," she said. "You said before we'd be drinking the big sister."

"One of the five *premiers grands crus* of Bordeaux," Charlie offered for my benefit. "Sorry. Am I telling grandma how to suck eggs?"

"No," I said. "I'm appreciating the education."

"The most feminine of the first growths. How old do you think, Angie?"

Angie again. That was what Jacinta had called her. Much less twee than Angel. If I had thought of her as Angie, there would have been fewer songs that pushed the memory button. But who knows what people call each other behind closed doors? And she had once sung, "Just call me Angel."

Angie was assessing the wine, swirling it in her glass like a pro. "It's old, but still quite firm. Not *really* old. Twenty, twenty-five years."

Charlie retrieved the bottle and handed it to Angelina. "Wow," she said, and passed it to me for inspection. Grand Vin de Château Margaux, 1966.

"One of the three good vintages of the sixties," said Charlie.

It was also Angelina's birth year.

"How did you find this?" I asked.

"After we got married, I started buying the vintage at auction. We have one every birthday. This is the last bottle of the Margaux."

Not saved for the next birthday. Surely there was a message in that. And given the precedents, Angelina should have had no trouble nominating the vintage without all the swirling and sniffing.

"Solves the problem of birthday presents," I said.

"I wish," said Charlie. "I made a big mistake. The first birthday we were together, before we were married, I bought her a ring. Thanks to lack of imagination, I bought her a ring on the next birthday, and at that point she decided it was a tradition."

"I did not."

"Right. One year I bought her something else and the face just dropped, didn't it? Wisely, I had a ring in my pocket just in case."

"Stop it," said Angelina. "You're making me sound—"

"Just making sure all the facts are on the table." He went off to get the apple tart.

I looked at Angelina and laughed. "You've been spoiled."

"True," she said. "He's very, very nice to me."

Her tone suggested something was missing, but the dynamic between them was a long way from poisonous. Claire would have been envious. Most married couples would have been envious. God knows what Richard would have made of him, running back and forth from the kitchen.

We had Calvados with dessert and slipped briefly into a mellow silence.

"So," said Charlie, directing his question to the ceiling. "How was the tart?"

"Brilliant," I said.

"As good as you remember?"

"Behave," said Angelina.

"Sorry. It's easy to forget the proprieties. Shame on me."

We were on the brink.

"Charlie," I said, and then didn't know where to go.

"Adam," he said. "Sorry, I was teasing. I'm sure you'll understand the temptation."

He waved us both up from the table toward the sofa and chairs, carrying our brandy balloons. He and I took the chairs, and Angelina sat in the middle of the sofa.

"Nothing worse than not knowing what's going on," he said. "I don't know what Angie's said to you, but she has free rein as far as I'm concerned."

At one level this was a relief, but where was the guy coming from?

"If I did have a problem, it'd be between Angie and me, not with you. I don't subscribe to the ethos that blames the third party. Now drink your Calvados and tell me, if you want to, whether you think she's changed."

"Charlie! Cut it out." Angelina sounded only half serious.

The simple and honest answer was: "Not in any way that matters to me." I was not going to share that with Charlie.

Instead, I said, "Am I going to be out of line if I say that I once dated the sexiest woman on the planet, but I think you got the better deal?"

They both liked that.

"I do have to thank you for teaching her to appreciate the finer things in life," said Charlie, patently not talking about 1966 claret.

"Coming off a low base," I said.

He laughed. "I'll do you a deal. No more personal questions if you play something on the piano. I believe that's what started it all."

This was a good deal. There were all kinds of questions I still wanted to ask but instinct told me that Charlie had revealed all he wanted to at this point. *These are the rules—if you don't like them, don't play.* Did they have an open marriage? Was he letting her play out a fantasy? Perhaps he had some physical impediment. Diabetes and impotence would go with the weight. It was an explanation that they might not want to share with me. It also fitted with Angelina talking Charlie up.

I played a couple of exploratory chords on the Yamaha. Sweet sound. I had just the song—an old music-hall number my dad used to play.

*I went to see a lady*
*I've been there before*
*Shoes and stockings in her hand*
*And her feet all over the floor*

*Champagne Charlie's my name*
*Champagne Charlie's my name*
*Champagne Charlie's my name by golly and*
*Roguein' and a-stealing is the game.*

I sang it through, and they both joined in on the choruses. At the end we were all laughing.

"Good song," said Charlie. "Okay, guys—I'm going to bed."

"Me too," I said. "Thanks again for the wine. And the meal."

I turned toward my room, walked a few steps, then looked back at Angelina. Charlie was nearing the top of the stairs. Angelina stood up, turned off the light, and followed me.

# 27

I was sorting through a jumble of feelings as I walked down the hallway to my bedroom with Angelina. Surprise was one of them. I had not known whether Charlie's reference to Angelina having a free hand extended beyond the one occasion—and, if so, whether Angelina would take him up on it.

The heat of desire had gone, as had the fear of discovery, not to mention the shock of it happening. With the recent exception, I had never contributed to anyone's infidelity. I had never physically cheated on Claire or, long before that, Joanna. E-mailing Angelina behind Claire's back was not exemplary, but it was far less than my dad had done. His playing around had given my mother a lot of grief.

I would like to say that my family history had weighed heavily on me as I considered whether or not it would be appropriate to screw Angelina against the front door on my arrival at her family holiday house, and then reprise the performance a day later. Truth was, the moral questions had barely crossed my mind. Part of it was the speed at which it had happened; part of it was that it was no more than the logical endpoint of something that had been building for months; and part of it was that at some level I thought of myself as having a special, permanent relationship with Angelina. *I went to see a lady / I've been there before.*

It was warm, and we lay on top of the bed, Angelina's head on my chest, almost at right angles to me. I ran my hand lazily through her hair, felt her cheeks, her shoulders, her breasts. "Tell me," I asked. "Why did you get in touch?"

Long pause. "You really want to know?"

My finger traced a scar on her belly that had not been there twenty-two years ago. "That's why I asked."

"If you keep doing that with your hand, I'm not going to have a chance to answer."

I moved back to her navel.

"This is going to sound embarrassing and superficial, but when I turned forty-five I said to my mother, 'They say women disappear after forty-five,' and Mum said, 'That's a lot of nonsense. You don't disappear at all. Men just stop noticing you.'"

Angelina laughed and so did I.

"Your mother hasn't changed."

"Not true, actually." She paused again, but must have thought the better of bringing her mother into the bedroom. "Anyway, I wanted to know if you would still notice me."

There had been a long gap between her turning forty-five and her e-mail to me. She was not far off forty-six now.

"That was all?"

"I'm using 'notice' in a broad sense."

"Well, now you know," I said.

"It was nice that you wanted to flirt with me," she said. "I wasn't planning to take it any further."

"That worked well."

"Are you really okay—I mean, with Claire? As okay as you can be? I'm sorry, it's been all about me and Charlie, but I didn't want to . . . No, no excuse. We've just been self-centered. We've had a lot going on and haven't exactly been . . ."

"It's all right. I told you: we ran out of steam." I wanted to talk with Angelina about the twenty-two years of my life she'd missed, over drinks and meals and walks in the sunshine, but I was not going to get the opportunity unless I got a grip on the present situation.

"Where's Charlie coming from?" I said.

"With this?"

"No, with tomorrow's wine matches."

"He's all right with it."

"So he said. Do I have to point out that most husbands wouldn't be?"

"He's not most husbands. There are some things that are between him and me, and this is about . . . this . . . not anything more. You're okay with that, aren't you?"

"This" and "that" evidently meant sex, but I was not prepared to accept that it was only about sex. It never is. Angelina had implied as much: *things between her and Charlie*. And, more significantly, there was the feeling between us that no amount of talking—or not talking—was going to deny.

After we made love, she lay still for a minute or so before climbing out of bed.

"I've got to do my teeth and stuff, and I really should go back to Charlie," she said.


Tuesday morning, I woke at dawn with a combination of adrenaline and stale alcohol in my system. I knew the treatment for a hangover, but it was tough medicine to take. No choice today, though. The last two days had turned on the sunshine in my life, and I needed to be in the best possible state to bathe in it.

In shorts and T-shirt, I jogged down to the village, then up the narrow road leading out. I needed the run; aside from the walk to the village with Charlie, I had hardly been out of the house. The sun was coming up, and there was still a bit of mist around in the valleys. I stopped at the church, which was not quite at the top of the hill, that prime location being reserved for the cemetery. The doors were open, and I stepped into the imposing space, so unlike modern churches and surely much bigger than the village could fill. Built for a future that didn't happen.

Back down the hill I was cruising, not pushing it. I had learned Grieg's "Morning Mood" on the piano as a child, and it was playing in my head as I passed the shops in the main street, closed except for the *boulangerie* at this hour. In the clarity of the morning and the music, I collected my thoughts and gave myself a talking-to.

I did not know everything that was going on, but I was accustomed to that in my consulting work. I could deal with a bit of ambiguity as long as I knew the key things.

I knew how I felt about Angelina. From the moment at the station— the moment on Skype, in fact—the connection had been back. I was sure it was there for her, too, regardless of her insistence that it was only about sex. I knew that Charlie and Angelina's marriage was in trouble, and that Charlie was prepared to let Angelina and me be together, at least temporarily. It was apparent that Angelina wanted that.

What I did not know was Charlie's motivation. But in the end, if Angelina chose to leave him, it didn't really matter.

By the time Charlie made an appearance, I was showered and had made an early start on the database work. I walked into the kitchen where he was wearing a voluminous Chinese robe, brewing an Angelina Special on the espresso machine. He sprinkled chocolate and cinnamon on top and passed it to me.

"Her Majesty awaits."

I knocked on the bedroom door of the woman I'd made love to the previous night.

"Adam?"

It was odd to hear her calling me that rather than Dooglas. "Who else were you expecting to knock?"

Their bedroom was at the front of the house, opening onto the long balcony and its views over the hills. Charlie's bedside table had enough pills to open a pharmacy. On Angelina's side, her laptop was on the table and her blue dress from the previous night lay in a heap on the floor.

She looked delightfully unkempt with the morning sun on her face and smiled when I gave her the coffee. "Give me a kiss."

I bent down and kissed her softly on the mouth.

"See you downstairs," she said.

Charlie and I did the croissant run, and he advised that dinner, subject to my approval, would be in Fleurie, half an hour's drive away. The alternative was a Michelin three-star restaurant, but it was a longer drive and heavier cuisine.

"Gotta watch the weight," said Charlie, with five size-six croissants in the bag. "Saw you coming back from a jog this morning. I'm working up to it. Had a bit of a scare a while ago."

I waited for him to elaborate.

"Bit of chest pain. My GP thought it was indigestion, but he sent me to the cardio just to be sure. I'm on the exercise bike, wires stuck all over me, and I start feeling a bit off—more than a bit off—so I say to him, 'I'm not feeling right, I think I'd better stop,' and he says, 'Just one more minute.' He's not looking at me, he's looking at the monitor, and I'm thinking, Well, you're the expert, you can see it on the screen, I must be okay, and the next thing I'm on the floor and he's calling an ambulance."

"Jesus."

"I almost met Jesus. They had to give me CPR on the floor of his office. Heart stopped twice. Poor buggers in the waiting room: they saw me walk in and then I'm carried out on stretcher."

"Quadruple bypass?"

"Just a couple of stents. But it was touch-and-go for a while."

"How long ago?"

"Few months," he said as we turned into the gate.

# 28

The three of us spent the day typing at our laptops in the living room.

In the evening Charlie drove us to the restaurant in Fleurie, where we were welcomed by the apparently famous proprietor, a woman *d'un certain âge* who responded in English to Charlie's French. We ordered one of the degustation menus and Charlie ate half of Angelina's meal in addition to his own. His cardiologist would not have been happy. Certainly his wife was not, but she limited her protest to a few defenses of her plate.

I asked about the Victoria Parade bar. It was long gone, but Jim's Greek Tavern was serving the same food with continued success. Charlie and Angelina ate there occasionally, and yes, she always thought of me when they did. I caught a glimpse of annoyance in Charlie's expression at being informed that, on their nights out, I had been with them in spirit.

Charlie showed what seemed to be a genuine interest in my job. He had done some work for an Australian IT consultancy that was gobbling up smaller players, and I mentioned Claire's software company. He had not heard of it—no surprise there—but neither had he heard of the buyer.

"A lot of that going on," he said. "Small players innovate but don't have the capital or the market reach to grow. So someone buys them, the product gets developed, and the founders get a check. Everybody's happy."

"Any advice for her?"

"Hire me. Seriously, you'd be amazed how much stress people go through doing something they're not good at when a pro can sort it out in a day or two."

I had been on the receiving end of that stress.

"Okay," he said, "two things about negotiations. Research the other party. Find out what they want. And know your BATNA." He didn't wait for me to ask. "Best Alternative to a Negotiated Agreement. What you'll end up with if the deal falls over—if the opportunity hadn't come along in the first place. The rule is: don't make a deal unless it's going to give you a better future than you'll have without it."

"Hard to argue with that."

Angelina pulled out her phone and made a fuss of doing something with it.

Charlie waved for the bill. "You'd think so. Ever bought a house at auction? People get me to bid for them, and they say, 'Pay whatever you need to, we have our hearts set on this place." And I say, 'What if there's another negotiator with the same instructions?' And—"

*Madame* arrived with the bill, Charlie put a card on it without looking, and she stuck it in the machine. Angelina was already getting up and Charlie signaled her back into her chair. He wanted to finish the lesson, and not because he thought I was in the market for a new house.

"I say to them, imagine the house is not available. Or they lose the auction. I *make* them do it. What will they do with the money they set aside? And sometimes we have an hour or so of dreaming and planning, and they have a proper BATNA. Couple of times I've had buyers who decided the BATNA was so good that they told me to forget the auction."

"So," I asked, "which one do you work on, the deal you're looking for or your BATNA?"

"You've got to keep your options open," he said. "You do all you can to advance both."

*All of the above.*

Angelina, designated driver, drove us home, and Charlie poured cognacs. I noodled around a bit on the piano, a little after-dinner music, and then Angelina and I went to bed together.

We kissed for a long time. When had I last kissed a woman properly? Even during my Friday-night visits, Claire and I had hardly kissed at all.

I found myself almost in a trance, lying next to Angelina, my senses concentrated and elevated. If Charlie had enlisted me as a sexual surrogate, in the wake of his heart problems, this could not have been what he had in mind.

Eventually Angelina fell back on the pillow. "I need a glass of water," she said. Then, after an odd pause, "Do you want one?"

"Thanks."

Angelina went off to fetch water, and it occurred to me that Charlie would have been the one to do the fetching if he had been in my place.

Back with two glasses, she sat against the bedhead, knees up. "It's weird," she said. "I told you yesterday about my job and you haven't said anything."

The honest answer would have been "That's because I've been too focused on doing this—and that. Which, as you pointed out last night, is what I'm here for."

I decided to take it up to her.

"I guess I haven't worked out how equal opportunity commissioner squares with the red number you wore on Sunday night."

"It wasn't what you expected, was it? The job, not the outfit."

"I think that's an understatement."

"All right, then. You know nothing about my capability to do the job, but you do know that something doesn't sit right about me having it. Which is what my job is about. Getting rid of that attitude."

"Point taken."

"But you're right. The powers that be had mixed feelings about appointing someone who people remembered as an actor, who might actually have worked in an environment where people were really discriminated against and exploited, over a public servant or legal academic. Until I pointed out the hypocrisy."

"Fair enough."

"Equal opportunity for women isn't just equal opportunity for women who dress in an approved way or have particular political views. I can wear whatever I want. I don't imagine wearing briefs and a T-shirt to bed disqualifies you from being a database architect."

"All right," I said, "but if I'm in a position of leadership, I'm supposed to embody the values that advance the cause rather than those of people we're seeking to enroll or protect."

I caught a flicker of surprise that the computer guy with the Manc accent had managed to say something articulate on her territory. Back in Australia, we had always matched it intellectually. Our paths had been different, but I did not feel I needed to concede ground now.

"How long did it take?" I asked. "To qualify?"

"As a lawyer? Eight years. Plus articles."

"Bloody hell."

"It was a five-year course, and I'd done the first year, but I did it part-time while I had the kids."

The kids had been absent from our conversations. As a childless person, I was less primed to inquire, and Charlie and Angelina might be sensitive to that, but they had volunteered virtually nothing. I recalled Charlie's condemnation of his ex-wife for bringing his daughter into their negotiations. Perhaps there was a tacit agreement to leave them out of the current games.

"It wasn't as tough for me as it was for some," she said. "I had Charlie and he's always earned a good income. He was a big support. He was fantastic. After I qualified, I did a lot of pro bono stuff. Unpaid."

I smiled. "I know what pro bono means."

"Sorry. So I haven't contributed much to the coffers."

"The price of fame," I said, thinking that she hadn't personally paid too much of a price. *Is the Château Margaux '66 to Madame's satisfaction?*

She laughed. "I think everyone in Melbourne knows who I am."

"What happened with Richard?"

"He dumped me."

"He *what*? *He* dumped *you*?"

"That's how my family reacted. In the end, I think they'd have coped with *me* walking out; they probably wanted me to. It's a long story, but he couldn't work for eighteen months. *Mornington Police* finished and my parents were propping us up financially."

"Your parents were supporting him and he walked away?"

"Pride. Mum and Dad were so good about it, but he couldn't deal with it. He was unbelievably angry. With me, them, the whole world. To tell the truth, I felt for him."

I had always assumed that Angelina had come to her senses and walked. On the contrary, she had stuck by someone who had been disgraced, ungrateful, and angry.

"What happened to him?"

"Went to Dubai. Looks after one of the sheiks. That's all I know."

"It takes a lot for you to give up on a marriage, doesn't it?" I said.

Instead of answering, she put one hand under each breast. "What do you think? Used tea bags? That's what my sister calls hers."

"I told you, you're beautiful. How much affirmation do you need?"

"You should know. I've had kids. It takes a toll on your body. Does it feel different to you?"

"Only in a good way. Does it snow here?"

"Why? Not in June. We've had it in April."

"Too cold for lemons, then."

"Sorry?"

"Where's the lemon tree?"

"Why?"

"There's no lemon tree. Charlie set us up. He probably watched the whole thing from the garden."

She seemed more amused than perturbed by the revelation. "He would."

"What about you? Were you part of the plan?"

"No way! You didn't really think that, did you? You were there."

"But he knows about your fantasy? About being caught."

"We've been married almost twenty years."

"And is this the first time it's happened in reality?"

She laughed. "Second."

"Go on."

"We were on holiday, and Charlie had tied me to the bed."

"As you do. With what?"

"Proper stuff. Leather things around my wrists and ankles. And my throat. A choker with metal studs from the bondage shop in Brunswick Street."

"Faceup or facedown?"

"It doesn't . . . You're getting off on this, aren't you?"

"It's a provocative image."

"Right. Well, I was faceup. Spread-eagled. We were making a lot of noise—I was making a lot of noise—and there's a banging on the door and I'm saying to Charlie, 'Cover me up,' but I'm lying on top of the bedclothes, and he can't get them from underneath me because of the ropes. So he's fiddling around and next thing I hear the door latch click and there's someone else in the room."

"Was he hot?"

"How would I know? I couldn't see a thing through the blindfold."

"Of course, the blindfold."

"And Charlie had this CD of Ravel's *Boléro* on, so I couldn't even hear them properly, but this guy's threatening to call the police, and Charlie's telling him that it's all a game and he hasn't kidnapped me or anything, and he's pointing out stuff . . ."

Charlie coolly explaining bondage to the bellboy while Angelina lies naked on the bed.

"Was it as big a turn-on as you'd imagined?"

"What do you think? It was horrible." She paused and smiled. "At the time."

"Happy holiday memories?"

"Something like that. You know, I wonder if there was anybody at all. I mean, there was a voice, but Charlie . . . He could have recorded something. There was the music playing; it was all a bit confused."

"He'd go to that amount of trouble?"

I knew the answer before I asked the question.

"So what's going on with Charlie now?" I said.

"In case you hadn't noticed, he spoils me. He gives me whatever I want. And I wanted you."

"You discussed it?"

"I said I'd like you to come over, and he agreed."

"It took you twenty years to ask?"

"I told you," she said. "I turned forty-five."

"Nothing else? Nothing happened to Charlie?"

Angelina sat upright. "Has Charlie said something to you?"

"He said he had a heart scare. I gather it was bad at the time, but . . ."

Angelina took a few moments to answer. "I guess we both saw it as a wake-up call. It was a factor."

She sat back against the headboard, hands behind her head, face set. She had withheld something.

"Was there a problem? With sex? After the heart attack?"

"I said there was some stuff I can't talk about. Okay?"

"Not really," I said. But there was a bigger question. "Where is this all going?"

"I don't know."

Great. That made two of us, possibly three, in a runaway train, sipping cognac in the dining car.

I doubted that was the way Charlie saw it. Whatever his agenda, his equanimity was a constant, and almost reassuring for that. I pulled Angelina back to me, kissed her for a while, then held her until we both fell asleep.

I was woken by the door opening. There was light in the hallway, and I saw Charlie in his robe. He walked to the bed, scooped Angelina up, and walked out, leaving my door open behind him. She began to protest as Charlie noisily climbed the stairs. The bedside clock showed just after three A.M.

"Fuck you!" she called out, but I heard more surprise than anger.

Had I misread Angelina? Had she really just set out to make Charlie jealous, even with his permission? *Prove how much you love me by letting me have another man, then prove it again by not being able to cope with it.*

If that was the case, then I would have no further role to play. And I would have to rethink everything that I had felt about her and us in the last three days.

When I woke again in the morning, I could hear Charlie in the kitchen. I slipped on my jeans and T-shirt. Might as well get any unpleasantness out of the way.

He spoke over the sound of the espresso machine. "Sorry to disturb you last night."

He handed me Angelina's coffee. "Something you should know. This is her special cup. Note the thickness of the rim. Too thick is not good. Neither is too thin. And she hates the ones that slope outward toward the top. No lips, either."

I wasn't sure how far his tongue was into his cheek.

I gave him the cup back. "I think *you* qualified for the coffee run."

Had I crossed the line? Maybe. Halfway to the stairs, Charlie turned around. "When I get back, we should talk."

# 29

Charlie started our chat on the walk to the village.

"What are you making of all this?" he said.

"Well, the food and wine have been brilliant," I said. "And the company."

"Sex not so great?"

"You're married to her. I don't have to tell you."

"I'll take that as a positive report. Are you in love with her?"

"Yes, I'm in love with her," I said to Angelina's husband, admitting it to him and myself at the same time. What else could I call the feeling that had come back in the first few seconds of our Skype conversation, hit me again on the platform at Mâcon, and colored everything since—the emotional dimension that had been strong enough for me to walk away from Claire?

I wasn't thinking about the consequences of sharing it with Charlie. The words had demanded to be said and I felt some relief in saying them, even to the man who had told me almost nothing about his own feelings.

"You've got two years on me," he said. "You poor bastard."

"I haven't spent them all pining. And I have to say I'm not feeling like a poor bastard. I'm feeling like I'm being welcomed where I should be thrown out."

Charlie was looking over the fields as he spoke.

"So at the end of the week, you're hoping you'll walk away with her. Part of you is. At some level, and after a decent period of time and considering et cetera, et cetera. You're in love with her."

He looked back toward me.

"I want her to stay with me. In case you were wondering. But it's not anything you or I can do much about, unless one of us opts out and denies her the choice."

He was rating my chances higher than I did, much higher than I had the previous night when I had thought the game was over. If sleeping with me was part of a plan to make Charlie jealous or more appreciative of what he had, then Angelina had surely achieved it. If it was a problem with sex, then Angelina's outsourcing of it with Charlie's consent seemed like a civilized approach that should maintain the marriage rather than threaten it. Maybe Charlie had agreed, but couldn't deal with it. That would sit with his three A.M. intervention.

Angelina had said that she did not want a relationship. She had said the same thing in 1989.

"So we wait and see," said Charlie. "And enjoy the holiday and the company while we can."

The runaway train metaphor came to mind again. Eat, drink, and be merry, and await the inevitable. On the other hand, this was the man who had invented a lemon tree. I did not see him as a fatalist.

"Let's get another coffee," he said, and we walked into a bar that could have been out of a 1940s movie—eight thirty in the morning and old men in berets drinking white wine from little glasses.

We ordered *petits noirs*, which confirmed Charlie's assessment of the local coffee.

"Why do you love her?" said Charlie. "She's not an easy person. And you're seeing her on holiday. Dressed to impress. You should know that she's not so relaxed when she comes home after a bad day at work. Or gets a drubbing in the tabloids. Or if I try to serve her Australian chardonnay."

"She seems to have got a bit pickier since I knew her," I said.

Privately, I blamed Charlie. He indulged her. I suspected that she would readily revert to generic red wine in old Vegemite jars at Jim's

Greek Tavern. Or, for that matter, a pork pie and a pint in an English pub.

"She's actually pretty tough," said Charlie, half answering my question. "We go camping with the kids . . ." He stopped. "You know we have kids, right?"

"Of course," I said. "Three." That was all I knew. "Who's looking after them?"

"Angelina's niece."

Presumably the babe in her elder sister's arms at the family Christmas, who would now be in her early twenties. It *had* been a long time.

"Angelina talks to them most days," he said, "but Stephanie's almost eighteen, and Samantha's seventeen. Adam's fourteen."

Adam. She called her kid Adam. My reaction must have been written all over my face.

Charlie was laughing. "Sorry, mate, sorry—just having a lend. His name's Doug. Douglas. After my dad."

His face was dead straight now. Mine could not possibly have been.

"Might have been better to call him Adam," he said. "Angelina hated Douglas—the name. *Hated* it. She started off calling him by his middle name, Anthony. *Her* dad's name. And it stuck. Someday he's going to tell us that being called different names by his father and mother screwed him up in some serious way. It's the only thing we'd ever really argued about, but my dad had cancer and I was bloody about it—fucked if I'd call him Anthony. Her old man's a decent enough bloke, but no balls. If he'd stood up to his wife, the family might have been less of a fuck-up."

I stayed with Charlie's family. "What sort of cancer?"

"Liver. It's a bastard. Three months and gone."

"My dad's was lung. Could as well have been liver with the amount he drank. Same result."

"You were close?"

"He left when I was fourteen, so not really, not as adults. But we both played piano. I don't know if it makes sense to you, but it was a connection between us."

"Makes perfect sense."

It was hard not to like this self-deprecating guy who could open a bottle of champagne when he discovered his wife with another man and the next day drag her back to bed. But there was one important thing we differed on.

"How wedded are you to croissants for breakfast?" I asked.

"Not specially. It's more an excuse for a walk to the village. Angelina has fruit and muesli anyway." He must have been eating four.

"How'd you feel about a full English breakfast?"

"Bring it on."

On the way out of the bar, I picked up a card for the local taxi company. I wasn't planning any excursions, but it gave me some independence—and an escape route, if I needed it.

We purchased the makings of breakfast at the *boucherie*, and I had to move fast to pay ahead of Charlie.

"What do you think's going to happen?" I asked as we walked up the hill.

"At the end of the week?"

"Yeah. You're being amazingly . . . calm . . . about it."

"Because I think she's going to stay with me. I'm not saying it's perfect between us, but we've got kids, a house—we've got a life together. I try to support her and what she wants to do."

He stopped, picked a handful of cherries from a tree overhanging the road, and tossed them in the shopping bag.

"If you're seeing something wrong, I think it's because we've reached a limit. The way we work relies on me pulling rabbits out of the hat for Angelina. Not just rings on her birthday but trips, surprises. For her fortieth birthday, I got everyone from her past together—all the actors, everyone—and we all went to this place in Thailand. I offered to fly you out, but she said no."

"So I'm this year's bunny?"

"I think 'rabbit' has a certain appropriateness. But you see what I mean. What do you offer after that?"

"So what does she do for you?"

"Appreciates it all. I'm not being flippant. Why do you play piano for nothing?"

There was a question that could have provided material for twenty years of psychotherapy—or about five seconds of my mother's free alternative: *You've always been a show-off.* Perhaps the same applied to Charlie. I let him go on.

"She does do things for me. For my fiftieth birthday, she booked a studio and made me a recording of 'Because the Night' with a band. You know the song? Patti Smith."

I nodded and didn't bother to elaborate on the authorship.

"For my forty-fifth, she gave me a portrait of herself by an Archibald Prize winner. Naked. It's in my study on the wall in front of the computer. Kids never, *ever* use my computer." He laughed.

"I've got a room like that," I said. "Had a room."

"Your man cave?"

"We inherited Claire's mother's house, and one bedroom was set up as a shrine to her sister who'd died when she was three."

Charlie nodded. He was puffing with the effort of walking and talking.

"Now it's my office, but Claire's never set foot in it. Not to dust, not to get a stamp, not for anything."

"Who cleaned it out?"

"Me. She wouldn't go into the house before I'd got rid of everything. At that stage we were still trying to have children, so . . ."

"Not much fun for you."

"I still have nightmares."

"You know what they say," said Charlie. "Who must do the hard thing? He who can."

We walked for a minute or two in silence until the path leveled and Charlie got his breath back.

"From my point of view, if she does want out, if I've got it wrong, better to do it now. Get it over once and for all, everyone move on."

For the first time, there was feeling in his voice.

Not many men would be able to match Charlie in the rabbit-out-of-hat stakes. Some might have the money, but few would be prepared to contemplate this week's indulgence. So what? Most marriages survived without escalating birthday surprises and visits from ex-lovers. Charlie's indulgence and Angelina's apparent need for it spoke of some longing, some hole that no amount of 1966 Bordeaux could fill.

As we reached the house, he said, "If you're wondering why I'm so relaxed about having you around, it's because you've always been around. You didn't have to do anything. It's better to have you here in person. Do your worst and we'll see what happens."

# 30

The kitchen had everything I needed, and I had three pans on the go. Eggs, tomatoes, champignons, bread, lamb's fry, bacon, and black pudding. Charlie was squeezing oranges.

Angelina came downstairs, empty cereal bowl and mug in hand, just as everything was ready.

"*What* are you cooking?" she said. "I could smell it from upstairs." Her tone suggested that the charms of frying bacon were lost on her.

"Adam's making breakfast," said Charlie. "Got room?"

Angelina looked in the pan. "What's the round stuff?"

"*Boudin noir*," said Charlie with relish. "Blood sausage."

"Yuck. Yuck yuck yuck yuck *yuck*."

Charlie was laughing his head off.

"Bastards," she said, as though we had done it deliberately to annoy her. She looked at Charlie. "You realize how much cholesterol is in that?"

"No more than three croissants with butter."

I was on his side.

"Come on," I said. "Have a tomato or a mushroom."

"I've had breakfast. I need to Skype the kids," she said, and walked off.

"Wooo," said Charlie, loudly enough for her to hear.

After breakfast, I set myself up in the living room. Charlie took Gilles's Renault for a shopping expedition to the Macon hypermarket, calling out a good-bye to Angelina, who had retreated upstairs.

I was deep into the database by the time Charlie returned, with no appearance from the lady. Meanwhile, there had been an e-mail from Mandy.

> *If you're thinking of doing something about the situation you've created with Claire, you might want to act sooner rather than later. Claire's inferior (least developed) function is S—under stress she's likely to turn to the Sensory. BTW, as you should know, yours is F—under stress you are likely to make bad emotional/value decisions.*

Even though I was not thinking of going back to Claire, the message got under my skin, a reminder that the world beyond our village was already moving on. Would "the Sensory" translate as an evening listening to music at the pub or a call to Concertina Ray?

Angelina came down while Charlie and I were unpacking the shopping. "What's for lunch?" she said. Charlie patted his stomach. "We just finished brunch. And very good it was too."

"*You* just finished brunch. Don't worry, I'll have an apple." She walked off without taking anything.

"PMS," said Charlie.

"I heard that," came the reply from the hallway.

"You were meant to. Come back and get your apple."

I guessed that if I had not been there, he would have offered to make her a sandwich, but pride prevented him doing so in front of me. It cost him. Angelina disappeared upstairs.

Midafternoon, Charlie came over to where I was working. "What are you doing?"

"Trying to repair the engine on a 767 while it's in flight," I said.

"Nothing too difficult, then."

"No people involved, so no."

He laughed. "Can you take some time out?"

I closed my laptop. "I'm at a break point. I skipped lunch, so I can call it quits for the day."

"Go a beer?"

"That'd be brilliant."

We sat in the courtyard and drank in silence for a while. Storm clouds were forming and something had been brewing in my head.

"Charlie," I started, "tell me if I'm way out of line here, but—"

"Just say what you want to say. I won't take offense." He passed me another Heineken. "If there's one thing you learn in my job, it's that more information is always better. Always. People think they'll win a negotiation by holding back stuff, but a lot of the time there are things that you want that the other party is able to give you relatively easily. Sometimes in a way you don't realize."

He was on a roll, and I let him go.

"Like Claire, selling her business. I had a company out of Silicon Valley wanting to buy a consultancy run by this charismatic—and egotistical—guy, and it was all about how much they had to pay him to stay on. Which he was equating with how much he was valued. Truth was, they wanted him to go. So did he. Turned the whole deal around when I found out."

"They tell you these things? They trust you?"

I shouldn't have bothered to ask. It was only a few hours since I'd told him I was in love with his wife.

"Most of the time." He paused. "I'll deny this with my hand on a Bible, but a couple of times I've left my iPod in the room while I went to the gents'. With the voice-record function on. Only ever used it in the cause of a mutually satisfactory outcome." He sipped his beer. "So what can you tell me to help us out?"

"I was thinking. If what you said this morning happens not to be the way things turn out . . . I mean, you've got kids at home, right? I'd be happy to talk about . . . finding the best way forward. For all of us."

It didn't come out the way I had planned, but there was probably no good way of saying it. I was expecting Charlie to come back with something sarcastic, but instead he said, "Thanks. I'll keep it in mind." Then he laughed. "We're doing our best. When you do mergers and acquisitions you often come in at a point where the writing's on the wall, even if neither party realizes it. Our job is to help everyone see it. And then make it work." Then: "Tell me a bit more about Claire. If you want to."

"We've only just split—a few days ago."

"That was the ostensible reason for you coming here—to debrief, cry on the shoulder of an old friend. Don't worry, I wasn't fooled. But you and Claire *have* broken up?"

"Yeah."

"You both okay with it?"

"To tell the truth, I haven't had much time to think about it."

It sounded callous, put that way. I added, "It had been winding down for a long time. For both of us."

"And you said no kids?"

"We tried. She's a great person, not least for putting up with me. We used to work together. No bad days, no tantrums, always looking ahead."

"So?"

"I didn't put in enough. It wasn't hearts and flowers. Or rings and birthday vintages."

"Because you couldn't let go of someone you once loved. Right?"

I said nothing. Was he right? Had my nostalgia for Angelina been a cause rather than an effect of our declining relationship? Maybe Charlie was just projecting his own fear of having to live without her.

"You poor bastard," he said again, apparently taking my silence as agreement.

"If it was true, then it'd be poor Claire," I said.

"Who loves you so much she'd rather you left her if that makes you happier."

It might have been true once, but the reason for our parting had been the opposite: putting our individual interests ahead of our relationship.

"I want to share a bit of personal philosophy," said Charlie, now two beers in. "In this world there are givers and takers. I'm going to guess that Claire's a giver."

"Which would make me a taker."

"That was my starting point. But it's not a bad thing. Givers and takers need each other. For some of us, giving genuinely feels better than receiving. So we need appreciative recipients. I get as much of a kick from the look on Angie's face when I give her something as she gets from getting it."

He may have been thinking of the look of relief when he poured pink champagne instead of murdering her and her lover.

Charlie's philosophizing was interrupted by the appearance of the taker.

"Sorry I was grumpy before. I've got an article due. Can I get you some wine or anything?"

"Sit down and I'll make you a margarita," said Charlie.

"Just a weak one. I'm not finished yet."

Charlie went to the kitchen and returned a couple of minutes later with the margarita and two more beers. "You want to hear a joke about a Frenchman, an Australian, and a Pom?" he said.

"No, no jokes—I hate jokes," said Angelina.

She stayed anyway, and Charlie told the sangfroid joke—complete with accents and embellishments. I laughed, but Charlie was watching Angelina. He had managed to bring up the topic without giving anything away.

"I've got a question for you," she said. "How many people are there in the story?" Luckily the question was directed at Charlie, because my instant response would have been three.

Charlie paused and nodded. "Fair point. I've got a better one."

"Enough," said Angelina. "You guys drinking beer together and telling jokes, it's a bit bizarre."

"One more," said Charlie. "There's this New Zealander . . ."

"Tell me this doesn't involve sheep," said Angelina.

"It involves sheep. Otherwise, I'd have made him a Pom. So this Kiwi is being interviewed . . ."

Charlie told a long version, complete with New Zealand accent, which sounded to me much the same as his Australian accent.

"'. . . and those sheds out there, I built all of them. But do they call me Murray the Shed Builder? No. And those wood piles. Do they call me Murray the Woodcutter? No.'"

I finished it for him. "'You screw *one* sheep . . .'"

Angelina got up and walked away.

Without our audience, we reverted to our discussion of givers and takers.

"I think you're being simplistic," I said. "I do—did—the cooking; I earned as much as Claire did . . ."

"But pleasing her wasn't the central motivation of your life, was it?"

"Not of hers, either," I said.

"I don't know her," he said, "but you might be surprised."

Charlie was right: he didn't know Claire. She would have been the first to admit that her software baby had dominated her life—and overshadowed our relationship—for the past four years. More to the point, I wondered at his characterization of Angelina. Had she become a taker only to accommodate Charlie?

Angelina returned and asked us to tell another joke. Really.

"There's some riddle about men not knowing where to find the clitoris. Right?"

"What's the difference . . . ?" Charlie and I began in unison.

"You go," said Charlie.

"What's the difference between a pub and a clitoris?" I said.

"Every man knows where to find a pub," said Charlie.

"That's the one I was thinking of. I just couldn't remember how it went," said Angelina, and turned away.

"Hey, hey," said Charlie. "Explanation."

"I interviewed a surgeon—a urologist—about discrimination in the surgical training program, and it turns out she's done this amazing research on the clitoris and I thought I'd do a separate column on it. Where do you think the clitoris is?"

This was, on the face of it, a curious question to ask her husband and lover. If either of us did not know how to find it, she would have been aware of the problem.

Charlie took up the challenge. "Most people think it's just a little nub, but it's actually quite big, and effectively surrounds the vagina. That's why women have so-called vaginal orgasms. Freud was wrong to differentiate them from clitoral orgasms."

"How did you know that?" said Angelina.

"Wide reading."

"Well, most gynecologists and surgeons—who are predominantly male—don't know it," said Angelina. "So I can start my column with your joke."

"We're expecting an acknowledgment," said Charlie. "*This column would not have been possible without the help of two men.*"

"Screw you both," said Angelina, and waited for a moment, as if daring either of us to respond, before walking away.

"Angie's got a bit to do, so dinner at eight," said Charlie. "I'm in charge of food. She's in charge of entertainment."

"What do I do?" I asked.

"Whatever she wants you to."

# 31

Back in my room with a couple of hours to spare, I turned on my laptop to do some work, then changed my mind. I wouldn't have shown up at the client's premises after three beers, and I owed it to them to apply the same rules to working remotely. I gave myself a mental pat on the back for behaving ethically, then logged into Claire's e-mail account.

Mandy's message had raised a suspicion and a quick browse of Claire's inbox confirmed it: Ray Upton, who I presumed was Concertina Ray, the garden gnome. But the initial e-mail had been from Claire:

*Is that invitation for a drink still standing?*

Straight back from Mr. Upton:

*Would you indulge me and allow me to treat you to dinner?*

And then, a minute later:

*Perhaps you would care to stay in London, post-prandially.*

Bastard. I Googled "Ray Upton," hoping to find "notorious pedophile" but instead got "Adjunct Professor Ray Upton: Lecturer in

Entrepreneurship and Small Business, Cranfield." The photo matched, as did the bio, which mentioned membership of a contemporary folk group that had released a modestly successful album in the 1980s. Claire could do better.

I could hear the shower running upstairs when Charlie put his head in with the offer of a pre-dinner martini, made with the gin I had brought. The storm clouds were closing in and we sat in the living room watching the sky darken. The temperature had not fallen.

"I've done a little research on Claire's suitor," he said.

It took me a few moments to register that he was referring to the prospective buyer of her company.

"They're sound, but she should know about their strategy, which they're not being particularly open about. Basically, they're looking to unearth one or two stellar products: an Amazon or a Facebook. They're buying a raft of companies and they'll let them sort themselves out. Only a couple are going to survive."

"How do they know any of them are going to be stellar? Why not keep the solid ones—"

"The way it works is this. They keep the principals on, offer them huge bonuses if they achieve crazy-high results in the next couple of years. Nothing to lose, the principals work hard, but above all they take risks. Most fail. A couple go gangbusters. Maybe."

Our discussion of company acquisition strategies was interrupted by Angelina making a grand—and careful—entrance down the staircase in a shiny black outfit: a short, tight dress, buttoned all the way to the bottom, bare legs, and strappy stilettos. Red lipstick. Martini in hand. Not quite the dress code for an at-home dinner in a French farmhouse. It was also a long way from what a woman of Angelina's sophistication would choose unless she was consciously playing a role.

I caught a glimpse—more than a glimpse—of the nervousness that I had seen when she had appeared in my bedroom in the similarly extreme red number. This was apparently what being in charge of the entertainment entailed.

We had something that I'm sure was very good for dinner, accompanied by wines of no doubt excellent quality. The food was on a platter and the wine was in a magnum. Charlie led a conversation, or at least delivered a lecture, about erotica, arguing that the artist must find the line that divides the permissible from the forbidden. It was reminiscent of the treatise on rosé champagne that had followed his discovery of us *in flagrante* two days earlier, and about as subtle as his wife's outfit. If Angelina was in charge, she was using a management technique unfamiliar to me.

Charlie waited until dessert to acknowledge explicitly that something was going on. "This is her perfect dynamic. Center of attention. Two men."

"Stop it," said Angelina.

"What she really wants is to be caught," he said. "She likes to be watched."

"*In fantasy,*" said Angelina.

"So she tells me," I said, meaning, *All right—I'll play along for now.*

"It must be show time," said Charlie.

"Don't push me," said Angelina.

I had no sense that this was a practiced routine. Angelina was on edge; Charlie was studiedly cool. I was wondering what was going to be expected of me.

Perhaps I'd led a sheltered life. My musical career had not reached the heights that attracted groupies and the database world is not known for debauchery. Sex had always been strictly one-on-one. My image of a *ménage à trois*—my best guess as to where we were headed, at least in a general sense—was of two footballers with some hapless fan in a hotel room, everyone drunk, and those with any moral fiber regretting it afterward, especially when the story appeared in the *Daily Mail*.

A polite withdrawal on my part would put an end to it. But Angelina had the same option. Curiosity—or compulsion—kept me there for the time being.

Charlie stood up, poured something into two balloons, and gave one to me.

"What about me?" said Angelina.

"You've had enough," said Charlie.

Angelina took the bottle and poured a slug into her wineglass. Charlie smiled and turned out the lights. The room was still illuminated by the setting sun.

Angelina walked to the CD player on the sideboard while I followed Charlie's cue and sat on the sofa—at the opposite end. The opening chords of "Because the Night" filled the room, and Angelina stepped into the space between us and the fireplace as her recorded voice sang with a worldliness that had been missing that first night in the bar.

She faced us, awkward for just a moment, then took a drink and plonked her glass on the sideboard. With that gesture, she must have summoned the actress within, because, when she turned back, she seemed to have disconnected from us and dedicated herself to the performance.

But if Angelina had to psych herself into this, who was it for? I was more puzzled than turned on, as removed as Angelina apparently was. And Charlie? I had no sense that he was getting off on this, except in some sort of intellectual way.

Again, I could have walked away. But Angelina was clearly intent on going through with whatever she and Charlie had set up, and I wanted to know what it was and why. I didn't want to deal myself out of the game. Nor was I about to abandon Angelina.

She danced, gyrated, running her hands over her thighs, outside and inside. Then she carefully undid the buttons of her dress, let it fall to the floor, and turned her back to us while she unfastened her bra and threw it aside. She turned to face us with her hands over her breasts, and I realized that the dynamic had changed once more.

The distancing had been temporary, a way in for her. Now she was present, connected to both of us and unquestionably turned on. And because she was, so was I.

There was a flash of lightning and, almost simultaneously, a clap of thunder. The music stopped for a few moments as the power cut out, then came back on, the song restarting from the beginning. If

God or Thor was trying to warn us against sin, He was going to have to do better than that. Seconds later the rain came, in noisy torrents.

Angelina walked up to Charlie and put one high-heeled foot in his lap, dropping her hands to her sides to balance herself. He undid the shoe, taking his time about it. She put her bare foot back on the floor and presented me with the other. The shoe was fastened around the ankle, and a tighter fit than the one I had struggled to remove the day we arrived at the house. Charlie steadied her as I eased it off.

She lay on the floor, on the rug, and Charlie followed, running his fingers lightly over her toes. In her twenties she had loved having her feet tickled and licked, but I had not tried it this time around. There was a foot going begging, so I joined the two of them on the floor. Charlie produced a sleep mask, the sort they hand out on planes, and put it over Angelina's eyes. He returned to her other foot and the two of us began working in unison. Twenty-two years had only intensified her response, or perhaps it was the doubling of the guard.

As wind and rain pounded against the windows, Charlie kissed the top of her foot, then moved his mouth up her body until he reached a nipple. I followed suit to the accompaniment of the Angelina Brown songbook: "Both Sides Now."

As Angelina's voice sang that she didn't really know what love was about, I went up and Charlie went down. I kissed her lips, ran my hand over her belly, and at the crucial moment, squeezed a nipple, hard, letting her break the kiss with her tongue still in my mouth.

We pulled back, as Angelina lay on the floor, and sipped our Calvados.

"Not done yet," said Charlie to Angelina. "Who would you like?"

"Up to you."

Charlie looked at me and nodded. *After you.* I could not have imagined any other answer. Charlie may have played the same role as I had in Angelina's fantasies, but I could not see him performing in front of me.

Angelina pulled the blindfold off and positioned me on my back, so that she would be looking directly at Charlie, who had moved to the armchair. I found it easier than I expected to ignore his presence.

It felt good, as sex does, but the emotions weren't there. I was a prop, perhaps more of a voyeur than Charlie.

"Look at me," said Angelina. She was speaking to Charlie.

"I'm watching you," he said, and whatever I was doing was irrelevant as Angelina arched her back, hands on her breasts, looking directly at her husband, until her pleasure carried me over the edge as well.

She subsided on top of me and we rolled over, feet toward the fireplace. I sensed a huge release of tension, above and beyond the sexual, a tension I had not realized was there, in the way that you only notice a steady background sound when it stops. It was coming from Charlie as much as Angelina. Even through my own post-coital haze, I understood why. This was it, the end of the line, the limit of what Charlie would or could offer Angelina.

"Bedtime," said Charlie from a few feet above. "Where do you want to sleep?"

"Right here is fine," said Angelina, sounding as if she had smoked a large joint. After a few moments, she hauled herself to her feet, collecting her clothes on the way, and walked toward the stairs. Charlie drained his glass and followed.

As I lay in bed, on the verge of sleep, I went over it in my mind, trying to square my role as a pawn in their sexual games with my instinct that there was something between Angelina and me that went beyond what had just played out.

But my last thoughts as I fell asleep were of Ray Upton seducing Claire over dinner, and me sitting watching, powerless to intervene.

# 32

We all slept in. I eventually made the trip to the kitchen and decided to risk Charlie's wrath by taking on the espresso machine.

I knocked at their door.

"Who is it?" said Angelina, and laughed. "Come in."

It was odd to see her in bed with another man. I knew that she was sleeping with Charlie, but this was the first time I had seen it. How had Charlie felt the previous night, watching his wife having sex on the floor with me? Perhaps much the same as I did now.

I walked to the far side of the bed and deposited Charlie's double shot on his bedside table. He still seemed half asleep. Angelina half sat to take hers, smiled, and sent me an air kiss.

"Ta for the coffee," Charlie mumbled as I left.

It was raining again, but softly, and the temperature had dropped. We spent the morning at our computers, scattered around the living room.

For the first time we did not do the croissant run, which was no loss to me.

Angelina brought out some fruit and at lunchtime fetched some charcuterie from the fridge. I didn't comment on the change of chef.

Midafternoon, Charlie opened a bottle of Burgundy. I put my work aside, and sat in one of the armchairs, listening to the rain and watching the fire.

At some stage, we all fell asleep. Angelina woke me as she got up. "I'm going upstairs," she said, and Charlie followed her.

It seemed my job was done. Whatever their problem, Charlie had solved it in his customary way, with outrageous generosity. Whether or not Angelina appreciated the gift in its own right, she had to acknowledge Charlie's message: *I'll do anything for you.*

After so much, so quickly, there had been an ending. I went outside and sat in the courtyard looking at the blue spruce until the rain started again. I didn't feel like working. I slipped upstairs and shut their bedroom door, then played the piano for a while.

The sun was setting when Angelina and Charlie reappeared.

"What were you playing?" said Angelina.

"Chopin." It was "Tristesse," one of my few classical pieces. No words.

"It was nice. Thank you." She turned to Charlie. "I'm starving."

"I don't feel like cooking," he said.

The statement would have been innocuous if it had come from someone other than Charlie. Angelina let it sit for a few moments before replying.

"We should go into the village."

The restaurant was closed, but for three customers they could manage *coq au vin* if we didn't mind them eating their own meal at the same time. They were a couple, younger than us, with children who came for good night kisses in their pajamas.

At some point during the meal, we lost Charlie. We had been talking about old times in Melbourne, and I realized he had not said anything for a while. He was playing with his drink, watching us reminisce as though we were the long-married couple. I caught his eye and was about to change the subject when he stood up.

"I need to call New York before they close for the weekend. Catch you at home."

Neither of us pointed out it was Thursday, not Friday. Angelina stood as if to follow, but he waved us back down.

"Sort out the bill. I need fifteen minutes."


Angelina and I walked home in the semidarkness.

"Is Charlie okay?" I asked.

"I don't know. Things are a bit complicated."

"You want to give me a few more clues?"

"What happened with you and Claire?" she said.

I let her get away, temporarily, with the change of subject. "Not enough rabbits."

"You've been talking to Charlie. Whatever went wrong with your relationship, it wasn't that. It's not true of us, either."

"Last night—"

"We were talking about Claire."

"I asked you—"

"It's important to me. To what's happening with us now. You've hardly told me anything. Except that you wanted to have children."

"That was the plan, and we didn't really make a new one. I think we just let it go. Grew apart. Did our own things."

"Did my being in touch have anything to do with you breaking up?"

I was about to dismiss the question with a quick "Of course not," as I had when she e-mailed me at the time, but she pushed the point.

"I really need to know."

"Why?"

"Because . . . it makes me partly responsible. I thought you were a safe option—as safe as it gets—for both of us."

"You're not responsible, beyond reminding me that there was something out there better than the way Claire and I had ended up. I thought, even at this age, that it was worth trying for again."

"You're talking about you and me, back in Melbourne?"

"What we had back then."

"Is that why you came here? After twenty years?"

"Twenty-two, if you're counting."

"You must have known it was only the remotest chance. . . . I can't believe you held on to it for so long. I'd stopped being sure it was ever there for you, and now you're saying it's been there for twenty . . . two years."

"Of course it was there. I told you I loved you. I meant it. I do now."

We were out of the village, on the narrow road to the house. Angelina stopped, turned, and looked at me. I looked straight back.

For a moment her eyes said *I love you too*, and then she turned away.

"Adam. You're crazy. We had an affair. I loved you too, but . . . twenty-two years."

"I've had a life. A pretty good life. I did love Claire. We had a lot of good times. But every time I heard a sad song, it was you I was thinking of."

It was true, but not something I had said aloud before, possibly because it would have sounded as pathetic as it did to me now.

Angelina started walking again. "God, I feel so . . ."

"Flattered?"

"Touched. Guilty. For bringing you here, when you were thinking . . . more than that."

"What you should feel is brassed off that I didn't make a commitment back in 1989. If that was what you wanted."

"Of course it was what I wanted. Remember I wrote to you? I told you, I screwed up. But I was also saying . . . You knew what I was saying."

She squeezed my hand and held on to it. We did not speak for the rest of the walk back to the house.


Charlie had apparently done whatever he had to do, with time left to open a bottle of plum liqueur and pour three glasses. The faraway look had gone.

"Your turn on the entertainment," he said.

"I think I'll stick to piano."

"Sounds wise. I gather you two used to do a dog-and-pony show in Fitzroy."

"Not really. Only a few times."

But I walked to the piano, sat down, and started "Brown Eyed Girl," the song I had been playing the night we met. Partway through, Angelina came and stood beside me, and joined in on the sha-la-las. She didn't touch me; we didn't exchange glances or say anything beyond the words to a song whose lyrics held no special message, but the mood between us had changed, in the same way that it had changed the night Richard walked into that cheap Chinese restaurant and Angelina began to contemplate, for a time at least, letting him go.

When we had finished she touched my shoulder and said, "Do you know 'Because the Night' by Patti Smith?" and I said, "And Bruce Springsteen," and she said, "Loovely," and I played the first bars and she sang the first line, then broke off.

"Then we did 'Both Sides Now,' remember?" I said.

"Of course I remember."

Of course she remembered. But what was Charlie making of this recounting of special moments? He was the one who had asked for the recital.

Angelina sang the first line of the Joni Mitchell song, with its reference to angel hair that I had no reason to notice that first time, and I picked up the tune on the piano.

All week there had been a certain equality between Charlie and me. If anything, the power had been with him. He could step in, and had stepped in, at any time, with the bottle of champagne and the three A.M. caveman act. I may have been the more active player in the *ménage à trois*, but Charlie was calling the shots, sitting in his armchair, all but smoking a cigar.

This was different. There was something between us that brooked no interference. Angelina stood so close to me that we were touching as she sang about old friends and change and life's illusions.

"Do you remember what you played as we left?" she said when we had finished.

I launched into "You're Gonna Lose That Girl" and Charlie started laughing.

"You never told me that," he said.

"If I had, you wouldn't have found it so funny tonight," she said.

"Can you play 'Angie'?" he said.

No surprise with that one. I was a couple of verses into the Rolling Stones' song about dreams going up in smoke and it being time to say good-bye when Angelina knocked my right hand.

"That's enough."

"What's the problem?" said Charlie.

"Not tonight, okay? We're having a nice time."

"It's just a song," he said. "Don't get your knickers in a twist."

"Sorry," said Angelina, to me. "No big thing. Play something else."

"One more."

"Your call," said Angelina.

I knew what I wanted to play, but was not sure I could remember all the words. I had listened to it a few times on the Eurostar.

I played a Freddie Sharp. Somewhere in space, my dad said *the black keys play louder*, and I sang "Angelina" with his and Bob Dylan's voices in my head.

I may have missed the verse about the valley of the giants and the milk and honey. But I did not miss the parts about compulsion and loss and vengeance. Nor did I forget that it was this song that had brought me to her door.

Angelina was pressed against me as I sang the final verse, an apocalyptic vision that had nothing and everything to do with how I was feeling: white horses and angels and unknown riders and tell me what you want and it's yours.

Playing the piano like the percussion instrument it is, I sang the last line of the final chorus with everything in my soul, a soul that only seemed to exist in the presence of the woman beside me.

*Oh Angelina.*

Charlie had beaten a retreat.

I drew my hand back from the keyboard and put it on top of Angelina's, on my shoulder.

"Just tell me what you want," she said.

It wasn't a hard question to answer. "I want you."

# 3 3

I folded Angelina into my arms. Tears were streaming down her face and I was almost in tears myself—the tears of release, of finally being able to feel instead of watching, waiting, wondering. As I held her, I felt the anguish that had fueled my singing dissipate and, in its place, a rising sense of pure joy at the possibility that I might have Angelina again.

Her feelings could not have been so simple. Choosing me over Charlie would mean leaving a long-term relationship and all the memories that went with it. I had done the same a few days earlier, but at least I had a little time and distance, and no children to consider. Charlie was still upstairs.

I took Angelina's hand and led her to my room, closed the door, and suddenly, desperately, wanted to make love to her. She sensed it, and kissed me, and then I was undressing her, with a familiarity that owed more to our time in Australia than the last few days. She wanted it too, perhaps to swamp the pain, perhaps to remind herself that there was substance to what she had chosen, or perhaps just to let go.

We started gently, but gently was not what either of us needed, and in a minute our clothes were scattered on the floor, and we were falling onto the bed. She rolled me over, too close to the edge, and I managed to knock over not only the table lamp but the entire bedside cabinet.

We both collapsed in giggles, hysterical, unstoppable giggles, which did what the sex was meant to have done. In that moment, Angelina did not feel like the equal opportunity commissioner who couldn't drink Australian wine; she felt like my partner, my best friend, the twenty-three-year-old I had loved when I was twenty-six. I kissed her all over while she was still laughing, then swung out of bed to right the cabinet.

I put the lamp back, and as I switched it on to check that it was still working, I saw a black iPod nano on the floor. It was running, with the microphone icon on the screen.

"What are you doing?" said Angelina.

I put a finger to my lips and showed her the iPod. She took a few moments, as I had, to realize what it meant, then I caught a flash of anger before she turned her head and lay facing away from me, presumably to give herself space to think through what Charlie had done—and why.

It was a gross invasion of privacy, but what privacy were we entitled to? For a few minutes, I fantasized about putting on a show for Charlie, pretending to do all sorts of outrageous things. A day earlier that might have been fun. Now it would only be cruel.

If he wanted to get off on hearing his wife having sex with another man, well, he had already watched us the previous night, and quite likely from the garden the first time on Monday. An audio recording would not add anything new.

Charlie knew of Angelina's penchant for exhibitionism and had delivered what was probably the definitive version of her fantasy. Angelina had said nothing in bed that would surprise him. The most damning conversation had taken place in the living room.

Maybe he wanted to bottle my accent for future use.

It was probably none of the above—just Charlie's desire to know what was going on. We had that in common. "Do your worst," he had said, "and see what happens."

He had expected to win and had played hardball. It was possible that in the joy that was suffusing me there was an ounce of triumph. Charlie would surely have felt it if the outcome had been the other way. I powered off the iPod and felt Angelina shift on the bed behind me. When I turned back, she was facing me, but her eyes were closed.

I watched her as her breathing slowed. After a while I walked to the kitchen for a glass of water, then came back and watched her for a bit longer.

At 5:30 A.M. I touched her shoulder. "Do you want to see the dawn?"

"I want to, but I'm so tired. Watch it for both of us."

I kissed her, then went outside and climbed the steps to the balcony and watched the sun rise on a new day while Charlie and Angelina slept. My mind began to settle. I thought about what I was facing: moving to Australia, taking on kids, dealing with Charlie. I could do all of this. Angelina knew who I was; I knew who she was; we loved each other. We would make it work. I went back to bed and slept properly for the first time.

I woke a little after 8:30 A.M. Angelina was still asleep. This was only the third day of my life that had started with the woman I wanted to be with forever.

I kissed her eyelids, prompting a flicker of movement, and tried to center myself in the moment, to block out everything else. It didn't work. Was I afraid that in the light of day she would reconsider her offer?

A few minutes later, Charlie put his head in, carrying a tray with coffees, orange juices, a croissant, and Angelina's fruit and muesli. Our clothes were still all over the floor.

"You gave Angelina a good shake last night," he said. "I was expecting to hear Gilles thumping on the wall."

Had we been that loud? Then I realized he was talking about my performance of "Angelina," which he must have heard upstairs, louder than any noises from my room.

"You know the song?" I asked.

"'Course I know the fucking song," he said. There was a touch of aggression in his voice, not unwarranted for a man who had brought breakfast in bed for his wife and her lover, and then had his knowledge of popular music questioned. I felt Angelina waking.

Charlie reached the door, then turned, looking at a scene that might play out, unseen by him, for the next forty years.

"I'm going to the Autun market," he said. "Might get lunch in Beaune."

"Do you want us to come?" said Angelina, still full of sleep.

"I owe Adam one. For the other night."

I guessed he was referring to his caveman effort. He hardly owed me for that. But maybe for the lemon tree. And the iPod bug. And recruiting me as a rabbit.

"Don't forget we're leaving tomorrow afternoon," he said. The message was clear enough. *You'd better get this thing sorted before then. For all of our sakes.*

A few minutes later we heard the front door close. I opened the bedroom door to let some fresh air through. It was warming up again.

We finished our breakfast, and Angelina lay back. "No hurry," she said.

I took her soft naked body in my arms, she nuzzled into my shoulder, and my hand slipped down her back.

As morning light filtered through the window, we made love, slowly, exquisitely slowly, for maybe forty minutes, something I had not done for years. We were both in some suspended place, close to the edge, but not so close that we had to consciously hold back.

We could choose to finish any time we wanted, but we were just rocking softly. I say *we* because I was so connected with Angelina that I could anticipate every movement. It's a cliché about two becoming one, but this was as close as I had ever got. When I wasn't kissing her, she was making noises, soft in tone but loud enough to have bothered anyone in the house. When we both started to ramp up the intensity, it was simply the best sex I had ever had, Angelina screaming, from her gut rather than her throat. And me, uninhibited for once by the possibility of Charlie hearing, matching her in volume.

I fell asleep again for a few minutes, and when I woke, I asked the question. Did she mean what she said before we went to bed? And all that it entailed?

She kissed me. "I can't talk without another coffee."

I ambled into the kitchen, naked, and Charlie was sitting at the table. He saw me and I instinctively covered myself for both modesty and defense.

"Gilles took the car," he said.

"I'll get something for dinner," I said, keeping the conversation focused on the practical.

"If you want. Ta."

"I'll head out anyway, when Gilles gets back," he said, and his voice cracked. The big happy guy who had scored a try against the All Blacks was fighting back tears. I had to give him credit for knowing his wife better than I did: he must have read the decision in her face when he delivered breakfast.

I wanted to put an arm around him, but being naked and the source of his problem militated against it.

Angelina was sitting up when I returned to my bedroom. Instead of commenting on the absence of coffee, she waited until I reached the bed, then said, "I love you."

It was the first time for twenty-two years. It was all she needed to say. I had what I wanted, what I had ostensibly come to reclaim, but had not dared to believe was attainable. Despite fantasizing about the idea, despite the undeniable reality of our rekindled love, in the depths of my being I had not expected Angelina would be prepared to leave Charlie for me.

I kissed her, over and over, and we might have spent the rest of the day in bed had it not been for Charlie's presence. Angelina wrapped herself in my towel and went upstairs to shower.

As I shaved over the vanity unit, a song came into my head unbidden, the song I had sung to give me the confidence to do what I had now done. "For Once in My Life." A song of joy, of celebration, of triumph.

My mouth had begun to form the words when I caught myself in the mirror. It was only a glimpse, just for a moment, and maybe something every man experiences at some time in his life.

I saw my father.

My face had thinned with the loss of weight and beard, and age was doing its work. I was four years younger than he had been when he died, eight years older than he was when he walked out on my mother and me. I had been fourteen—the same age as Angelina and Charlie's son was now—when my father decided to put his own interests ahead of ours.

I looked hard for a while. At myself, not the flash of my father. There was something unpleasant in my eyes, a coldness that didn't fit with the way I saw myself. I was looking at a man who was destroying a twenty-year marriage with three kids who were oblivious to it but who would be sat down by their parents in a couple of weeks and told the bad news. I doubted they would be making fine distinctions about the responsibility of third parties. At some point I would need to look them in the eyes, too.

I trailed the razor in a long stroke down my cheek as I felt the energy drain out of me.

The garage door made its opening noise. A few moments later, the kitchen door slammed and the car drove away.

I walked down the hallway to the living room and checked the kitchen on the way. Charlie had indeed left. Angelina must still be upstairs. I sat at the piano and let my unconscious mind choose the song and take me to that place where I could feel something other than emptiness.

When I was thirteen, my dad had collared me after school while my mother was still at work.

"Been drinking, have we?"

How the hell did he know that a few of us had sampled some bag-in-box red wine the evening before? He had not been around when I came home, a little bevvied but by no means drunk, and I had managed to avoid my mother.

He laughed. "Bit of advice for you, lad. Think about what you sing in the shower. Didn't have you picked for a Dean Martin fan."

I realized, with some embarrassment, that I had begun my day singing "Little Old Wine Drinker Me."

"It's like requests," he said. "You give away more than you bargained for. Hope you've learned your lesson."

It wasn't clear if he was referring to the drinking or the injudicious song choice.

Now I wanted to give voice to my feelings, or at least tease them out, as I had when I listened to "Angelina" the night I left Claire. I noodled around and found myself playing a Jackson Browne song.

The lyrics came easily, about fantasy replacing the real world, about the light of the past, about the angels being older. About nets coming back empty. The specifics didn't matter. A thousand songs would have done, songs about lost love. *Lost* love. It was already over. I couldn't do it.

Angelina had come downstairs and was standing beside me, listening. She was barefoot, wearing designer jeans and a pink singlet, looking so unreasonably beautiful.

"I was serious last night," she said. "I thought I told you twenty years ago, but you didn't seem to hear me. Or want to hear me." She put a hand on either side of my face, looked into my eyes, and said, "I love you, Dooglas. Adam. You are my soul mate. If you want to be with me, I want to be with you. Do you understand me?"

"I understand you," I said.

But I had heard the fade in her voice. Because she had heard the sadness in the song? Because she had arrived at the same place as me? Or because she felt, even as she said the words, that they belonged to another time?

There was sunshine coming through the window. "Can we go for a walk?" I said. "I love you too, but we need to talk. Charlie was crying this morning."

She pulled back and shook her head, walked to the window, and looked out for a long while. I sat silent on the piano stool.

Finally, she turned back. "I'll get my shoes."

# 3 4

We took the road up the hill, past blackberry bushes and purple lupines with yellow, white, and dark orange butterflies fluttering around them. It was warm but not hot, dead still, and the bushes were full of buzzing insects. I just wanted to concentrate on the feeling of Angelina's hand in mine and her presence beside me.

It seemed she was feeling the same way. We did need to talk, but we knew that once we began the spell would be broken. We walked up to the cemetery, where there was a wooden bench at the side of the road, with views over the countryside, and sat, still holding hands, holding on to the moment.

"You know that line in *Casablanca*?" she said.

"'Play it again, Sam'? He never actually says it—"

"No, 'We'll always have Paris.' It's really quite a profound statement. About how you look at your life. Whether you live in the moment or whether everything you've done, everything you've said and heard and felt, is there forever."

I kissed her, she kissed me back for a little while, and we looked over the fields for a bit longer.

I was not Rick in *Casablanca*, doing the thinking for both of us. She had done her own thinking. Perhaps I could have steered her in the other direction, but that was hypothetical now. Nevertheless, with a man's distrust of the unspoken, I wanted to talk it through—not the emotions but the practicalities. I wasn't sure whether to start with the strengths of her marriage or my limitations as an alternative to Charlie. There was one obvious way that involved both.

I was about to say "Tell me about your kids," but she must have sensed it and put her finger to my lips.

"No. Not yet. I want to have one day with you when all we talk about is what we used to have and how we feel about each other now. Like there's nothing else."

So we did that, through late morning and lunchtime, walking all the way to the next village and back, talking about Shanksy and the warehouse apartment and Christmas dinner at the Browns.

"My mum loved you," she said.

"Right."

"She thought you were hilarious, with your jokes about Margaret Thatcher. She was so over Richard, by the end. They went out of their way to help him and he couldn't even manage a thank-you."

Arguments about the vagaries of memory notwithstanding, there is only so long two people in their forties can sustain a conversation with reminiscences from a three-month affair of two decades earlier, stopping to kiss and saying variations of *I love you*. By midafternoon, it was only making the elephant in the room more apparent.

"So, what's all this about, then?" I asked.

"How do you mean?"

"You and Charlie. This wouldn't have happened if there wasn't something wrong already. And I don't believe it's about Charlie having a heart problem. You're not that calculating."

"You don't know how calculating I am."

"You knew that actress was waitressing at the restaurant, didn't you? The one who got the part ahead of you in L.A."

She laughed. "You do know. But you're right. I'm not abandoning Charlie because of his health. I looked after Richard when he didn't have a job. I took him back because he needed me."

"So, what's wrong with you two? Tell me if I'm missing something, but you seem like a pretty happy couple—except when you're talking about leaving him."

"When was the last time you slept with another man's wife, under their roof, with his knowledge? And swapped notes with him over a beer afterwards? Or shared a drink while she stripped?"

"We were consenting adults. I thought we all had quite a nice time."

She stopped and looked at me, perhaps frustrated with more than my attempt to make light of the situation.

"It's not the issue. Is that what a happy couple with teenage kids looks like to you? Or do you think there might be some underlying problem?"

She had a point. A year ago, Sheilagh and Chad had got into some experimentation with other couples. Sheilagh had been full of how their lives had been revitalized, but in hindsight it was the beginning of the end. Decadence heralding decline and fall.

"You know I have this sexual fantasy," she said. "But that's what it is—a fantasy. It shouldn't have got to the stage where the only way we think we can rescue our marriage is to do stuff that in the end is going to drive us apart."

"It's that bad?"

"It's been rocky. Since before I Skyped you. I'd decided that this week I was going to make a choice: go on trying to fix it or call it quits. Charlie, too. We've been giving it our best shot in our own perverse ways. I wasn't thinking of you as an alternative, but then you split with Claire, and I thought having you here might help bring things to a head. If I'd had any idea you'd loved me for all that time I wouldn't have. But . . ."

"So you used me?" I said, doing my best to sound as if it didn't matter.

"I didn't think you'd have a problem with a week of fine wine and sex. Especially as it turned out to be more sex than I'd intended. I thought you'd be on my side, but Charlie's been working on that. He's an expert. But, really, I had no idea. You'd never written—you'd never given me any indication."

"Tell me about Stephanie and Samantha and . . . Anthony."

"How do you know their names?"

"Charlie told me. If we'd ended up together I'd have had to know them. I'd have been their stepfather."

Would have been. I had slipped into past tense, and Angelina nodded slowly. It really was only going to be this one day.

"Did he tell you about Anthony?"

"The Douglas thing? Seemed a bit of an . . . overreaction."

"We both overreacted. It was a tough time. His dad was dying and my parents split up. And—" She put her hand up to stop me interrupting. "Did he tell you about Samantha?"

"Is she the older one or the younger?"

"Three months younger. She's Jacinta's daughter. Jacinta died when Samantha was two."

"Oh, shit. I'm so sorry."

I had stopped in the middle of the road. I wanted to hold Angelina, to comfort her, but the time to do that had long passed. I wanted her to hold me, and could not ask her to. The years had pulled us apart in ways I had not imagined.

Angelina waited while I took it in and then answered my unasked question. "Depression and drugs. Don't really know which came first."

"Overdose?"

Angelina shook her head. "Jumped off the Westgate Bridge. How do you make sense of that?"

"Fuck."

"I mean, you know about us and heights. Me and Dad and Meredith. Jacinta had it too. What was she saying? *This is how much pain I'm in: bigger than the biggest fear you can imagine.*"

"But too late."

"Way too late."

"That's why your parents split up?"

Angelina nodded. Her mother in a cartoon with the caption *You had one job.*

"Samantha barely remembers her mother. It's been a bit of a challenge with two girls so close together. Tough for Stephanie, too."

I was finally beginning to see beyond the twenty-three-year-old to the person she had become and the journey she had taken to get there. With Charlie. He had supported her through tragedy, adoption, and a new career. He must have seen his children born, driven

Angelina home from the hospital with the new babies, got up in the night for them. He had taken on Angelina's sister's daughter as well as losing his own. They had twenty years on me. If my life with Claire had been less rich than theirs, it was my own fault.

What could I offer that warranted Angelina walking away? A year or two down the track, she would think that Charlie had done more for her than I would ever do. And she would be right.

There was the other thing.

"How did you feel when your parents split?" I said.

"Pretty devastated. It was a bad time, anyway. Samantha's dad wanted custody, but he was a complete dropkick. We were lucky we had my dad on our side."

"And you were how old? When your parents split up?"

She managed a laugh. "Thirty. Thirty-one. I didn't need my parents to take me to the school play anymore."

"I was fourteen."

I knew I was about to wade into deep water, but I needed to say something.

"It could have been a lot earlier. My dad didn't beat my mother or anything, but he cheated on her. And put her down. She put up with it—I know she had the right to leave and all that, but she didn't, and I'm eternally grateful to her for the time I got to have with my dad."

I had never said this to anyone, least of all the person who needed to hear it.

It seemed Angelina needed to hear it, too. Having held herself together as we talked about her troubled marriage, her sister's death, and our own impossible love, she burst into tears at the story of my mother's fortitude. It was lucky we had found somewhere private to fall apart.

The day was starting to cool by the time we headed back toward the village.

"This morning was the best sex I've ever had in my life," I said, and she laughed.

"Me too. At forty-five. That's something, isn't it?"

We walked in silence for a few minutes.

"I love you so much," she said.

"I love you more than you can possibly imagine," I said.

"I doubt it. I have a good reference point. Say it again."

"I love you, Angelina."

"I love you, Dooglas. But we're not going to be together, are we?"

"No. Not in this life."

Angelina looked away for a few moments. Her eyes were still red from crying.

"It's probably a good thing. It's probably a good thing that I married Charlie, regardless of what happens now. I really love my kids, you know."

"Tell me something great about them," I said, meaning *Tell me about the twenty years you spent as a family.*

We detoured and walked for another hour while Angelina talked about her kids: stuff they did as toddlers, school, their friends, Stephanie's snowboarding achievements, Anthony's acting lessons, Samantha's plans to study law.

It hurt. It was unlikely I would ever have children, and there was a hole there. And, with every memory, Angelina was slipping away. A transient and impractical fantasy built on nostalgia, the romance of a torch carried for twenty years, and a drunken bonding over the piano was fading in the light of the day.

In the village, we bought a shoulder of pork and some charcoal for the kettle barbecue.

"Not finished," I said as we climbed the hill to the house. "Now tell me about Charlie."

"I don't want to."

"You said you were deciding whether to leave him. I'm your sounding board. Start with the good things."

We had to walk back to the house, where we dropped the shopping, then down a muddy track to the lake and back, to make room for stories of Charlie's devotion that had surely been recounted around dinner tables countless times. I was not the sort of person who could fill that space. Whatever Angelina said about Charlie's indulgence, she had become accustomed to it. As Sam Spade might have put it, she was high maintenance, and I wasn't a maintenance man.

A few days earlier I had wondered if all this giving and taking was compensating for some deficit in their relationship. Or if it was a deficit in itself—some sort of codependence. Apparently it was, but for twenty years it had worked: adoration in exchange for appreciation— or idolization. If the problem was that Charlie had run out of rabbits, I was not going to be able to top him. He had done all he could to make himself unmatchable.

"And the bad things?" I said.

"Don't worry. I understand what you've done. It'd be a horrible waste if I didn't do my part. There's nothing I can't get through. Just me being selfish. No surprise there."

"You're going to stay with Charlie," I said, "give it your best shot?"

"If he'll have me."

"He will. I promise."

Charlie had said it: *At the end of the week I want her to stay with me.*

"And if he won't? Will you be there for me?"

"He will."

Christ. If she wasn't secure with Charlie's ring-every-birthday, special-coffee-in-the-morning, let-me-organize-your-ex-lover-to-shag-you level of adoration, how the hell would she have coped with me?

Then, because it struck me that there might be some substance to her fear, given what Charlie had been exposed to this morning and for the past few days, I added, "And you have to promise to do something."

"Write to you every year?"

"When Charlie gets back, you have to talk to him. Tell him in words of one syllable, because he's a guy, that you love him. Exclusively. Unconditionally. You expect that of him, right? It cuts both ways."

She took a long time to answer. We were almost back at the house, and had stopped in the road, facing each other. I had thought this would be unbearably hard for me. Focusing on Angelina had got me through. But I could see that the promise to recommit to Charlie was harder for her than I was expecting it to be. Which made it harder for me to watch.

"Okay."

"Promise you'll do it?"

"Promise."

"It's going to be okay for you?"

She took a deep breath, looked out across the fields, and exhaled. "It's going to be great. It's been great. I'm such a screw-up. Thank you."

I had the resolution I had come for and perhaps left a relationship for—a confirmation that we loved each other but could never be together. Two of the three components were not news: I had already known at some level that I loved Angelina and had not expected we would be reunited. Angelina loving me in return meant that when I next listened to a sad song I would know that the longing I felt was reciprocated. Did that halve or double the pain?

"Hey," she said, as we approached the gate. "Do you want to talk about Claire?"

*Claire.* That would have been the coffee I got in bed every morning, even when I was sleeping in a different room and she was the one working, and the hand across my belly with *you're looking trimmer* and *stay* and finding the piano tuned the morning I left her and the trip to Paris after I'd lost our house and the *talk when you're ready.*

"Same sort of stuff," I said.

# 3 5

Charlie was pulling up as we arrived back at the house. Despite accepting my offer to prepare dinner, he had bought a substantial quantity of food, which he dismissed as appetizers. I guessed it was instinctive for him to react to adversity with generosity.

Angelina headed upstairs, and I went to the kitchen to offload the shopping and grab something to eat. We had missed lunch.

Charlie cornered me. "How was your day?" he said.

"Best talk to Angelina," I replied, trying not to sound aggressive.

Charlie put a big hand on my chest and pushed me against the wall like a rag doll.

"I asked you, how was your fucking day?"

"Good," I said stupidly. "We broke up."

It was a hopeless choice of words but I had been under some pressure. To my enormous embarrassment, I felt tears running down my face. Charlie let me go, then put his arms around me, and I heard Angelina walking into the kitchen.

Charlie and I separated, and looked at each other goofily. Did people ever grow up?

Charlie shook his head. "Margarita and two beers?"

"Don't overdo the Cointreau if you're using those round lemons," said Angelina. "They're sweeter." Then she checked herself and laughed.

"Dinner at seven-thirty?" said Charlie.

"Fine," I said. I was famished, but I needed the time-out more than food.

I knew that I had made the right choice, even with Angelina wanting me, being prepared to walk away from her husband and her family, and with Claire out of the picture.

What about the other, extreme option? If Charlie's heart succumbed to the croissants, it would be a different matter. I would be the white knight on a steed instead of the home-wrecker. But I wasn't going to spend my life wishing for that.


In my room, I booted up the laptop and composed belated apologies to work. I could catch up on Sunday. I was about to send the e-mail when it struck me that I did not want to return to my mother's in Manchester. The job paid well, and would easily cover accommodation within commuting distance. I added a query about whether it was too late to withdraw my notice.

I was browsing Claire's e-mail, losing any claim to moral superiority over Charlie's bugging, when the reply from work popped up.

*As long as you don't come in too often ;-)*

I felt surprisingly moved by this backhanded compliment.

But Claire's inbox confirmed what I had expected. Dinner tonight in London with Concertina Ray.

I sent her an e-mail:

*How's the deal going? Make sure you and the guys have worked through your BATNA. Good luck.*

The reply came straightaway:

*Thanks. Deadline Monday. The weekend to decide. Leaning toward yes. We haven't talked, but assuming for purposes of decision that you are not a part of it. Let me know if you want to discuss. Love, Claire.*

I lay on the bed. What about Claire?

Claire had been my Charlie. Her message said she had not given up on me, but *Leaning toward yes* meant leaning toward moving to the U.S. Yet she still seemed prepared to take my wishes into account.

Angelina was no longer an option. *Say it again.* Angelina was no longer an option. Where did that leave Claire?

Not twenty-four hours earlier I had been ready to make a life with another woman. I had told Angelina—and myself—that I left Claire for the prospect of something better.

I e-mailed back: *Best to assume I'm not part of it.*

I decided not to add any warnings based on what Charlie had told me. It would only appear that I was trying to talk her out of the deal, which would be as good as saying that I wanted her to stay in the UK. I did not want to let down a second person who had imagined a future with me.

My meditations on what to do with my own life were brought to a halt by Angelina putting her head in the door. She had been crying.

"I did what you wanted me to do. Made it right with Charlie. I want you to know it wasn't easy."

"Do you think you needed to?"

"I *know* I needed to. I knew that already."

"For him or you?"

"Him. Which means ultimately both of us, I guess."

She turned and left before I could say anything more.

I leaned back into the pillows, trying to work it out. What had been so traumatic about confirming her commitment? Was I missing something?

A few minutes later, Charlie called me from the kitchen. "Hey, Adam, you still want that beer?"


We sat outside. Charlie had put out a plate of the best anchovies and olives I had ever tasted, with crusty bread.

"More Spanish than French," he said. "Save some room for dinner."

The beer and food made me feel a bit better and a load seemed to have been lifted from Charlie, at least since the morning. Angelina came down after about forty-five minutes, with the puffiness gone from her eyes but still looking flat.

Charlie fetched fresh beers, and had been forward-thinking enough to make a double mix of margaritas, which apparently contained the correct amount of Cointreau. I tasted Angelina's and it seemed fine to me.

"So," said Charlie. "Have you guys got it out of your systems?"

"Yes," I said, and gave Angelina a look.

"You read anything by John Irving?" said Charlie.

"*The World According to Garp*?"

"That's the man. But I'm thinking *Hotel New Hampshire*."

"I might have seen the film."

Charlie laughed. "I doubt this bit's in the film. The hero's in love with his older sister. They can't keep their hands off each other, even though they've never gone the whole enchilada. Then one day she calls him up—they're adults living in apartments—and says, 'Come on over and have your way with me.' So he races across New York and screws his big sister. And when he's done, she says, 'Do it again, and again.' Until he's begging for mercy. And they've both *really* got it out of their systems."

"Cigarettes," I said. "When I was fifteen, my mother caught me smoking and made me smoke the whole pack. Until I threw up. Probably saved my life."

"They don't make mothers like that anymore. She'd probably get put away for child abuse by the morality police," said Charlie.

"When's dinner?" said the equal opportunity commissioner. "I'm going to eat all that bread if you don't take it away."

"Dinner," said Charlie, "will be at seven-thirty. And afterwards, we shall take the *Hotel New Hampshire* cure."

"Charlie. That's enough."

He smiled. "I speak metaphorically, of course. Nobody's going to have to screw their soul mate. We're going to play music until we've all had enough."

"What do you mean, *we?*" I said.

"I've got a blues harp," said Charlie. "Careful what you wish for."

My beer bottle was almost empty, but I raised it and clinked it with Charlie's. Angelina waited a few moments before joining in with her cocktail glass.

"Amen to that," I said.

It would have been simple enough for Charlie to say, "Since this is your last night together, feel free to have a sentimental musical send-off." But that would not have been in character. He had to frame everything as a game.

It was hard to see how Charlie had taken the resolution of the marital crisis. He played his cards close to his stent-reinforced chest; a lot could change beneath the veneer before any cracks showed on the surface. Angelina was looking more composed. Which left me.

Back in my room, I looked in the mirror again. Maybe I was fooling myself, but I didn't see Freddie Sharp looking back.

Dinner was a *tour de force*, in keeping with tradition, except this time I made a contribution. The Jamie Oliver recipe for pork shoulder, which I had always bought in a ready-to-cook pack, was on the Internet, and once I'd committed it to memory I only needed one surreptitious look at my phone to recheck the marinade ingredients. As a seasoned consultant, I was able to translate my last-minute cribbing into an impression of expertise good enough to convince my client, and put him on the defensive by raising an eyebrow at the lack of allspice berries.

The kettle barbecue had only been used once. The coals had cooled before the cooking finished, and Charlie had decided it was a bad job. I offered him some instruction and he was a willing student. An Australian taking lessons on barbecuing from an Englishman, albeit via California and Randall. Could it be any clearer that he did not feel competitive toward me?

Well, yes. The hors d'oeuvres threatened to kill our appetites. All week he had been sending me a message with the food and wine: *This is what you would have to match.* And to Angelina: *This is what you would be missing.*

Charlie was being less pushy with the wine than usual, and when Angelina waved an empty glass at him, he said, "Steady, it's a long night."

As we picked the meat from the not-too-rare-but-still-moist quail— blasted, at my Internet-informed suggestion, for fifteen minutes at three hundred degrees Celsius over the hot coals—I asked, "So, what do you eat on a Friday night at home?"

"Not too different to this," said Angelina. "But Thursdays we always eat out at the same place."

"I know it sounds boring," said Charlie, "but we both work crazy hours, and if we didn't lock in something, we'd never get around to having time for ourselves. Angelina would never get out of her work clothes."

"Your idea, right?" I said.

"We treat it like a business meeting. No canceling without rescheduling, and the guys at the restaurant know us and look after us."

She smiled, the first time I had seen her smile since the walk. "Family dinner on Sunday nights. Compulsory attendance."

I excused myself to go to the bathroom, then went to my room and checked my e-mail. Claire had replied.

*Message received. I'd still like to talk sometime. We should stay friends. Going to London Sunday to talk with VJ and Tim pre The Big Meeting on Monday.*

I mailed back a *Good Luck*.

I walked back to the smell of roasting pork, and the voices of the couple who were going home to date nights and family dinners and everlasting love.

"Thought we'd lost you," said Charlie.

"Taking a bit of time out," I said. "Reflecting on what you two have managed to do. If I'd done half what you've done with Claire . . ."

"You'd want to think it was enough, wouldn't you?"

Angelina's lips tightened. Charlie's point was clear. It almost hadn't been enough.

"Charlie," I said. "You know I love Angelina. She's a fantastic person and I've often wished I'd married her, even though it would have been a mistake. For her, in particular. The time I spent in Australia . . ."

I was drifting from my point, like a drunk. Do not start the next sentence with *I just want to say*.

"I just want to say that if she has to be with someone else, I'm glad she's with you."

The smile he gave me in response was unmistakably ironic.

# 36

As promised, we adjourned to the piano after dinner and Charlie lined up not one harmonica but a fleet of eleven, one for each key.

It had cooled a little, and Charlie lit the fire again. "All right," he said. "This is how we play Fuck Your Sister."

"We're not playing anything if you're going to call it that," said Angelina.

"Smoke Till You're Sick, then. We play every song that means anything to you two until you don't want to hear them anymore. Are we all in agreement? This is your doctor speaking."

"Some doctor," said Angelina. "Doctors have drugs."

"Fortunately," said Dr. Charlie, "drugs Charlie supplies."

He disappeared to the cellar.

Angelina looked at me. "You okay with this?"

"I'm okay."

Charlie came back with a bottle. I use the word loosely: I judged it as about a double magnum—a jeroboam in champagne country.

"This is what is known as a *pot gascon*. Two and a half liters of Armagnac."

If I got nothing else from the week, I had another bottle size to add to my pub quiz repertoire.

"Did I get the year right?" He tilted the bottle toward me. It was a 1963 vintage. My birth year.

"You certainly did. Shit, don't open it for me."

"It keeps. And we're not here forever."

I fetched balloons from the dresser in the dining area and Charlie poured three big measures. So much for going easy on the drink.

"So," he said. "What's on first?"

I'd had some time to think about it. While almost every love song reminded me of Angelina, we had few *mutually* special songs. Charlie didn't need to know that.

"Australian song," I said. "Nick Cave." I played "The Ship Song," released a few months after Angelina and I had parted. It was more acknowledgment of reality than cry of pain. But Angelina took over the singing and it became apparent that there would be no easy options tonight. It was equally apparent that what we were doing had nothing to do with working it out of our systems. No, this was a test: *Do your worst, Adam, do the one thing you do better than me, the one thing you and Angelina have that she and I don't, and let's be sure that she won't crack.* A few hours after she's cried an apology and a promise of uncompromised love. I may have seen a hard man in the mirror this morning, but I was surely looking at another one now with his elbow and his brandy balloon resting on top of the piano.

Fuck you, Charlie.

I played a few chords, hit a couple of wrong notes, and stood up, consciously putting a lid on my anger.

"I think that Armagnac's finished me. Sorry."

"It's okay," said Angelina. She squeezed my arm. "I'd still like to sing a few songs with you. It's our last night."

She sat at the piano and sang Sarah McLachlan's "Angel," about waiting all your life for a second chance. She played nicely, and her mature voice suited the song—as well as ripping my heart out.

Enough. I was over having our feelings laid out for someone else's assessment. I took the stool back.

"This was one my father used to play," I said, and sang "For Once in My Life." Angelina, of course, had never met him. Nor had Claire. His memory was now shared only with my mother.

I sang about not letting sorrow defeat me, about being able to make it through, and, in memory of my dad, the man who I did not want to be but who right now I was happy to have in my corner, I fudged the augmented fifth. I felt a bit better.

It was after midnight.

"One more song each," said Charlie. "Ladies first."

Angelina took my place at the piano again. It was a good thing, because, though I was familiar with the song, I would have stepped away. Edith Piaf's "Non, Je Ne Regrette Rien." Angelina knew that I had played it at my father's funeral. What message was she trying to send?

She sang the French song in English—"No Regrets"—which for me weakens it. A song in a foreign language that you understand but are not fluent in has a special poetry, and the English version is not an exact translation. Gone is the beautiful ambiguity in the line about lighting the fire with your memories.

Angelina was well into the song before I realized that it was not about me at all. She was looking at Charlie, and Charlie was looking right back.

If it was a staring contest, she won. Charlie dropped his eyes and turned away from the piano as Angelina sang the last verse. He topped up his glass, then walked back.

"That was the song we played at my old man's funeral," he said.

There was no cosmic coincidence here. For men of our fathers' generation, "No Regrets" was up there with "My Way" on the funeral hit parade.

"Your turn, Adam," said Charlie.

Angelina interrupted my attempt to think of something to take the tension down.

"Play the one you played last night. 'Angelina.' "

That wasn't going to do it.

"I said it was Adam's choice," said Charlie. There was an edge to his voice, the edge of someone who has had one drink too many. It had been a hell of a day for me, but surely worse for Charlie, even if he had ended up with the better outcome.

"Happy to take advice," I said.

I sang it through, just as a song, not a cry of anguished love. This time I remembered the verse about doing my best to love her but being unable to play the game.

"Got a musical challenge for you," said Charlie. "A bet, if you like. What's the most original rhyme in that song?"

"Original or outrageous?"

"That'll be the one."

"'Angelina' and 'subpoena.'" It's a song of perfect rhymes. No "Ditta" and "bitter."

"Agreed. So the question is: Who was the first lyricist to use that rhyme?"

"What do I win?" I said, and immediately regretted it. I could see us both doing something appallingly stupid.

I looked at Charlie and pleaded with raised eyebrows: *Don't do it.*

Angelina was standing stock-still. I had never heard the rhyme outside this song, but I am an experienced user of limited information. Three times a week.

I could think of only three contenders, unless it was a show tune, which was a strong possibility. That's where you find the witty rhymes. It would be a lottery among the Lerner-and-Loewes and Stephen Sondheims.

The trick option was Dylan. Most people wouldn't have asked the question if that was the answer. But Charlie wasn't most people.

Then there was the parody-or-comedy-song option. The leading contender would be Tom Lehrer. "Poisoning Pigeons in the Park." Except he only made three studio albums and my dad had them all. That rhyme was not there. Sammy Cahn, maybe. He used to do songs to order. Maybe for some famous legal colleague.

My final option was the undisputed king of rhyming. Better still, I knew where the lyric would fit. Write it down, Sheilagh.

Charlie still had not told me what he was wagering. Please don't say Angelina. Because then I'll have to fake a wrong answer.

"Angelina," said Charlie. "Get it right and you can sleep with her. One last time."

All right. Just sex. That wasn't a problem at all. I would just have to deal with the emotional consequences later.

"W. S. Gilbert, in *Trial by Jury*," I said.

I think astonishment would be a good word for the expression on Charlie's face.

"Fuck," he said. "I wouldn't like you on the other side of an acquisition."

"I believe I get a say in this," Angelina said. Her tone made it clear that Charlie had crossed the line.

"No," said Charlie. "You don't. If you wanted a say, you should have said so before Adam answered the question. Anyway, you've chosen every other night."

Big difference between choosing and having someone else choose for you. Of course I wasn't going to sleep with Angelina if she didn't want it. She knew that. Perhaps it was on that basis that she let it go, at least for the moment. She was simmering.

Charlie got to choose the final song. No surprise there. I wondered what he would request if he was drunk in a piano bar. I imagined him walking up with a twenty in one hand, scotch in the other. It would have to be a song of his unstinting, self-sacrificing love for Angelina. Nothing obscure. "You Are the Sunshine of My Life"? "Wonderful Tonight"?

" 'Bird on a Wire,' " he said. "Leonard Cohen. Do you know it?"

Deduct half a point. The title is "Bird on *the* Wire." Written in Greece, circa 1968. Kris Kristofferson said he wanted the first two lines on his gravestone. Joe Cocker did a nice cover. Which is to say, I know it.

"Bird on the Wire" is not a song of love for another. It is a song of reflection, perhaps of apology, but mostly of self-justification. For the first time all week, Charlie was giving away something significant.

I played an intro, and after Charlie half sang, half talked the first couple of lines with me, I let him go on alone. He slowed it down, sang around the lyrics a bit, repeated lines, putting a lot into it. Angelina had backed away from the piano.

The second verse is the only part of the song that expresses unal-loyed affection for another, the sentiment I had expected Charlie to opt for. He sang an alternative version. The knight who had saved all his ribbons for his loved one was replaced by an accusation, an excuse, and an ugly image: of the singer being twisted by their love.

I glanced at Angelina. Her expression was blank, closed. In the time we had spent together as lovers, I had never seen her look that way—and I was glad I hadn't.

When Charlie finished singing about the pretty woman who had tempted him, about swearing to make up for it, he added another verse, one that I didn't know:

*Don't cry, don't cry any more, I've paid for it.*

So Charlie had had an affair. Angelina had a better reason than turning forty-five or Charlie's heart problem—or me—for wanting to leave her twenty-year marriage. And she had not told me.

Christ—maybe she didn't know. Or not until now. Was Charlie, at the end of the week, saying: *There's this one extra thing that may affect your decision?* Only after Angelina had passed the point of no return.

Whatever the truth, Charlie had had the last word. I was begin-ning to wonder if the week had ever been about Angelina and me.

Then Angelina said to me, "Do you know 'Angel of the Morning'?"

She had positioned herself between the piano and Charlie, and we were lined up as we were on that July evening in 1989, with Charlie in the place of Richard.

This would be our last song together. I took it up a semitone to A sharp.

Angelina sang, in a voice given timbre by time, but still with the purity that you don't hear in speech:

*There'll be no strings to bind your hands.*

I did not look to see Charlie's expression, because in my mind I was living that exact moment again.

*Play another chord and I'll break your arms.*
I played the F.

*Not if my love can't bind your heart.*

The first time, she had surely sung it for Richard. The second for me. Now?

Angelina put her hand on my shoulder, pressing with the beat. Was she thinking of the Barrett Browning sonnet, too?

I picked up the music, and we played and sang like it was 1989. Angelina was gripping my shoulder so tightly I could barely go on as she asked someone, one of us, to slowly turn away from her.

It was late. The fire had gone out. Charlie had not touched his harmonicas. No one spoke.

I didn't need to say that I would not be claiming my trivia prize.

Angelina, tears running down her face, turned to me, kissed me gently, and, in front of her husband, said the words she had said to me fifty times before, long ago and far away.

"Good night, Dooglas."

# 37

Charlie strode up the stairs ahead of Angelina. It was an unfortunate slip of the tongue, but he seemed to have an unlimited capacity to forgive. Had it always been that way or only since he had needed Angelina to reciprocate?

I made it to my room before the familiar emptiness hit me: the feeling I'd had in the morning when I realized it wasn't going to happen; the way I'd felt as I walked to the plane in 1989; the phone call earlier that year—"You're Alfred Sharp's son?" No tears, no *feelings*, just emptiness. Drained. Hollowed out. Gutted.

It was late, I'd been drinking for hours and had hardly slept the night before, but sleep was not going to come. If I didn't do something my mind would start churning over the decision I'd taken—*we'd taken*—reviewing it in the light of what I had just learned, reassessing it in the face of Angelina's tears. We had come so close to waking up together every morning for the rest of our lives. Only a day ago, I had held it, believed in it. And now: nothing.

I put my earphones in but could not think of anything I wanted to listen to. I hit the Random button and an unfamiliar song began, probably from one of Stuart's CDs. Piano chords, slow, melancholy lyrics about having nowhere to go. Not what I needed. I was about to skip to the next track when the drums came in.

I lay back, volume up, listening to anthemic rock, cherry-picking the lyrics that connected—*hold on if you can*—giving myself up to the music the way Claire used to. The three-minute rush that is a great rock song did its magic, and the emptiness began to give way to love and pain and even a little optimism, the energy to go on. Whatever I had lost, there was still music. I was a mess, but it was better than nothingness.

Back in the day, safecrackers used to sandpaper their fingertips to make them more sensitive. That's how I felt when the song ended: raw, exposed, and vulnerable. Alive. If I walked outside I would feel the grass and the rain with new skin. I wanted to hold on to this, to take it home with me.

And I was ready to go home.

I logged on to the SNCF railway Web site and booked an early-morning ticket to London.


I woke to the alarm, called the local taxi company, and padded upstairs for a shower and a sober review of the previous evening.

Charlie's motivation—or his primary motivation—was now clear. "Okay, I bonked the intern or the housekeeper or your best friend; now you can have one in return and we'll be even. And you won't be able to take the high moral ground anymore."

Of all the men in the world that Angelina could have a free pass with, she chose me. I would have chosen her.

The factor none of us had considered was that Angelina and I would fall in love again—or, at least, fall back into the love we once had.

Showered and dressed, I knocked lightly on their bedroom door, and pushed it open. I could hardly leave without saying good-bye to Angelina.

Charlie was out to it, snoring. Angelina's side of the bed was empty.

There were two other bedrooms upstairs, and I found her in the one that doubled as her wardrobe, sprawled on top of the covers in her blue nightdress. I touched her shoulder and she stirred, but it took a cupped hand to the side of her face to wake her.

"Adam?"

"Are you okay?" She looked wrecked.

"What time is it?"

"Six forty-five. I'm on the eight-thirty train."

"Oh shit. I've hardly slept."

"The Douglas thing?"

"We had a fight. Another fight." She lay back and looked at the ceiling. "I'm so over it." She reached up and pulled me down toward her. "I don't want you to go."

I didn't want to go either, at that moment, with no thought of the consequences. But we had done the hard yards the previous day and I did not want to walk them again. This was hurting us both for no good purpose.

"You're going to sort it out. We talked about this. I've got a taxi booked."

"Cancel it. I'll take you to the station."

She got to her feet, grabbed underwear, jeans, and a sweater from a chest of drawers, then pulled the blue nightdress over her head, looking right at me.

"You've got time for a shower, if you want," I said. "I'll make you a coffee."

I went downstairs and turned on the espresso machine.

What we needed right now was a psychologist. Or maybe we only needed Mandy and her Kübler-Ross grief model. Angelina had got stuck in Denial with Richard, but this time she seemed to have moved on to Bargaining. Or would it be: *Angelina's psychological type is compelling her to make a decision—an* emotional *decision—and you guys keep changing the parameters.*

My mother would have had none of this mumbo jumbo. I could see her looking down at Angelina on the bed. *For goodness' sake, how old are you? Go back to your husband and sort it out before he throws you out on the street where you belong.*

Angelina joined me in the kitchen, looking more composed but fragile.

"I'm sorry. I was upset. I know we talked about it. But there are things I couldn't tell you that make a difference. You need to know—"

"Charlie had an affair?"

That stopped her.

"Did I talk in my sleep? He told you? My God, he told you."

"When did it happen? Before or after the heart attack?"

"After. With one of the women at work."

Right on both counts. Men are pathetic.

"An affair or just a bonk?"

She managed a laugh at the word from the past. "Charlie would say just a bonk, but I don't think she would have. It wasn't only once. She was twenty-nine. *Twenty-nine.*"

"How did you find out?"

"I know him. I asked and he fessed up."

If Charlie had listened to that Lenny Bruce performance, he would have known: *never* confess. So much for the world-class negotiator. Didn't he remember what Richard had done to her?

"So . . ."

"I was pretty hurt. I wanted to leave him, and I told myself that he was right: we shouldn't throw away all the good things et cetera, et cetera, et-fucking-cetera. But I wasn't nice about it. I made it difficult for him. I made him fire the little bitch."

"I'd have thought that would be pretty hard to do. You can't fire people for screwing a colleague."

"Really? I must tell the guys at work. I'm a fucking equal opportunity commissioner. I told you I made it difficult for him. But I didn't want her around. She didn't get fired, technically. She got a fat check and a new job. For almost wrecking a marriage."

"And you haven't forgiven him?" Because you can give up your career for your wife, buy her a ring every birthday, adopt her sister's child, but screw *one* sheep . . .

"I know if he could take it back, he would. It was half my fault. After the heart attack, I didn't want to have sex. I was afraid he'd die."

"You ever cheat on him? Ever?"

"Never," said the woman to her lover. "But I guess we're even now."

"Is that what this is all about?" I said.

"It's part of it. Not all. It could only have been you. I wanted to tell you about it, but he made me swear not to tell anyone. Otherwise, he'd leave me. *He'd* leave *me*. He's been screwing some *kid* and I'm trying to hold it together for the sake of our marriage and he's the one giving *me* ultimatums."

"You're still angry."

"Not so angry I can't think. I kept my promise, my promise to you yesterday, but if he's told you . . . I can't believe he told you . . . then you understand. Yesterday I told him I forgave him. And I meant it. I had to make myself mean it. That's what I had to do for our marriage to survive."

Of course. Charlie had not been hanging out for Angelina to renounce me, but to forgive him. Had saying the words convinced her that she could never really do so?

"I don't believe you want to lose Charlie." I would not have believed Mandy wanted to lose Randall, either. Plenty of men think that other men should be forgiven the occasional slip-up.

I looked at my watch.

"You really want to go?" she said.

"I have to."

Did she realize how close I was to giving in to my emotions and Bob from Idaho, both screaming at me: *Take her, take the chance*?

Charlie had extracted a promise of silence on the infidelity; he had got forgiveness; now he apparently wanted an apology for the Douglas fiasco of twenty years ago. Why should I have to play God and decide that their wounded marriage was worth more than a chance of us being together? Why should I override Angelina's adult decision?

Because I *knew* Angelina. I knew that instinct would drive her to the dramatic decision, to singing "I Will Survive" and walking away. Even against her own best interests. Which made her no different from Mandy or a million other betrayed spouses. What would her best

friend say? Probably tell her to walk. But she had known all this yesterday and had made a choice.


We hardly spoke in the car.

On the platform, she put her arms around me as the train pulled in.

"I asked you something yesterday," she said. "Do you remember?"

"We said a lot of things yesterday," I said. "It was a big day."

"It doesn't matter. There's nothing else we can say, is there?"

"No."

We'd had our chance. I hoped no song would ever re-create what
I was feeling at that moment.

# 38

On the train to Paris, I waited for the ache of the farewell to subside and be replaced by some sort of relief at closure.

The week had woken something in me, but it had come with a hard lesson. There was a place for lost love, and it was not in a French farmhouse with a married couple struggling to get through a crisis. Lost love belongs in a three-minute song, pulling back feelings from a time when they came unbidden, recalling the infatuation, the walking on sunshine that cannot last and the pain of its loss, whether through parting or the passage of time, reminding us that we are emotional beings.

The countryside and villages rushed past, we pulled into Paris and I changed trains, but the ache did not go away. Instead I felt unsettled. Something didn't fit: the feeling, as I held Angelina on the platform, that she was still hoping I might change my mind.

I did not believe she loved me as much as she loved Charlie. Twenty years ago, maybe. But not now, even after his affair. My sense of unease began to turn into a conviction that she was not going back to Charlie at all, that the Douglas fight had been terminal. She would not have told me, because that would be acknowledging that I was second choice.

A line from the Killers' song I had played in my room the previous night, about shining in the hearts of others, was running around in my head, trying to reassure me that after all these things I had done I could hold my head up.

At the Gare du Nord, waiting for the Eurostar to leave, I found myself thinking about Claire. I would have only myself to blame if the next time I heard a sad song I was transported to a moment with her that I had failed to appreciate. Or to one that I *had* appreciated: the evening at the Buddha Bar after the lotto debacle, when she had somehow understood that the biggest threat to our relationship was not her own anger but my shame—that I was ready to leave so as not to have to face her again.

The penny dropped.

I was on the train. I had transited Paris, bypassed the baby grand in the waiting area, checked in, queued for security, formally exited France, cleared UK immigration, shuffled with the crowd onto the platform, boarded the train, and found a place for my bag. I was as good as home. I had only one question to answer: How much did I love Angelina?

I had likened the day that Angelina reconnected with me to my father turning over a 45 of the Beatles' "Hey Jude" to play the flip side, with the simple clarity of the piano giving way to the fuzz and confusion and excitement of electric guitars. Ask anyone about "Revolution" and that's what they'll remember—the guitars. But listen to it again and you'll hear the electric piano of Nicky Hopkins, the ring-in, low in the mix for a while, but in the end resurgent, bringing it home.

I raced back through immigration, officially reentered France, crossed Paris to the Gare de Lyon, and bought a ticket on the TGV to Mâcon, back to where I had come from.

I had an hour and forty-five minutes on the train to think. It was long enough to work out what had been going on, or near enough. The key to negotiation, as the man at the center of it all said, is to know the other party's goals.

I had known the first of Charlie's goals within minutes of meeting him. He needed to be liked. By everyone, even me. He also wanted to keep his marriage, but I had relied too much on that goal. Now I knew another, perhaps related to the first: he needed to escape his shame.

Charlie's marriage, his persona, had been built on his worshiping Angelina, and she in turn idolizing him for that. He had slipped up in the worst possible way. My guilt about losing twenty thousand pounds to a bad investment must have been nothing to what Charlie felt when Angelina looked at him.

The week now made more sense. Charlie had acceded to us being together, knowing that his affair had made Angelina vulnerable. She didn't have Claire's superhuman capacity to put her emotions aside and make the right call for everyone. Then, after trying to bring Angelina down to his level, pushing her as far as she could be pushed, he had found his shame was still there and had then done everything to make Angelina leave—including encouraging her backup option. Without ever dropping the good-guy persona.

*All of the above.*

He wanted his marriage to survive. But only if he could get past the shame. And no forgiveness, no matter how complete, could do that for him.

What about Angelina? She knew Charlie. She knew what was going on. She had tried to put aside her own anger to rebuild his ego. *His* ego. All those stories about what a hero he was. She had bought into his game of bringing her down. Then she had taken the huge step of forgiving him.

But before she had had a chance to recover from the emotional toll of doing that, Charlie had asked her, through the Smoke Till You're Sick sing-along, to violate her memories. And finally the insult of the Gilbert and Sullivan bet.

Maybe Angelina's forgiveness was a two-edged sword: in the act of forgiving him, she was showing herself to be a better person. What Angelina did in an attempt to get the marriage back together could not be equated with Charlie's self-serving fling. Charlie may not have processed this—just realized he could not win and lashed out.

Whatever the reason, Angelina had lashed back. *Your father may have died with no regrets, but will you?*

That would have done it. It cut to the core of his problem. Charlie had an even bigger need to be liked—*admired*—than I did. His only option was escape. Angelina knew it.

*Dooglas* gave him a final, wretched chance to seize the high moral ground on his way out.

Which left the third party. I was supposed to be the catalyst who would, by sleeping with Angelina, square the ledger and serve as a peace offering—a gift—from Charlie, in line with tradition. And walk away unchanged.

Angelina and I were never meant to fall in love again. But I had been primed to do so from the moment I decided to leave Claire. In the face of Angelina's crumbling marriage, and the convoluted games it had descended to, our shared memories and the support I had offered must have seemed like a breath of fresh air—and a way out.

I remembered what Angelina had asked me the previous day and had tried to remind me of on the platform: *If Charlie was not around, would you be there for me?*

I had said yes. She had not held me to it. She had let me think that they would sort it out.

Their marriage was over. Angelina and I loved each other. She was waiting for me to work it out and step up. Again.

I jumped off the train in Mâcon, headed down the platform to find a taxi, and almost ran into Charlie, waiting at the first-class end of the train for the last of the passengers to alight. He had two big suitcases and was alone.

I stepped between him and the train. It's fair to say he was as surprised to see me as I was to see him.

"I need to talk to you," I said.

"I have to catch this train. Angelina's still at the house."

"You've left her?"

"You're free to see her. As you've been for the last week. Now, I need to get on the train."

Given our respective physiques, if Charlie insisted on getting on the train I was not going to be able to stop him, short of doing something that got us both arrested. That was my Plan B.

I started with Plan A. "If you don't talk to me, I'm going to broadcast your affair all over the Internet."

I wasn't going to need Plan B, though we might end up getting arrested anyway.

"You fucker. You little fucker. She told you? Texted you? Bitch. That's why you came back. Fucking—"

He was furious with everyone except the person who had created the problem. I had not made the journey on a false premise.

I stepped back as the train was about to leave. He had a choice: get on board or grab me. He chose the latter, but there is only so much you can do in view of a platform full of staring passengers and the railway attendant. He must also have realized that the first thing I would do after waking up in the hospital with both arms missing was dictate a message about his infidelity.

He put me down. "You're not happy with wrecking our marriage? You want to humiliate me as well? And her, you know. It doesn't reflect well on her."

"I don't want to humiliate you or Angelina," I said. "I'm here because I want to tell you something relevant to both of us. I'll see you in the coffee shop in fifteen minutes. When we're both in a mood to negotiate."

I was not planning any negotiations. But I needed his professional persona. Mr. Safe Hands. Mr. Win-Win. Mr. Incredible.

# 39

There were some seats separate from the café and Charlie joined me from the booking desk carrying—not wheeling—his two suitcases. I had coffees waiting.

"So," he said. "What do you have to tell me that justifies me keeping a dozen senior executives cooling their heels in Milan?" He sipped his coffee and winced. "If you think you need some sort of dispensation from me, you've got it. So has Angelina. I've already told her I won't come between you."

"I'm not here to see Angelina. She wants to be with you. I think you know that. You're the problem."

He didn't argue. He was a smart guy, the sort of guy who spends the fifteen minutes after losing his cool thinking about why it happened. But now it was up to me. Between Paris and Mâcon, I had managed to think of only one way of persuading him.

I told him a story. About the lotto debacle. With a little artistic license, because the original facts were not going to equate to Charlie's cheating on a relationship that had been built on his adoration. So it was not a lotto syndicate but futures trading. I had quit my job and spent my days writing thirty thousand lines of code, an infallible system. I'd had some bad luck but never lost my faith. Good money went after bad; I took the imaginary savings my mother had from my dad's nonexistent life insurance; I lost Claire's mother's house, the one she currently lived in. Everything short of mugging a nun and stealing the collection.

At that point in the tale I was beginning to feel relatively virtuous by comparison with my fictitious alter ego. Or Charlie, for that matter.

I told him about my confession and my shame, and about Claire organizing the trip to Paris. Here there was no need to embellish.

"A pretty special person," he said when I finished.

"Luckily," I said. "Because I didn't have the guts to deal with my problem myself."

Charlie went to speak, then stopped himself.

I remembered something Claire had told me from her sales training. *Don't buy it back.* Once you've made your sale, stop selling, or you'll risk the buyer getting pissed off and changing his or her mind. *Don't buy it back*, she would say after I had persuaded her to go to the pub instead of the Masala Garden, and was then tempted to enumerate all the advantages of her wise decision.

Still, I was not sure I had made the sale. I wanted to say something more anyway. For Angelina.

"All the things you did, she saw through. She played her part in whatever game you set up because she wanted you to get through it. Including everything she did with me."

I knew the last bit was only partly true. Her *I love you* might not have happened without the marital crisis, but it had nothing to do with any games with Charlie. I could only assume Charlie didn't know about that. He was nodding slowly.

I had one more thing to say, a final bit of advice for the great negotiator. "There's a saying we often quote in IT that insanity is doing the same thing over and over, and expecting a different result."

"Einstein."

"Attributed to. So maybe, if you want to keep your marriage, you'll have to do something different instead of more of the same."

It struck me that Charlie had just kept amping up the rabbits-out-of-a-hat game when he needed a paradigm shift. It also struck me that I was at risk of buying it back.

"I'm going to get a couple of beers," I said.

From the bar, I saw Charlie stand up and use his phone. He was on it, pacing around, for nearly half an hour, time that I used to drink both beers and confirm I had missed the last connection to London.

When he had finished the call, I brought two more beers over. He was still standing.

"I've spoken to Angelina," he said. "She's—"

"—a special person, too," I said. If my mother had been listening, she would have told us both to get a grip.

"You need to get to London?" said Charlie.

"I'll have to wait till tomorrow," I said. "And thank you, but no, I don't think it'd be a good idea to spend the night at your place."

"Can you call a taxi? Your French is better than mine."

He gave me his phone and followed me to the sign with taxi details.

"Home?" I said.

"No, Angelina's going to catch me in a couple of days. We can share one to Lyon airport. My shout."

It was a ninety-minute ride to Lyon. The last flight to Milan had gone, and Charlie booked two seats to London: "Best place to get a connection tomorrow."

In the departure lounge, Charlie fetched glasses of champagne for both of us, but we kept our toasts to ourselves.

"So," he said as they announced a delay to our flight, "are you going to take your own advice?"

"About?"

"Claire."

"Different story."

"You sure? You just spent a week with another woman. You'd have to be a psychopath to be able to go back to your partner without feeling bad about yourself. But if you tell me you're not going back because you're still in love with Angelina, I'm going to puke."

Enough already. I had bailed this guy out, sacrificed the chance to be with the love of my life, and now he was calling it all into question.

"You don't think I love Angelina?" I said.

"You didn't love her enough to take her twenty years ago. I saw the letter you sent. 'I'm not coming back. I'm with someone else. Love, Adam and Claire.' You chose Claire. Angelina was there if you wanted her. I was her second choice. Claire was your first choice."

Jesus Christ. Maybe that was the letter I should have read over and over. I had loved Claire. But she had to compete with a memory of a person—and a love—that was forever young. I had still felt guilty at not being there for Angelina. Perhaps it had been that guilt, rather than happy memories, that lay dormant before turning into nostalgia.

Charlie laughed. "Made me try harder."

"She doesn't see you as second best now."

"That's what time and hard work does. Love is a verb. Your turn now. I mean, what are you going to do? Find someone else like Claire and not make any mistakes? No shared memories? Find out she doesn't like your English breakfast? Or Bob Dylan? You've fixed half of it. Don't you have the guts to deal with your own problem yourself?"

Charlie was on the phone again, and I pulled out my laptop to pass the time. For no conscious reason, I found myself Googling Bob from Idaho. I had heard nothing from him since Singapore, 1990. To my surprise, I found him, easily. He had a Web site devoted mainly to technology topics, but there was a personal section.

He was gray, but instantly recognizable. He had recently posted pictures of his fortieth wedding anniversary gathering, with children and grandchildren. His wife, the heart-stoppingly beautiful Polish lady, was an elegant contrast to the slightly shambolic American who looked as though he still couldn't believe his luck.

I had always thought of Bob as the man who seized the day, a role model for what I had failed to do. But after forty years, he was something more: the man who, with his wife, had turned that opportunity into a life. Time and hard work.

Charlie and I had seats together in business class.

"All right," he said. "Are we good on sorting it out with Claire, or do I have to waste time that I could use to help with her buyout?"

It's always easier to solve other people's problems. I ignored the first part of his question.

"Monday's D-Day and she's meeting with the other directors tomorrow to make a decision. If she sells, she'll probably need to move to the States. In which case, the part about us . . ."

As I was about to state a position I had held for most of my life, I felt diminished in the presence of this guy who had abandoned his profession to support his wife's Hollywood ambitions.

"Forget that," I said.

"She's having her strategy meeting tomorrow?" he said. "Where?"

"London, I suppose."

"Can they use some help?"

# 4 0

I left Charlie to get a taxi at Paddington and took the Tube to Liverpool Street.

At the end of a day that had begun in a Burgundian village and included a return trip to Paris, a long taxi ride, an international flight, and the 10:30 P.M. train to Norwich, a black cab deposited me outside the place I had called home until a week ago.

I had texted Claire, asking if I could stay the night, and she had responded with an unadorned *OK*.

She opened the door in jeans and a jumper. She'd had her hair done but, I reminded myself, she had been on a date the previous night. Elvis appeared at her feet, saw me, and fled. Perhaps it had been a long week for him, too.

"How was she?" said Claire.

"Can I come in first?"

She let me in and we stood in the kitchen. Her expression was not giving anything away.

"I told you, I stayed with a couple of Australian friends in France," I said. "Middle-aged married couple with teenage kids."

"And was the woman's name by any chance Kylie?"

Aha. I now knew the source of her information. Kylie was the name I had used with my mother.

"No," I said. "It was Angelina. Charlie and Angelina. They're both lawyers. She's an equal opportunity commissioner in Melbourne. They've got three teenagers."

Claire was clearly wrong-footed.

"Nice people," I said. "They work incredibly hard on their marriage. After a major screw-up on his part."

I fished her present out of my bag. I had wrapped it myself, that service not being on offer at the souvenir shop at Lyon airport.

She sat on a stool at the counter to unwrap it, then did her best to smile at the eight-euro coffee mug that was supposed to rekindle our relationship.

"You got the right spelling," she said.

"That's the advantage of buying in France. They know how to spell Claire. We should go there more often. Pay for it by upping my hours. There's a card."

She opened the envelope. On the card, I had written, *I will make coffee for you every morning for the rest of our lives.*

I had considered adding *if you'll marry me*, or *even if you don't marry me*, but it had not sat right. There was still a lot of work to be done, but I wanted to do it with Claire.

She shook her head. "I'm really sorry, and it's my fault too, but it's all a bit late. The sale's probably going through, and if it does I'll go to the U.S."

"We should talk anyway," I said. "You first. Whatever you want to say about me. Or us. It's probably not going to be a surprise."

"Actually, it may be," said Claire. "You want to know something funny? Way back, when you went to Holland, your mum took it upon herself to fill me in on Kylie. You know how she is: 'I shouldn't be telling you this, but you need to know—it's affected him.'"

I laughed at the accuracy of Claire's impression and my mother's observation.

Claire managed a smile in return. "It wasn't much more than what you'd told me. Just a bit about who she was, which I really didn't need to know. But *Kylie*, an actress in an Australian soapie, and a singer. I couldn't remember you telling me her name, and then I thought maybe you might not have because that would give it away."

It took me a few moments to twig.

"You thought I'd been dating Kylie Minogue."

"*Very* briefly."

And I thought I'd been out of my league with Angelina. "Why didn't you tell me? It's hilarious."

"I didn't want you to think I was an idiot. Or betray your mum."

The unreality of it struck me, and I began laughing, and Claire joined me until we were both laughing uncontrollably at the idea that I had had an affair with an international pop star. I really did love Claire. She deserved better than what I had given her. Even in the last ten minutes.

I took a deep breath.

*Remember Lenny Bruce. Remember Randall. Remember Charlie.* Do not *ever* confess.

"Her name wasn't actually Kylie. You were right about France. She was the one I told you I reconnected with."

"Angelina?"

"'Fraid so."

"Was her husband there, then?"

"All true. The kids, the working hard on the marriage. The Château Margaux and the guinea fowl with foie gras."

"And how was reality compared with fantasy?"

"She was older."

"That's not what I was asking."

"I think we both worked out that we had made the right decisions."

"So you're over her?"

I could have protested at the ludicrousness of the question, but I was doing my best to be honest.

"I'm through it. I'm not going back."

Claire walked to the fridge, opened it, closed it without taking anything out, and sat down again.

"Adam, I don't want to make the same mistake again. When we got together, I could see you were still bruised, but I should have given you a chance to talk. Your mum was right."

"No surprise there."

"You know me. I'm not the one to start the touchy-feely discussions. You're the emotional one." She laughed. "Relatively speaking. Given we're IT people."

"Not soapie stars. Or Californians."

"We're still human beings. Mandy was telling me about this four-dimensional—"

"Physical, intellectual—"

"I thought we were doing pretty well on practical, which is my domain, but you've been letting the team down on emotional. I need you to keep us human. Music used to be our safe place for that, and you've been keeping it to yourself."

"I should have gone back to Australia about fifteen years ago and done what I've done this week."

The outcome would likely have been the same, possibly without the three-way sex.

"While we're being honest," said Claire, "there's something I should tell you. You may want to take your mug back."

"You slept with Ray?"

"Ray? God no. What makes you think . . . Have you been looking at my e-mails?"

I'm sure my expression made a reply unnecessary.

"Serves you right. I saw him to talk about the deal. He was quite useful. Knew all about BATNAs. I think he wants to be mine. Do you want to open a bottle of wine?"

It was late, but it seemed that she needed a drink to convey whatever bad news was in store for me. Perhaps she thought I would need the drink.

I found a bottle of Argentinean malbec, opened it, and filled two glasses. It had probably cost a tenth of what Charlie had paid for the stuff he had been serving in France and tasted just as good. Better. It was nice to be home, if I could forget that it might be a short-lived state of affairs.

"I did something I'm pretty ashamed of," she said. "And, if you're going to make a new life for yourself, you should know."

Christ. What was the worst case? As soon as I asked the question, the answer flashed into my head. Randall. She'd slept with Randall. Claire was the other woman who had destroyed Randall and Mandy's marriage.

I was right: it *was* the worst case. And there was no way in the wide world it was true. I laughed out loud at the ridiculousness of it.

"What are you laughing at?"

"I imagined you'd slept with Randall."

"Before or after he was with Mandy?"

"After. What are you saying?"

"Neither. But he did try. Before I met you. I introduced him to Mandy instead. He never mentioned it to you?"

How many secrets were out there? How many of our friends had had one-night stands, affairs, lost loves that they never confessed?

"Whatever it is, you really don't need to tell me," I said. "Unless you want to get it off your chest or it's somehow relevant now."

"Both," she said. "I had a fertility test. Back when I was trying to get pregnant. I just wanted to know. And it *was* me. My tubes were blocked. They could have tried to do something about it, but it would have been difficult and I just didn't want to do it. I didn't want to tell you that, in the end, I was the one choosing not to have children. Maybe you'd have left me to have children with someone else. And now . . . you need to know it wasn't you, in case . . . I'm so sorry."

She was crying, crying over something that had happened maybe fifteen years ago, over the whole screw-up that was us and children: getting over my own fears, persuading her to try, failing and never properly finding our way back to a vision of a relationship for the two of us.

I stood and put my arms around her as she sat on the stool, and she put hers around me.

"You should have told me ages ago," I said. "We'd agreed we weren't going to do IVF or anything, anyway. I wasn't going to leave you, and I don't want to now."

"Adam, I can't—"

"I knew. I did it, too. Got tested. Same reason. Just wanted to know. If it had been me, maybe we could have done something straightforward to sort it."

"Why didn't you tell me?"

"So you wouldn't feel the way you did."

Claire let go and I stepped back, making space. "God, we were idiots," she said. "It's taken this to get us to say what we should have said . . ."

"So where does that leave us?"

She got a tissue from the bench and wiped her face. There was no anger or malice in her expression, just sadness.

"I think it leaves us with a better understanding of what happened. I'm sorry to put it like this, but nothing's changed from what we said a week ago. It's not about anyone else, it's about me moving. About that being more important to both of us than our relationship."

"I said I'd make you coffee every morning. I suppose if you're in the States I'll have to go there to do it."

She stared at me. She *did* know me, and she had not expected this.

I picked up the coffee mug. "Get the best deal you can and I'll fit in. If you want me to."

"You hate America."

"I love you."

She looked and looked and looked. It wasn't the *I love you*. It was the willingness to move, which in the last few hours had changed in my mind from a deal-breaker to no big deal. If we were going to undo the deadlock, one of us had to step up—simple logic that would have changed my life twenty-two years earlier.

"You want to go back to what we had?" said Claire.

"It suited both of us, didn't it?"

"Must have. Why would two smart people like us have set it up any way except the way we wanted? Maybe we both thought there were more important things than our relationship."

"I may have changed," I said.

I was conscious that my desire to reboot our relationship arose only partly from reaching a resolution about Angelina. I wanted us to have some of what Angelina and Charlie had, despite the fact that what they had was codependent, perhaps pathological, and, until a few hours ago, terminal. It seemed worth it for the good bits.

"I have to say, the coffee in bed is a persuasive argument," said Claire.

"Dinner out together once a week," I said. "I'll cook all the time. And work most of the time. And we should go to France. Before we go to America."

I was starting to paint a picture that I liked. We could skip the foie gras.

"All right," she said. "But two more things."

"Two?"

"Two." She stood up and I followed her to the sitting room, bringing the bottle with me. She waited until I had topped up both glasses and taken a seat on the sofa opposite her.

"If you're not really over . . . Angelina, I need to know. And we'll work it through to whatever the ending is. Like we should have done last time."

"I got over it last time. It was just nostalgia until we got in touch again. And for a little while I thought I could turn back time."

"It must have been a big week. I don't know what happened, or how much you're planning to tell me, but if you need to, let's do it now. I don't want it drip-fed to me over the next twenty years."

"If *I* need to? What about you?"

"You know something: I used to believe that couples should share everything, no secrets, but you get older. When I look at Mandy and what she's gone through, I wish Randall hadn't been such a coward and had just lived with it. Or maybe confided in you or a counselor or someone who'd never tell Mandy. If he hadn't dumped it on her . . ."

"You don't want to know?"

"Not for me. I don't need any more detail. Stories about people I've never met that I'm sure they'd rather I didn't know. But if it's important for you to share it . . ."

"If I need to, I'll pay for a therapist. Not Randall's."

"If it makes you feel any better, I'm assuming you slept with her. I'm not going to base the rest of my life on it." She looked away for a few moments, then looked back. "Or anything you might have said to her. I'm not Mandy. Second thing, then."

She walked to the piano and lifted the lid.

"You can sing for your supper. Every night. Keep your promise to your dad."

Easy. No. *This* was a big deal. In fact, it was a huge deal. I had avoided playing with Claire in the house. The emotional nexus between me, music, and a woman had, for at least the last few years, belonged to the Angelina relationship. Claire must have guessed this. Or maybe she just wanted me to deliver on my emotional sidekick responsibilities.

I had begun to think of how to overcome my resistance, when I realized it wasn't there. I wanted to play. Maybe that would be the legacy of the last few months.

I walked to the piano and, as I had done a day ago and a world away, I let my unconscious mind choose the song, just as you start walking without thinking about putting one foot in front of the other.

I played a chord, an F sharp, three fingers across the black keys, and the opening line of a Tom Waits song filled my head.

I played it: "San Diego Serenade," a simple melody, a three-verse litany of loss, about not knowing what you have until it's gone. Just my middle-aged voice and my dad's piano. I wasn't playing the song for Claire or for Angelina; I wasn't directing the words at anyone. I was just playing music that allowed me to be an emotional being and let Claire join me in that place.

It was nearly two in the morning.

"Thank God I don't need to get to London till tomorrow after-noon," Claire said.

Ah. Charlie had a two P.M. flight to Milan. I explained about his offer and she texted her partners.

"We'd better go to bed, then," she said. "In our room. That's a third thing. You're never sleeping in Alison's room again. America or not, we're selling the house."

Then she kissed me and, despite being forty-nine and half-drunk and having made love to another woman all week, I felt a distinct reaction.

"We missed Friday," I said.

"Don't even think about it," said Claire.

It was an unexceptional way to end the most tumultuous week of my life.

Charlie would stay on until the Tuesday and guide Claire's team to a deal far beyond their expectations, giving himself another story to tell. Her commitment to move to San Jose for three years would be backed by a similar commitment to her software baby and a salary that I would not be able to match if I worked eight days a week.

Claire would return from London singing Charlie's praises as both a negotiator and a charmer who had flirted outrageously with her. And with some questions about a futures trading debacle she had never heard of. She would tell me that Charlie had canceled his visit to Milan because his daughter did not want to see him.

In California, I would meet up again with Randall, who would find me a job, after I'd given him a bollocking for hitting on Claire a quarter of a century earlier.

I would play piano in a bar, three nights a week, and find myself working hard to expand my repertoire to include songs from the last thirty years. There would be no space in my life for regular trivia nights, and no time or reason to sit in a room with a playlist of heartache. At the piano, I would be too busy getting a new song down to let the lyrics pull me into nostalgia.

One night, a guy who looked a lot like Jackson Browne would walk into the bar and take a seat in the back corner. I would play "The Pretender" and he would applaud enthusiastically and walk toward the piano. I would decide that if he wanted to play I would let him. He would continue past me to the bathroom, but I would be pretty sure it was him.

I would finally and clumsily thank my mother for doing the hard yards while I idolized my absent father.

Claire and I would agree to a regular date night, and talk about what was happening in our busy lives and sometimes what was going on in our heads. Afterward, I would play piano and we would share a connection that neither of us felt comfortable putting into words.

Without fuss, but to mark a commitment to growing old together, we would get married.

Four years after moving to San Jose I would receive an e-mail from Samantha Acheson, beginning with the words *I understand you knew my mother, who passed away*, and there would be tears running down my face before I realized she was referring to Jacinta. She was collecting memories from people who had known her, and I duly wrote an affectionate and nostalgic two pages of reminiscences. Samantha added that her parents were well and still drinking too much.

I would never see Angelina again. I would remember her—not the twenty-three-year-old, but the woman I spent a week with in France—when I heard a song of lost love, and it would be all the more poignant because at the Mâcon railway station I was only a semiquaver away from asking her to come with me.

For those times, I had another Jackson Browne song of love revisited, with a line about laughing in pleasure's ruins. I would play it in my head or on my phone, and remember the night that our rekindled passion left a bedside cabinet on its side and Charlie's iPod looking up at us. But it was the sentiment of the closing lines that would carry me through my sixth decade: Was it the past or the future calling?

And, as far as anyone can say for sure in a world where a one-word e-mail or a slip of the tongue in a French farmhouse or a cosmic ghost flipping the record over can change everything in an instant, it was going to be all right.

These are the versions that I had in mind when writing. See textpub
lishing.com.au/books/the-best-of-adam-sharp for a Spotify playlist.

"Hey Jude" (The Beatles)

"Like a Rolling Stone" (Bob Dylan)—the "Judas" moment is on *The
Bootleg Series, Vol. 4: Bob Dylan Live 1966: The "Royal Albert Hall" Concert*

"Someone Like You" (Adele)

"My Sentimental Friend" (Herman's Hermits)—a taste of Adam's
accent

"Walk Away Renée" (The Left Banke / The Four Tops, or, for
a spare version such as Pete the Project Manager sings, Linda
Ronstadt)

"Brown Eyed Girl" (Van Morrison)

"Because the Night" (The Patti Smith Group)—Adam is wrong:
Bruce Springsteen did record a studio version, eventually released
on *The Promise* in 2010

"Both Sides Now" (Joni Mitchell / Judy Collins)

"You're Gonna Lose That Girl" (The Beatles)

"You Are So Beautiful" (Joe Cocker)

"You Can Leave Your Hat On" (Joe Cocker)

"I Hope That I Don't Fall in Love with You" (Tom Waits)

"If You Gotta Go, Go Now" (Bob Dylan / Manfred Mann)—
Dylan's acoustic version on *The Bootleg Series, Vol. 6: Bob Dylan
Live 1964: Concert at Philharmonic Hall* is closest to how Adam
plays it

"I'm Henry VIII, I Am" (Herman's Hermits)—an overdose of
Adam's accent, in the same vein as their "Mrs. Brown, You've Got a
Lovely Daughter"

"Greensleeves" (Loreena McKennitt)

"I Am Woman" (Helen Reddy)

"Early in the Morning" (The Mojos)—the all-female Australian
blues combo that Adam and Angelina catch at the pub in 1989

"Walking on Sunshine" (Katrina and the Waves)

"Mr. Siegal" (Tom Waits)

"Imagine" (John Lennon)

"Angel of the Morning" (Merrilee Rush and the Turnabouts / Juice
Newton)—growing up in New Zealand, I first heard Allison
Durbin's version

"I Will Survive" (Gloria Gaynor)

"Great Balls of Fire" (Jerry Lee Lewis)

"Skyline Pigeon" (Elton John)

"Walking in Memphis" (Cher)

"Walk Out in the Rain" (Ann Christy)

"Against the Wind" (Bob Seger)

"Clair" (Gilbert O'Sullivan)

"Goodnight Irene" (Ry Cooder)—his version features an accordion

"Angelina" (Bob Dylan)

"Lola" (The Kinks)

"For Once in My Life" (Stevie Wonder)

"C Jam Blues" (Oscar Peterson)

"Champagne Charlie" (Leon Redbone)

"Summertime" (Billie Holiday / Janis Joplin)

"Angie" (The Rolling Stones)

Chopin: Étude Op. 10, No. 3, "Tristesse" (Vladimir Ashkenazy)

"Farther On" (Jackson Browne)

"The Ship Song" (Nick Cave and the Bad Seeds)

"Angel" (Sarah McLachlan)

"Non, Je Ne Regrette Rien" / "No Regrets" (Edith Piaf)

"Bird on the Wire" (Leonard Cohen)—the performance on *Cohen Live: Leonard Cohen in Concert*, 1994

"All These Things That I've Done" (The Killers)

"San Diego Serenade" (Tom Waits)

"The Pretender" (Jackson Browne)

"The Times You've Come" (Jackson Browne)

"Revolution" (The Beatles)

# ACKNOWLEDGMENTS

This book would not have been written, and nor would I be a writer at all, without the support of my wife, Anne Buist, who again provided inspiration, encouragement, and a critical eye.

Special thanks are due to Orest Bilas (late of Manchester) and Piano Man Pete Walsh.

My editors, Michael Heyward, Rebecca Starford, and David Winter at Text Publishing, helped me take the manuscript a long way from the draft I wrote between the Rosie novels.

My early readers were there before and during the formal editing process, and made innumerable valuable suggestions: Jon Backhouse, Tania Chandler, Eamonn Cooke, Judy Della-Vecchia, Robert Eames, Irina Goundortseva, Toni Jordan, Rod Miller, Helen O'Connell, Susannah Petty, Daniel Simsion, Dominique Simsion, Chris and Sue Waddell, Pete and Geri Walsh, and Janifer Willis.

My international publishers—Cordelia Borchardt (Fischer, Germany), Jennifer Enderlin (St. Martin's Press, U.S.), Maxine Hitchcock (Penguin, UK), and Jennifer Lambert (HarperCollins, Canada)—also provided helpful input.

Thanks also to Robin Baker, Peter Dawson, Susan and Martin Gandar, Emma Healey and Andrew McKechnie, David Hay, Kim Krejus, Sarah Lutyens, Karyn Marcus, Steve Mitchell, and Susan Sly.

Finally, I want to acknowledge the continuing contribution of the team at Text Publishing—in particular Anne Beilby, Alice Cottrell, Jane Novak, and Kirsty Wilson—and my publishers and agents around the world who have done so much to bring my books to readers and to enable me to continue working as a writer.